WILD STAR

TYSON WILD BOOK FIFTY FIVE

TRIPP ELLIS

Copyright © 2023 by Tripp Ellis

All rights reserved. Worldwide.

This book is a work of fiction. The names, characters, places, and incidents, except for incidental references to public figures, products, or services, are fictitious. Any resemblance to persons, living or dead, actual events, locales, or organizations is entirely coincidental, and not intended to refer to any living person or to disparage any company's products or services. All characters engaging in sexual activity are above the age of consent.

No part of this text may be reproduced, transmitted, downloaded, decompiled, uploaded, or stored in or introduced into any information storage and retrieval system, in any form or by any means, whether electronic or mechanical, now known or hereafter devised, without the express written permission of the publisher except for the use of brief quotations in a book review.

1

"Want me to get you anything?" JD said with a smirk, just to rub it in.

I scowled at him and sneered, "No. That's all you, buddy."

He climbed out of the passenger seat, closed the door, and hustled into the liquor store.

There were rows and rows of liquor bottles. Every imaginable brand of whiskey, rum, vodka, tequila, gin, and liqueurs, along with a nice selection of wine and beer. None of which I could indulge in leading up to the procedure.

I sat behind the wheel of the new-to-me 1984 white Ferrari 308 GTS. The targa top was off, and the Florida sun beamed down. The mid-mounted V-8 engine idled, and the bolstered black leather seats hugged my form.

I had gotten a hell of a deal on the car.

Too good to pass up.

The *bonus* I had to give Nancy Van Zant wasn't bad, either.

I hadn't owned a car in a long time. My sport bike fed my adrenaline addiction and got me around town, but I needed something a little more practical. Not that a classic Ferrari is practical, but I could throw a few grocery bags in the passenger seat or the front trunk. Justifying the purchase of a classic Ferrari under the guise of practicality takes all kinds of mental gymnastics. But it was a cool car in a rare color. I just hoped I hadn't bought a money pit.

Just a few more days, I told myself. I could deal with almost anything for a few days. Going without alcohol wouldn't kill me, and it was for a good cause. The possibility of saving someone's life made it a small price to pay.

A customer pushed through the glass double doors of the liquor store, stepping outside with a bottle in a brown bag. Our eyes met, and we both did a double take.

The customer froze for a moment, his eyes round.

He dropped the bottle and darted into the parking lot. It shattered, and clear liquid seeped through the brown bag and flowed onto the sidewalk.

The man hopped onto a sport bike, cranked up the engine, and backed out of the space just far enough to turn the front wheel and avoid the curb as he launched forward. He twisted the throttle, and the 600 cc engine growled.

I overcame my momentary surprise, threw the car into reverse, and launched out of the parking space.

I shifted into first, dropped the clutch, and mashed the gas. Tires squealed, and the V8 roared as I sped across the lot.

JD stepped outside with a box full of adult beverages. His eyes widened, and a look of confusion twisted his face. The breeze fluttered his long blond hair. He wore his typical uniform of a loud Hawaiian shirt, cargo shorts, and checkered Vans. For an instant, he looked like a boy who'd lost his mother in a crowded shopping mall.

I wasn't about to let Liam Vance get away. He was a wanted fugitive, and he had tried to assassinate us.

Tires squealed as I turned out of the parking lot, chasing after the sport bike. I slammed through the gears, working the gated shifter. The unmistakable howl of the Italian sports car sang its glorious note.

The Ferrari's V8 produced 240 hp.

It wasn't bad back in the day, but anemic by modern standards. Notwithstanding, the car wasn't short on thrills or handling. It was sex and steel in a sleek, curvaceous package. The smell of leather and oil permeated the air. The mid-engine gave it a perfect balance. Still, it was no match for the sport bike.

I tried my best to keep up, but Liam wrung the damn thing out. He pulled away with ease and zipped around slower cars, dodging oncoming traffic. He disappeared around the corner at the next intersection.

Traffic at the light held me up. It finally turned green, and cars flowed through the crossing. I made the turn, and by that time, the punk was long gone.

I called dispatch and requested additional patrol units in the area. At least I got a plate number on the bike.

I circled back around to the liquor store. The box of whiskey was on the ground, and JD leaned against the wall, waiting. I pulled into a parking space, and he grabbed the whiskey and hustled to the car. I popped the front trunk, and we positioned the bottles inside.

"Where the hell did you go?"

"You didn't see Liam walk out of the store?"

"Who?"

"Liam Vance. The asshole that tried to take us out."

Jack's face tightened. "And you let him get away?"

I rolled my eyes. "No. I didn't *let* him get away. He got away all on his own."

Jack frowned and shook his head.

"Don't worry. We're going to get that son-of-a-bitch," I said with a grin on my face.

We climbed into the car. I cranked up the engine and dropped the Ferrari into gear. I eased out the clutch, and we rolled out of the lot. We drove across town to 859 Sand Pine Way.

The sport bike was registered to Henry Wilkins.

We met Erickson and Faulkner near the cozy, one-story house with French gray siding. It had white accents and a maroon door. A white picket fence surrounded a tiny front yard with a few small fan palms. An American flag hung from a column.

The house and yard were well maintained. There was an extended gravel shoulder in front of the picket fence that was home to a white Sebring convertible. A 25-foot center console on a trailer sat in the red brick driveway. The house didn't have an actual garage. A green trash bin and a blue recycling bin stood near the curb. The sportbike wasn't around.

My first thought was that the crotch rocket had been stolen. But dispatch didn't mention a report of the theft.

We had a quick huddle with the other deputies, then stormed the property. JD and I pushed through the gate and marched to the front porch. Erickson and Faulkner made their way around the side of the house, and through a gate, into the backyard. It squealed slightly as they opened it.

I put a heavy fist against the door and shouted, "Coconut County! Open up."

2

The rotor blades of Tango One pattered overhead.

This was an average suburban neighborhood, not the type of place where you would expect to find an accomplice of an assassin. The neighborhood was well maintained. Parked cars lined the road and driveways. A gentle breeze rustled the trees, and the distant sound of children playing drifted down the block.

JD and I readied our weapons, and another patrol unit screeched to a halt at the curb. Deputies Robinson and Halford joined us.

Henry Wilkins pulled open the door with a curious look on his face. His eyes flicked from JD to me, and he tried to hide a flash of recognition.

Henry was in his late 20s with curly sandy-blonde hair that was a little shaggy. He had a scraggly beard and a thick physique. The guy looked like he put in the hours at the gym. He had bulging biceps and traps like mountain ranges.

He stood about 6'2" with caramel eyes and a friendly face. Henry looked like your average guy.

"Is there some kind of problem?" he asked.

"We're looking for Liam Vance," I said.

"Who?" he asked, his brow knitting together.

"He's the guy I just chased on your motorcycle," I snarked.

"You found my bike?"

"Momentarily."

He frowned and shook his head. "Yeah, man. That was stolen."

"Oh, really?" I said, thick with skepticism.

"Yeah."

I let him play this game for a little while. "When, exactly, did it get stolen?"

"I'm not sure. I just looked out and noticed it was gone a few minutes ago."

I glared at him, not buying a word of it.

"So, you don't know Liam Vance?" JD said.

Henry shrugged innocently. "No. Should I?"

"Yeah. I think you should." Jack pulled his phone from his pocket and displayed an image from Henry's social media profile—Liam and Henry had their arms over each other's shoulders, smiling for the camera like best bros.

Henry frowned and slumped.

"You're under arrest for aiding and abetting a fugitive," I said.

"What!?"

"Turn around and put your hands behind your back."

He didn't look too happy about it, but he complied.

I pulled out the cuffs and slapped the hard steel against his thick wrists. I ratcheted them tight and read him his rights.

Deputies stormed inside.

I escorted Henry down the walkway, through the gate, and stuffed him into the back of Robinson's patrol car.

Mendoza still hadn't returned to work yet. But he was progressing well. He had a personal injury lawsuit against the company that made the defective vests. I hated to break it to him that he was never going to collect. The money was long gone.

I returned to the house and joined in the search. We turned the place upside down and didn't find Liam Vance. Though, it looked like someone had been staying in the guest bedroom. The sheets were rumpled, and dirty clothes littered the floor.

We found a couple of pistols in a drawer in the master bedroom, along with a box of ammunition. We confiscated the items, and the lab would run ballistics.

We had already linked a weapon found in Liam's apartment to the drive-by shooting at *Diver Down* that was an attempt on our lives. We had more than enough evidence to put Liam away for quite a long time, if we could catch up with him.

Curious neighbors gathered outside to get an up-close look at the commotion.

Henry was taken to the station, processed, printed, and put into an interrogation room. We let him stew in the tiny room while we filled out after-action reports in the conference room. JD and I typed away on wireless keyboards connected to iPads.

Henry fidgeted in the claustrophobic interrogation room as we stepped inside. He sat at the table, fluorescent lights buzzing overhead. The walls closed in around him. Fifteen minutes in the cramped space was enough to make most people unsettled. An hour or two could drive some people to the brink. The anxiety, the anticipation. The fear of the unknown. The prospect of incarceration and the horrors that go along with it. Some people go to prison and never come out. A lifetime wasted in a 6x8 cell. Some get shanked in the yard. One thing is certain—everyone is changed by the process.

"You can't arrest me," he protested. "I haven't done anything wrong."

I laughed and took a seat across the table from him. "You gave a wanted felon your motorcycle."

"I told you. It was stolen."

"Your best friend stole it?" I said, incredulous. "From your social media profile, it looks like you guys are tight."

He paused, and his jaw tightened. "Look, what was I supposed to do? I didn't know he was in trouble. He asked me if he could borrow the bike. I gave him the keys. I never saw him again."

It was a load of crap.

"He's not staying at your place?"

Henry shook his head.

I sighed and shook my head. "How about we stop playing games, and you tell me where he's at?"

"I don't know," Henry said, shrugging innocently.

"I don't know if you've figured this out yet, but Liam will be charged with attempted murder. I think you know something about that."

He swallowed hard, and sweat misted his brow. "I don't know what you're talking about."

"Sure you do," I said. "I know you recognized us. I saw it on your face when you answered the door. In case you've forgotten, let me refresh your memory. We are the two deputies that you and Liam tried to gun down at Diver Down not long ago. You were driving the car."

His involvement was pure speculation at this point. I didn't see either of their faces at the time.

His brow crinkled. "What are you talking about!?"

"You know damn good and well what I'm talking about."

"First, you accuse me of helping Liam out. Now you accuse me of attempted murder?"

"I'm glad you've been paying attention," I snarked.

He scowled at me. "You can't prove any of this." He paused, his eyes flicking between the two of us. "I told you. Liam borrowed my bike. I didn't have any knowledge he was a fugitive. You can't charge me with anything," he said in a smug tone.

Henry sat back and acted like he was untouchable.

"I've got news for you. You're getting charged, and you're going to sit in the pod until you make bail. If you can't make bail, you'll sit there until your trial date. By that time, we'll have subpoenaed your phone records, credit card receipts, and talked to all your neighbors. Wanna bet someone saw Liam come and go?"

His face tightened again.

I continued. "You have one opportunity to save your skin. You help us find Liam and testify against him, and maybe you get off with a slap on the wrist."

He didn't like the sound of that. "I want to talk to a lawyer."

"I hope you know a good one."

The chair screeched as I pushed away from the table. JD and I walked toward the exit, and I knocked on the door. A guard buzzed us out, and we stepped into the hallway.

The sheriff joined us, having watched the interrogation from the observation room. "That punk knows exactly where Liam Vance is."

"My thoughts exactly," JD said.

"Put him with a cellmate in the pod who likes to talk," I suggested. "He'll gab to somebody. Monitor all of his calls. See who he talks to and what he says."

All phone calls made from the jail were recorded. No warrant necessary. No expectation of privacy.

Maybe we'd get lucky.

3

We left the station and headed back to the *Avventura*. With the targa top off, the wind swirled around the cabin, and classic rock blasted from the speakers. The unique dog-leg shifter pattern took a little getting used to, but I had to admit, I was enjoying the car. Who wouldn't?

We pulled into the lot and found a place to park near the dock. I killed the engine and hopped out. We grabbed the liquor and carted it down the dock toward the superyacht.

The sun angled toward the horizon, casting amber rays across the marina. Boats swayed in their slips. Riggings clinked against masts, and seabirds hung on the draft.

It was a nice sunset. The amber ball painted the sky multiple shades of pastel colors—pink, blue, and orange.

A gaggle of paparazzi loitered on the dock near the stern of the *Avventura*, waiting like vultures. They snapped photos, and cameras flashed as we crossed the passerelle to the aft deck. They shouted at us, "Can you get Logan to step out for a picture?"

We ignored them. They'd been hanging around ever since Logan had arrived.

He was arguably the biggest movie star on the planet. With him in your movie, you were guaranteed a box-office smash. Wherever he went, throngs of fans and hordes of press followed. When they found out he was staying aboard the boat, the paparazzi had been loitering, hoping to catch a glimpse or snap a candid photo of the star.

I figured they'd move on once they got their shot. They couldn't hound him forever like this. Or maybe they could.

We crossed the passerelle, and I slid open the glass door to the salon and stepped inside.

Buddy greeted me with a wagging tail and a slobbering tongue. The little Jack Russell bounced up and down excitedly, displaying his vertical leap. He wasn't short on energy. Harness that, and he could provide power for the whole island.

I knelt down and petted the little guy.

Logan entered the salon with that movie-star smile. "What happened to you guys? I thought you were just making a quick trip to the liquor store?"

"Things got complicated," I said as I stood up.

Jack moved to the bar and restocked it.

Logan had dark hair, ice-blue eyes, and a jawline that was made for the camera. He was the bright and shining center of the movie star universe. He was in Coconut Key doing *research* for the upcoming TV series based on our adventures.

We were still waiting on his costar, Brad Tyler, to arrive. The two were going to shadow us for a few weeks to get into *character*. They wanted to learn our methods, mannerisms, and lifestyle. This was all fun and games for them. Just another role. Another opportunity to play make-believe. But these guys had no idea what they were getting into.

There had been some production delays with the *Wild Fury* whiskey. The distillery that Jack had contracted to produce it on a mass scale was backlogged. We were back to drinking store-bought whiskey for the time being, and I was on the sidelines.

Jack poured two glasses, then moved from behind the bar. He handed one to Logan, who politely declined.

"No, thank you. I don't drink when I'm on a project. I like to stay in tip-top shape. Keep my wits about me at all times."

JD looked at him like he was crazy. "This is part of your training. I lost my drinking buddy this week." He pointed to me, then told Logan, "So, you better learn to keep up."

He handed Logan the glass, and the movie star reluctantly accepted.

JD lifted his glass to toast. "To wild adventures!"

The two clinked and sipped the fine amber whiskey.

Logan looked like he'd swallowed a mouthful of turpentine. He coughed and almost spat it out. Jack patted him on the back. "It's good for you, son. Put hair on your chest."

"I'm thinking that since Tyson is abstaining, I should too," Logan said, his mouth dry and on fire. "In the spirit of getting into character and all."

JD's face twisted, and he shook his head dismissively. "Nonsense. This is an anomaly. He's just giving his liver a breather. You want the full, immersive Coconut Key experience, don't you?"

Logan nodded.

"Then you're going to get the full experience. We want an authentic portrayal," JD lifted his glass again, and the two toasted.

They sipped their beverages, and Logan seemed to handle it a little better this time.

Commotion on the dock caught my eye. The gaggle of paparazzi swarmed to meet Brad Tyler as he emerged from a black Lincoln Navigator.

The driver hustled around, grabbed his bags, and escorted him down the dock.

The cameras flashed like machine guns, flickering in the evening light.

They asked dozens of questions, and Brad kept a cool, calm demeanor. He wore dark aviator sunglasses. His long, sandy-blond hair dangled at his shoulders. He was already in character, wearing a loud Hawaiian shirt and cargo shorts.

He was taking this role seriously.

Together, Logan and Brad would represent us on camera.

Brad strode across the passerelle with a beaming smile. The driver followed with his luggage.

I slid open the salon door and greeted him with a smile and a handshake.

"Tyson, it's good to see you," Brad said.

"Likewise. Thanks for coming."

He stepped into the salon, shook hands with JD, then looked at Logan. Without hesitation, Brad cocked his fist back and swung a hard right. His fist careened through the air and connected with Logan's million-dollar face.

Technically, it was a $20 million face. That was his quote for Hollywood blockbusters. I don't know how much he was getting paid for the TV show. I didn't ask. It was between him and the studio.

4

Logan Chase might have been the center of the movie star universe, but Brad Tyler gave him a run for his money. Even in his 50s, with his shirt off, Brad was the guy men wanted to look like and women wanted to climb on top of.

His fist careened through the air and connected with Logan's cheek. The smack of the impact echoed throughout the salon, and the force wrenched Logan's face aside. The blow sent him tumbling to the ground.

He lay on the deck dazed for a moment, partially from the hit and partially from the fact that Brad actually took a swing at him.

This was Logan Chase.

Nobody put a hand on Logan Chase that Logan didn't authorize. But the two were far from their handlers, personal assistants, agents, managers, and entourage of people. That was part of the deal. They would come to Coconut Key and live as we did. Do what we did. Follow in our footsteps. No pomp and circumstance.

JD helped Logan off the deck. You could almost see the stars swirling around his head.

Brad stood there with a smug grin on his face, proud of his accomplishment.

"What the actual fuck, man?" Logan said, wiping traces of blood from his mouth.

"I just thought we'd get that out of the way."

"What did you do that for?"

"You know damn good and well why I did that."

Logan stared him down for a moment.

JD and I stood in between the two to keep things from getting out of hand.

"I take it you two don't get along," I said.

"We have our differences," Brad said, amused.

"I wasn't aware of that. I was under the impression that you had no problem working with each other."

"Oh, I don't have a problem," Brad said. "Now that's out of the way. I'm over it."

"Well, I'm not over it," Logan snarled.

"You realize you two are supposed to be playing best friends," I said.

"It's called acting," Brad said. "And I didn't get my Academy Award for nothing."

JD pulled Logan across the salon. He looked like he was about to charge Brad.

I ushered Brad aside and said in a hushed tone, "Is this going to work? Do I need to talk to David about recasting?"

Brad looked at me like it was the craziest thing he'd ever heard. Actors like these two didn't get *recast*. They never got fired from sets. They were stars. Productions revolved around them.

But this show was different.

David Cameron was directing, and I had negotiated casting approval as part of my deal. Besides, I wasn't in the mood to put up with any nonsense.

Brad flashed that cool, disarming smile. "I promise. I'll be on my best behavior from here on out. Everything's going to be fine."

"What's the issue?"

"It's a personal matter between Logan and me."

"This better not be a problem," I warned.

Brad raised his hands innocently. "No problem here."

I don't think these guys were used to having people dictate terms to them.

I walked across the salon and joined Logan and JD. "Is everything okay over here?"

Logan paced around, his fists clenched, his jaw tight. He huffed through his nostrils. "That son-of-a-bitch is way out of line." He growled loud enough for Brad to hear.

"You want to take a swing at me? Here I am," Brad shouted across the salon.

I shot him a look.

He raised his hands in surrender.

"He assaulted me. I have witnesses. You witnessed that," Logan said to us, then shouted at Brad, "You're gonna be hearing from my lawyers!"

Brad dismissed the notion with a hand wave.

My face tightened, and I just shook my head. It looked like we were going to be babysitting two spoiled brats for the next few weeks. And I was going to have to do it all without alcohol. This was turning into a nightmare.

JD got Logan a bag of ice from the minibar to put on his face, and I took Brad up to the sky deck. "I'm serious. I don't have the time or the energy for this."

"My apologies. I was out of line. It won't happen again."

"Maybe you should apologize to Logan."

Brad shook his head. "Not till he apologizes to me."

"I don't think that's gonna happen."

"He knows damn good and well what he did. I'm completely justified. Like I said, I just needed to get that out of my system. I'm over it and ready to work." He smiled.

I glared at him.

There was a long, uncomfortable moment.

"I'm sorry," Brad said, relenting. "I think we're getting off on the wrong foot. If it will make you feel better, I'll go apologize."

"Yes, that would make me feel better," I said, patronizing him.

I followed him downstairs, and he marched across the salon toward Logan.

"Keep him away from me," Logan said, pointing.

JD stood in between them.

Brad raised his hands innocently. "I come in peace. I'm sorry. I was out of line."

Brad extended his hand.

Logan glared at him for a moment but didn't shake hands.

Brad feinted, and Logan flinched.

Brad broke into laughter. "Gotcha!"

Logan didn't think it was funny.

I gave Brad another stern glance, and he raised his hands innocently again. "Hey, I tried." Brad ambled to the bar and poured himself a drink. "You don't mind if I help myself, do you?"

The two couldn't have been more opposite. Logan was focused and intense. Brad was laid back and took everything in stride. He didn't have a care in the world.

Logan was on the phone with his agent in no time. "I want this asshole off the project. Now! Or I walk."

"Go ahead, walk," Brad shouted from across the salon.

"I don't have to put up with this," Logan said to his agent.

The agent's voice crackled through the speaker phone. I could barely make out the phrase, "Just calm down."

"I am calm!"

"You don't sound calm," his agent said.

"I don't sound calm because I just got punched in the face."

Brad smirked and shook his head. "Wah, wah, wah, keep crying."

Logan glared at him and told his agent, "You call David Cameron right now. You tell him that it's Brad or me. But we're not doing the show together."

"For crying out loud," Brad said. "I didn't even swing that hard." He moved from behind the bar and approached Logan. "You want to hit me? Go ahead. Hit me. I'll give you a free shot." He stood there, leaned in slightly, and stuck out his chin."

Logan glared at him. He told his agent he'd call him back, then ended the call and slipped his phone into his pocket.

The two squared off, glaring at each other.

JD and I stood between them.

"Okay. Suit yourself," Brad said. "You had your chance." He stepped back toward the bar. "I came all the way down here to raise some hell. So let's have a good time." He looked at Logan. "Put your big girl panties on and get over it."

Logan's jaw tensed, and his fierce eyes blazed into Brad.

"There's half a dozen paparazzi out there, and they all got a picture of me laying you out," Brad said. "That photo is going to be on the cover of every magazine and gossip blog around the world. The next story they write is either going to be how you stormed off set or how we put our differences aside. You can cry like a baby, or we can walk out there with smiles on our faces, like nothing ever happened. Which one do you think is going to make you look better?"

5

Brad and Logan flashed million-dollar smiles as they stepped onto the aft deck. Cameras flashed and flickered, and paparazzi drew closer to the stern.

JD and I took the lead as we crossed the passerelle to run interference between the paparazzi and the celebrities.

They shouted questions:

"Why did you hit Logan?"

"Have you two buried the hatchet?"

"Will you be able to work together?"

Logan smiled. "Everything's fine. We were practicing a stunt." He put his hand on Brad's shoulder. "We're both looking forward to this production. Now, gentlemen, we're happy to pose for a few pictures. Then I would appreciate it if you would give us our privacy for the rest of the evening."

The two movie stars posed on the dock, looking like best friends for the camera.

They answered a few questions, then we made our way down the dock to the parking lot.

Logan arranged for a driver to pick us up. A black Yukon pulled into the lot and drove around by the dock. The driver, Amir, hopped out wearing a suit and tie. He got the door, and we all piled into the vehicle. He was a little starstruck by the celebrities, and there was the usual exchange. The *"I'm a big fan. I love your work"* kind of thing.

The movie stars were gracious and accommodating and signed autographs.

"Where to, gentlemen?"

"There's an event at the museum that I was looking forward to attending," Logan said. "Cocktails and art. We could all use a little culture about now."

It was an exclusive VIP opening of a new exhibit. It wasn't hard for Logan to wrangle an invite.

He had taken a moment to cover the redness on his face with some makeup. But his cheek was still a little swollen.

The driver zipped us across the island to the museum. Logan had hired him for the evening. He dropped us off at the gala event and got our doors.

We climbed the steps to the museum entrance as other patrons filtered in. It was a swanky gathering populated with Coconut Key's elite. These were all big-time donors to the museum—collectors, local politicians, sports figures, and local celebrities.

We were all a little underdressed for the occasion, but that didn't really matter. I was used to the shiny gold badge getting us in everywhere without issue, but the movie star card was far more impressive. Wherever they went, the velvet ropes parted. The two movie stars greeted the security at the door with a smile, and they motioned us in without a second thought.

People milled about, socializing, waxing profound about the art that hung on the walls. Catering staff weaved through the horde of patrons with trays of hors d'oeuvres and glasses of wine. There were lots of wealthy older gentlemen and young stunners in tight cocktail dresses with long legs and spike-heeled shoes.

"Good call," JD said to Logan.

Logan smiled.

The two celebrities drew all eyes. Hushed whispers drifted through the crowd.

Like politicians, they nodded and smiled. They shook hands and received compliments.

It seemed like the attention would be fun at first, but I imagined it would get tiring after a while—never being able to walk outside without someone wanting to say something to you.

These guys were used to it. I think they thrived on it. They were loved and adored by all.

JD grabbed a drink from the bar and got a round for our shadows.

"To letting bygones be bygones," JD said.

Brad lifted his glass, and they all clinked.

I was the odd man out.

We were in public now, and they were both putting on a good show. There was certainly no question as to their acting abilities.

The event was for one of those modern art exhibits where the work elicited both curiosity and confusion and perhaps disdain. An orange duct taped to a canvas. A shattered toilet reconfigured into an abstract shape. A large canvas with a solitary swipe of paint.

We perused the art and mingled.

Like supermassive black holes, the celebrities drew in beautiful women. It didn't matter whether they were single or with significant others. The ladies drifted toward the stars, pulled by their inescapable gravity.

I began to think this whole idea was ill-conceived. We were practically invisible now. The idea of spending a week in their shadows grew less and less appealing.

The artwork was on loan to the museum from a private collector. I'm sure, for the right price, everything was for sale.

The murmur of conversation echoed through the cavernous space. High heels clacked against the tile, and classical music from a quartet flowed throughout the space.

"What do you see?" a gorgeous blonde asked in regard to the painting we were both looking at.

I didn't see much besides her tight dress and low-cut neckline which accentuated a glorious valley of all natural cleavage.

I refocused my gaze on the artwork and stared at it in deep contemplation. "I see a guy pissing in a pool."

She regarded my statement carefully. Her eyes narrowed, and she stroked her chin with folded arms. "What makes you say that?"

"Because it's a guy pissing in a pool."

It was literally an impressionist rendering of a man in a tuxedo, relieving himself in the sparkling waters of a luxurious mansion in the Hollywood hills.

"Yes, clearly. But what do you really see? What is the deeper meaning?"

"The guy in the tuxedo is probably the butler. He's urinating in the pool because he doesn't like his boss. This is the moment before the big party when all the guests are about to arrive and get into the water. It's his way of getting back at them for treating him like crap for all those years."

She chuckled. "That's a refreshing answer. Most people are afraid to state the truth."

"What do you see?"

Her gorgeous blue eyes flicked from the painting to me. She looked me up and down.

I didn't mind her looking.

She had full lips, classic bone structure, and a petite little figure that was a work of art in itself.

6

"I see it as an indictment of the commercialization of modern art," the gorgeous blonde said. "The crude subject matter. The garish colors. The blurred lines. I think the artist is challenging our perception. What is art? What is its value? Is it an asset? It can be bought and sold, yes, but to reduce it to merely an investment seems sacrilegious. Yet only the truly wealthy can afford a piece like this."

"Only the truly wealthy would want a piece like this."

She laughed again. "I suppose you're right. It's the most *valuable* piece in the exhibit," she said in air quotes. "As I said, your honesty is refreshing." She smiled. "I'm Astrid."

She extended her hand, and I took it.

She had soft hands, well-manicured nails, and smooth skin. Her hand was warm. I liked holding it.

"Tyson."

"It's nice to meet you, Tyson."

"Likewise.

"What brings you to our little soirée? You're not on the guest list." She muttered aside, "I know everyone on the guest list. Who are you here with?"

I nodded across the room to the dynamic duo.

She lifted an impressed brow. "You keep good company."

I shrugged. "Would you like me to introduce you?"

She contemplated the thought for a moment. "I must say, I am a big fan. I do enjoy their movies, but I'm quite content to remain engaged in our conversation. It has potential."

I smirked slightly.

Through a side entrance, two people dressed all in black hurried down the hallway. They each carried a bucket. I didn't think much of it at first.

A woman approached Astrid and muttered. "Is this your doing?" She nodded to the movie stars across the museum.

Astrid's gaze followed. "No. You'll have to thank Tyson for that."

The woman regarded me with an impressed gaze.

"Vera, this is Tyson…?"

"Wild."

"Tyson Wild, Vera Voss," Astrid said.

Vera extended her hand. "Pleasure to meet you."

"The pleasure is all mine."

Vera was an attractive woman in her early 30s with a stylish bob of chocolate hair, caramel eyes, and elegant features. She had a toned little body that the tight cream cocktail dress offered glimpses of. The strapless top teased a delightful valley of cleavage. A diamond necklace sparkled around her collarbones. She had a regal quality to her. The bling dangling from her ears and wrapped around her fingers, along with the designer handbag, screamed wealth and luxury.

"I'm sure Tyson can facilitate an introduction," Astrid said.

"Honey, I can make my own introduction," she said with a naughty glimmer.

I had no doubt she excelled at introductions.

The bucket brigade's intentions became obvious.

They approached the painting, reared the buckets back, and heaved them toward the pool pisser. A wave of red paint launched into the air from the buckets, careening toward the canvas.

Astrid jumped in front of the liquid, trying to block it.

Her act of bravery did little to avert the damage. A considerable amount of paint and splatter hit the canvas, and her tight black dress was now covered in crimson. Her skin and hair were splattered, and paint dripped down her dress.

The crowd gasped in horror.

The two art terrorists began babbling some nonsense.

I flashed my badge and shouted, "Coconut County! On the ground. Now!"

Two large gentlemen that hovered near Vera pounced on the little bastards, pinning them to the ground. The frail activists didn't stand a chance against the muscle-bound men.

JD rushed across the museum, and we took over and ratcheted cuffs around the perp's wrists.

I read them their rights as they continued screaming something nonsensical.

"Art is murder, man," one of them said. "Don't you get it?"

I had a hard time wrapping my head around it. I think they just wanted attention.

JD and I escorted them out of the museum and waited for a patrol car to arrive. Their county taxi showed up, and we stuffed them into the back of the patrol car. They were taken to the station where they'd get a complimentary night's stay and a free meal.

We hustled back inside, and I rejoined Astrid. "Are you okay?"

She smiled. "I'm fine. But I don't think my dress is going to make it." She took a deep breath and cringed. "As for the painting, I think it can be salvaged. Who knows, this might make it more valuable."

Museum personnel removed the painting from the wall and rushed it to another area where it could be cleaned and restored. Time was of the essence.

"I think that was my cue to get out of this dress," Astrid said. She looked herself over. "Although, maybe I should put myself on display. Maybe I qualify as modern art now."

She was definitely a work of art. Easy on the eyes.

"I think I'd like a police escort back to my house, just in case of another attack," she said with a diabolical glint in her eyes.

Who was I to turn the young lady down?

7

The driver grabbed a towel from the cargo area and covered one of the back seats. The paint was still wet on Astrid's designer dress. I helped her into the SUV, then hustled around to the other side and climbed in. The driver zipped us across the island to the posh estates of Stingray Bay.

Astrid had done well for herself.

We cruised through the expensive neighborhood, moving past perfectly manicured yards, towering palms, and large McMansions. The front façades were lit up with exterior lighting. Luxury vehicles were parked in circular driveways—BMWs, Porsches, Range Rovers, and every other imaginable brand of high-end vehicle.

Astrid examined the modern art masterpiece that was her dress. "I think that's going to leave a permanent stain."

"I'm afraid so."

She shrugged it off. "Oh well. I have other dresses, and this gets me out of the event early. If you've been to one, you've been to them all. At least I met someone new and interesting," she said, glancing at me with a mischievous glimmer in her eyes.

"It seems the night wasn't a total loss," I said with a grin.

"So, how do you know Logan Chase and Brad Tyler?"

"It's a long story. Short version—they're in town, doing character research for an upcoming television show based on the adventures of my partner and me."

Astrid lifted an impressed brow. "You sound important."

I gave a modest shrug. "We've had some interesting cases."

Astrid said to the driver, "It's just up here on the left."

He pulled to the curb, hopped out, and got her door. I jumped out, ran around, and escorted her to the walkway. The driver asked me if I wanted him to wait or if he should come back later.

"I'll call you," I said in a hushed tone.

A knowing smirk curled his mouth, and he climbed back into the car. He waited for a moment.

I escorted Astrid up the walkway to the front porch. Her keys jingled as she fumbled with them. She unlocked the front door.

"Would you like to come inside?"

I smiled. "Yes, I would."

We stepped into the foyer, and the driver drove away as Astrid closed the front door behind us.

Like most of the mansions in Stingray Bay, it had a grand entryway with marble tile and an arched staircase that led to the second floor. Vaulted ceilings echoed our voices.

There was a parlor to one side and a small office area to the other, with the living room beyond.

"Welcome to my humble abode," she said. "Be a doll, would you, and make us a drink? Whiskey, rocks. I'm sure you can find your way up to the master bedroom."

I was sure I could.

Astrid's spiky heels clacked against the tile as she marched toward the steps.

I moved into the living room, found the wet bar, and poured a single glass of whiskey.

By the time I got upstairs, the shower was running. The bathroom door was slightly ajar, and steam seeped out like a magical mist, teasing pleasures that awaited.

I didn't see Astrid, or the dress, in the bedroom.

The furnishings were lavish with modern, yet classic, styling. A four-post bed was the centerpiece with a tufted headboard. French doors opened to a large terrace that overlooked the pool and the backyard. Amber lights from homes across the canal glowed in the distance.

A large flatscreen display was mounted to the wall across from the bed. The corners of the room were alive with vibrant plants.

Astrid poked her head out of the bathroom and gave me a look. "Are you joining me, or do you need a formal invitation?"

That was all the invitation I needed.

I smiled and delivered her drink.

She took it, pulled open the door, and kissed the glass. The amber liquid flowed past her full lips as she stood there on full display. She had speckles of red paint across her face and hair. The red pigment had stained areas of her cleavage and dripped down her flat stomach. She looked like a scream queen just out of a horror movie.

Astrid was well put together. Perfect teardrop breasts, smooth skin, toned thighs, a landing strip to the promised land. A slice of heaven.

She watched with lecherous eyes as I peeled off my shirt. Her pupils dilated, and she lifted an eyebrow. She looked ready to devour me, and I was all game.

"Am I drinking alone?"

"Long story."

"You're not a teetotaler, are you?"

I chuckled. "No. I'm doing a good deed."

"Well, you're going to be doing dirty deeds in a minute. Get those pants off and get in here."

She took another sip, spun around, and slipped into the shower.

She had a nice spin. Pert, round assets.

I didn't waste any time shedding the rest of my clothes. I followed her into the steamy shower.

We lathered each other up, and I helped her get the paint off, making sure there wasn't any left in hard-to-reach nooks and crannies.

My hands traced the curves of her supple skin, the water beading on her glorious mounds.

I pulled her close, and our lips collided, our hips pressed together. She radiated desire.

We went at it hot and heavy in the shower, her breathy moans of ecstasy echoing off the tile. Pulse-pounding, slick, and steamy.

We did the dirty deed until the hot water ran out.

Afterward, we slipped out of the shower, toweled off, and made our way to bed. We rolled around the sheets some more. When it was all said and done, we lay beside each other in a state of post-orgasmic bliss. She snuggled close and stroked my chest, her delicate fingers tracing the ridges and valleys in my abs.

"What's this *good deed* you speak of? I must know more."

"I'm donating blood stem cells."

"That's mighty generous of you."

"A minor inconvenience for me. Life changing for someone else."

"Admirable."

"Seems like the right thing to do."

"I hope everything works out for the best."

"Me too."

"Do you know who you're donating to?"

I shook my head. "A friend asked me to register, but you never know who you might be a fit for. The whole process is anonymous."

I'd been connected with a recipient through the Match for Life Foundation. For the days leading up to the procedure, I was on medication to boost production of blood stem cells. It had the unwanted side effects of fatigue, muscle aches, and headaches. All of which I was experiencing to some degree or another.

"Has that kind of thing happened at the museum before?" I asked.

Astrid rolled her eyes. "It's becoming more and more frequent. Nobody has any respect anymore. They've caused millions of dollars of damage. Done irreparable harm to priceless masterworks of art. Surely there is a better way to protest. It seems like their cause changes every week. Sometimes I don't think they even know what they're protesting." She sighed wistfully and mocked, "Ah, to be young and angry."

"Sorry about the dress."

"It's okay. I think I have an idea. I'm going to spin this into a positive. When life gives you lemons..."

We chatted more and caressed one another. I passed out beside her and woke with the morning sun as it beamed in through the French doors, filtered by the sheer curtains.

My phone buzzed my pants that were on the floor across the room.

I carefully slipped out of bed.

Astrid stirred, stretched, then rolled over.

I padded across the floor, grabbed my phone from my pants, and swiped the screen. The sheriff's gruff voice barked through the phone. "I need you and that nitwit to get over to 1137 Hibiscus Court. We have another situation."

8

Hibiscus Court was only a few blocks over in Stingray Bay. I kissed Astrid on the cheek and said goodbye.

She peeled open her sleepy eyes and smiled. In a soft, morning voice, she said, "I had fun last night."

"So did I."

"If somebody throws paint on my dress again, I'll give you a call."

"You can call me even if they don't."

She smiled, and I slipped out of the bedroom. I hustled down the steps, snuck across the tile, and stepped outside into the morning air. I started walking over to Hibiscus Court and called JD.

He didn't answer on the first ring or the second.

Finally, his groggy voice filtered through the phone. "What is it?"

"Rise and shine. We've got trouble."

I updated him on the situation and told him to meet me at the location. "How are our house guests?"

"They made it through the night without slugging each other. How did things go with Little Miss Paint Splatter?"

"The paint came off with a little elbow grease."

"I bet it did," JD said. "You missed out."

"I'm not feeling like I missed out on anything, but I'm sure you'll tell me all about it."

I ended the call and hustled down the street. Red and blue lights flickered atop patrol cars parked in front of the McMansion. A crowd of curious neighbors had gathered, and deputies loitered around the entrance to the home. Camera flashes spilled out of the front door.

I walked across the lawn, stepped inside, and moved across the foyer.

In the living room, Brenda hovered over the body. She wore pink nitrile gloves as she examined the remains.

Dietrich snapped images of the gruesome scene.

The sheriff stood there with folded arms and a tight face.

Forensic investigators swarmed about.

The familiar howl of the flat-six rumbled to the curb outside, followed by a V8. Doors opened and closed, and soon JD traipsed through the house with the two movie stars in tow.

Daniels gave them a curious glance. He muttered in my ear. "What the hell are they doing here?"

"Think of it as an extended ride along."

The sheriff frowned, not fond of the idea. "Tell them not to interfere and keep them from contaminating evidence."

"You got it, boss."

He hated it when I called him boss.

JD joined us with his entourage, and we made introductions.

"It's an honor to be here," Logan said to the sheriff. "We really appreciate the department extending this courtesy to us."

The sheriff just glared at him with narrow eyes.

"We won't cause any trouble," Logan assured. He flashed that charming smile. But his smile faded when he took a good look at the corpse on the tile in the living room. "Is he...?"

"Yes, he's dead," the sheriff said dryly.

"What happened?"

"That's what these two numbskulls are going to find out," he said, nodding at JD and me.

"Who discovered the body?" I asked.

The sheriff nodded to the maid in the kitchen, speaking with Deputy Hayes.

"What do we know?"

"Gunshot wound," the sheriff said. "One to the chest, one to the head. By the looks of things, he startled an intruder. One shot took him down, the second shot finished the job."

"Forced entry?"

"A pane of glass is broken at the back door."

The house was opulent. It was a step above most in the neighborhood, and that was saying a lot. Imported Italian marble. Lots of large canvases of fine art on the walls. It looked like several pieces were missing. Statues stood atop podiums. Sleek, expensive furniture lined the living room. As was common in most of these McMansions, the kitchen was full of state-of-the-art appliances, and the open-concept design created volumes of interior space.

I snapped photos of the scene for reference, capturing angles of the bare walls where paintings had once hung.

"The victim's name is Cornelius Worthington III," Daniels said.

He was a handsome gentleman in his mid-50s with silver hair and a touch of his natural dark color around the temples. It was tousled now but looked like it had been coiffed to perfection before the attack. Cornelius had tan skin, chiseled features, and was in good shape for his age. The color had drained from his face and lips, and his skin took on a slightly greenish tint. His cream linen suit was now speckled with blood, and crimson pooled on the tile around the body.

"Time of death?" I asked.

"Judging by the body temperature, I'd put it between 8 PM and 10 PM last night," Brenda said.

"Next of kin?"

"He's got a daughter named Zephyr," Daniels said.

"Is that the daughter over there?" I asked, nodding to a gorgeous blonde in the kitchen, wearing hot pants and a tank top.

"No. That's the maid."

"The maid?"

"We might need to hire her around the boat," JD muttered.

I couldn't disagree.

"Anything else missing besides a few paintings?" I asked.

The sheriff gave me a flat look. "Do I live here? How would I know? Talk to the maid."

JD and I moved into the kitchen.

Irina was a petite woman in her early 20s with platinum hair, elegant features, and azure eyes. The girl had a dancer's body. She spoke in broken English with a thick Russian accent. She told me Cornelius left a key for her under a rock in the backyard and she came twice a week. When she entered the home, the alarm was off, which she said was unusual. "I saw Mr. Worthington in the living room. Fuck that. I left and called the sheriff's department. I waited in my car till they arrived."

"How long have you been working for Mr. Worthington?"

"A few years." She frowned, and her eyes filled with sadness.

"You know if there's anything else missing from the house besides a few paintings?"

She shrugged.

"When was the last time you were here?"

"A few days ago."

"Were the paintings here then?"

She nodded.

"What were they?"

"Ugly."

I chuckled. "Did Mr. Worthington have any enemies?"

She shrugged again and thought for a moment. "I can't think of anyone besides his daughter." She shook her head, indicating the relationship wasn't great.

"They didn't get along?"

"Da."

"You know why?"

She shrugged again.

"Do you have a card?" JD asked.

She dug into her purse and pulled one out. It read: *Irina Pavlova, Topless Cleaning Services.*

JD lifted an excited brow. "You taking on new clients?"

"It seems I have an opening," she said dryly.

"What are your rates?"

"Depends. What do you want me to do?" It was a question with a lot of possibilities.

"What's on the menu?"

"I don't do windows."

"What else don't you do?"

She gave him a flat look. "I don't fuck my clients if that's what you're getting at."

"We have a yacht that gets a little messy after parties," JD said.

"How big?"

"Big enough."

"Then you can afford my rate. Call me when you need something polished," she teased.

I thanked her for the info and gave her a card.

"We'll be in touch," Jack said.

We rejoined the others.

"Did the neighbors hear anything?" Logan asked.

Daniels shook his head.

"Shooters probably used a suppressor," I said.

It wouldn't make the report silent, but it would knock it down by 30 dB. In a house like this with good insulation, you might not be able to hear the shot from the outside.

We stepped outside and spoke with the crowd of neighbors. JD's jade green 1974 Porsche 911 was parked at the curb. Behind it, my white Ferrari 308.

"You don't mind if I let them drive your car, do you?" JD asked.

Logan smiled. "I'll take good care of it. Sweet ride."

I wasn't exactly thrilled about the idea, but Logan was good for it if something happened.

Word had traveled that the movie stars were on the premises, and there was a bevy of housewives that lit up with glee upon the sight of the two celebrities.

Logan and Brad greeted their adoring fans with charming smiles. The women swooned, and the movie stars shook hands and signed autographs.

Paris Delaney and her news crew were on the scene, and the cameraman rushed in to capture the celebrity interaction.

I spoke with an older woman that lived across the street.

"I saw him load three paintings into the back of his SUV last night," she said.

"What time was that, ma'am?"

"Oh, I don't know. I guess around 8 o'clock or so?"

I pointed to a white Land Rover in the driveway. "Is that the vehicle that you saw Cornelius get into?"

She nodded.

"Did you see him return?"

"No."

"And you didn't hear anything later in the evening? No gunshots?"

She shook her head. "Was this a robbery gone wrong?"

"We don't know yet. Did you see anyone else around the house last night?"

The woman shook her head.

I gave her a card and moved on to other neighbors. Nobody had seen anything, but we found one guy who didn't have too many nice things to say about Cornelius Worthington III.

9

Vince Adler was in his mid-40s and stood about 6 feet tall. He had shaggy sandy-blond hair that hung just past the tops of his ears, narrow blue eyes, and chiseled features. His jaw was lined with stubble, and by his expression, he didn't seem too upset about Mr. Worthington's demise.

I flashed my badge and made introductions.

The two movie stars hovered behind us, and Vince eyed them with curiosity.

"You live in the neighborhood?" I asked.

"Right there," he said, pointing to a house catty-corner to Cornelius's estate.

"You see or hear anything unusual last night?"

He shook his head. "I see the medical examiner's van. I take it that bastard's dead."

"That is correct. Mr. Worthington is no longer with us."

Vince smiled. "Well, it seems like there is justice in this world, after all."

"So you got along with Mr. Worthington?" I snarked.

Vince laughed. "I like to think of myself as an easy-going guy. I get along with a lot of people. Just not that scumbag."

"Care to elaborate?"

He hesitated for a moment. "He belonged behind bars."

"Why is that?"

Vince's face tightened, and he glanced around. "Let's just say he's lucky he lasted as long as he did."

"This sounds personal," I said.

"You're damn right it's personal."

There was a long moment of silence.

"Why don't we talk about this in private?" I suggested, noting his hesitancy to continue.

I told Logan and Brad to hang back. JD and I escorted Vince away from the crowd.

I asked in a hushed tone, "Tell me what's going on?"

His jaw tightened, and his eyes filled. He looked around to see if anyone else was paying attention. "What's the point? He got what he deserved."

"Did you give it to him?"

His face wrinkled. "What!?"

"You seem to have a lot of animosity toward the guy."

"I didn't kill him. But if I did, I'd be totally justified."

"Why is that?"

His face tightened, and his eyes flicked between JD and me. Finally, he admitted, "Cornelius molested my daughter."

That caught us by surprise.

"Was this reported?" I asked.

Vince's jaw tightened. "I wanted to. But Sabrina begged me not to."

"That's your daughter?"

He nodded. "She pleaded with me. Said it would ruin her reputation. I know the legal process can be grueling on the victims of sexual assault. I didn't want to put her through that."

"You don't strike me as the kind of guy to let that kind of thing slide."

Through a clenched jaw, he said, "It took everything I had to hold back from walking across the street and putting a bullet in his head."

"Totally understandable if you did," JD said.

"You sure you didn't walk over there last night and settle the score?" I said.

Vince's face twisted into a scowl. "I'm sure."

"Do you own a 9mm?"

"Yeah, why? Is that what he was shot with?"

"Tell me where you were last night between 8 PM and 10 PM?"

"Now, hold on a minute."

"You just told me it took everything you had not to walk across the street and kill the guy," I said flatly. "Now he turns up with two bullets in him. I'm gonna ask questions."

Vince's jaw flexed. "That guy did things to my daughter, and now I'm the bad guy?"

"We're just trying to clarify the situation."

"I don't see it as a situation. I see it as a fortuitous event."

"So, tell me where you were last night?"

"I was at home, watching TV."

"Can anyone else verify that?"

A frustrated sigh escaped his mouth. "No."

"Is your daughter at home?"

"She's with her mother and her new husband in the Platinum Dunes."

The divorce seemed fresh. It was a sore subject.

"How old is your daughter?"

"16."

"And when did this alleged abuse take place?" I asked.

"It's not alleged."

"You saw this firsthand?"

He glared at me. "I read the text messages between the two. It didn't take a rocket scientist to figure out what was going on."

"You confronted her, and she admitted it to you?"

"What does any of this matter now? He's dead, and good riddance."

"You mind if we take a look at your pistol?"

"You got a warrant?"

"I can get one."

"Then get one. Otherwise, stop harassing me."

He stepped away and marched toward his house.

"I think we made a new friend," JD said, his voice dripping with sarcasm. "We need to have a talk with his daughter."

"You'd have to be pretty stupid to walk across the street and shoot your neighbor with a motive that obvious, but you never know."

"Maybe he's not the brightest bulb in the box."

By the time we returned to Brad and Logan, Paris and her crew were filming, asking more questions.

"How long are you in town for?" the ambitious blonde asked the duo.

"A few weeks," Logan said.

"You said you're in town doing character research. Is this usual for you?"

Logan smiled. "I like to get to know the characters I play inside and out. It helps bring authenticity to the role."

Paris focused her attention on Brad. "It's my understanding there was a little drama between you two yesterday. You've had a long-running feud. Is it all in the past now?"

Brad slung his arm around Logan, and the two smiled. "Water under the bridge."

It was total BS.

Paris didn't buy it for a second, but she moved on. "What can you tell us about the crime scene?"

"Oh, it was grizzly," Logan said.

I interrupted. "That's all for now. We can't discuss ongoing investigations."

The camera swung to me.

"Do you have any leads?" Paris asked.

"Not at this time. We're asking anyone who may have seen anything to contact the Sheriff's Department."

I shuffled Logan and Brad away from the news crew and told them to keep their mouths shut when it came to crime scenes.

JD and Logan hopped into the Porsche, and Brad rode with me in the Ferrari. We headed back to the station. Fans smiled and waved as we pulled away.

A woman shouted, "I love you, Brad!"

He smiled and waved back.

Classic rock pumped through the speakers, and the wind swirled. The V8 growled as we cruised across the island. Brad soaked up the sun, his mirrored shades reflecting the brilliant ball.

I asked, "So, what's the drama between you two?"

10

"I don't want to talk about it," Brad said. "It's embarrassing."

I gave him a look.

"Okay, he banged my wife."

"I can understand why you're upset."

"They did a movie together. Sometimes people get close on set. It's a business where people expose their deepest emotions every day for the camera. Things can get *confusing*. Lines get blurred. Sometimes it's hard to tell reality from fiction. There was a lot of speculation in the tabloids. Needless to say, she's no longer my wife."

"I don't really keep up with the tabloids."

"It's all horseshit, anyway."

I grinned.

"You dated Bree Taylor, right?"

"For a minute."

"She was a really special woman."

"Indeed."

"Look, I gotta apologize again. I shouldn't have hit him. But we're all good from here on out. No more trouble. I promise."

I took it with a grain of salt. "I take it there weren't any incidents last night after I left?"

"We had a good time. We left the museum, went to Oyster Avenue, and JD showed us around town. Then we had a little gathering on the boat. I gotta say, this is a nice break from Hollywood. Except for the dead guy. That kinda sucks."

I called Isabella, my handler at *Cobra Company*. The clandestine agency had vast intelligence resources. She could find out almost anything about anyone. She didn't have to deal with pesky little things like warrants. I couldn't use the information she gave me in a court of law, but it could often provide valuable insight.

"I need you to track GPS data and call history for a phone," I said.

"Give me the details."

I did.

"I'll get back to you as soon as I can. It's a little hectic right now."

"Everything okay?"

Brad listened intently to the brief exchange.

"Nothing I can't handle."

She ended the call.

"Is that your clandestine contact?" Brad asked.

"I can neither confirm nor deny."

He laughed. "I actually read the pilot episode."

"Is reading the script unusual for an actor?" I snarked.

"It usually changes 10 times before the camera rolls. Sometimes I just wait till they hand me the revisions in my trailer. But this one is different."

"Why did you sign on to this project?"

"David's a genius. And it looked like fun. Something I could dig into. A real adventure." He paused. "How much of this is true, and how much is made up?"

"Let's just say the names have been changed to protect the innocent and the guilty."

"It doesn't really get THAT crazy, does it?"

"Stick around long enough, you might find out."

We pulled into the lot at the station, parked, and hustled inside. Of course, everyone wanted to meet the movie stars. There were smiles and handshakes and a lot of banter about different movies that the two had been in.

JD and I left them to entertain the rest of the deputies while we filled out after-action reports.

Brad and Logan joined us in the conference room as we were finishing up.

Brad had a sly grin on his face. Once the door was closed, he said, "Okay. Tell me about the redhead. Denise. What's her story?"

I cringed and exchanged a glance with JD.

"She's off-limits," Jack said.

Brad lifted a surprised brow. "You got a thing for her?"

JD pointed at me.

"She's a real smoke show," Brad said. "Something about a woman in uniform." He paused, still grinning. "What's the deal with you two?"

"It's complicated," I said.

"It always is, isn't it?"

"What's the plan now?" Logan asked, getting back on track.

"We'll start working on a list of suspects, talk to the next of kin, and take it from there," I said.

"I'd like to be as hands-on as possible. I really want to step into your shoes. Learn to think like you think."

"Remember, you guys are just observing. Don't get involved."

"What happens if something goes down in the field?"

JD and I shared a glance.

"If anything happens, keep your head down and stay out of trouble," I cautioned.

We left the station and headed across the island to the Trident Tower. Cornelius's daughter, Zephyr, lived in the luxury high-rise. It had an attached marina filled with luxury yachts and bluewater sailboats. There was a 24-hour valet, concierge, and all the amenities—weight room, pool, laundry, you name it.

Logan and I followed in the Ferrari as JD pulled the Porsche under the carport. The valet hustled to get his door and was somewhat awestruck when Brad Tyler climbed out of the passenger seat. The valet gave Jack a ticket, then grabbed my door. I slipped him a few bills and told him to keep it up front next to Jack's.

JD flashed his badge at the glass doors, and the concierge buzzed us in. The cute blonde stared at the two movie stars with googly eyes. It took her a moment to form complex sentences. She flashed a bright smile, extended her hand, and introduced herself. "So nice to meet you."

Both movie stars put on the charm, each trying to outdo the other.

"I feel so special," she said. "What brings you to the Trident today?"

"We're here with these two gentlemen," Logan said, motioning to us.

We smiled.

"I'm so embarrassed to ask, but no one's ever going to believe me if I don't have proof."

"Would you like a picture?" Logan asked.

She nodded with excitement and pulled out her phone. She handed it to Logan, then sandwiched in between the two. She beamed a smile, and Logan held the phone out. He snapped the photo, and the camera flashed.

"Take another one just for safety," she said.

He did. Then she thumbed through the photos to make sure they looked good.

"Thank you so much," she threw her arms around him and gave him a hug and kissed his cheek. Then she did the same to Brad. She smiled with glee. "Now I can say I've kissed both of you."

"We're just gonna head on up," I said.

With a naughty glimmer in her eyes, she handed them both a card. "If there's anything I can do to make your stay in Coconut Key more enjoyable, don't hesitate to get in touch."

"I just might do that," Brad said.

JD and I made our way to the elevators while the concierge chatted with Brad and Logan for another moment.

I pushed the call button, and a moment later, the door slid open. We stepped aboard, and the two celebrities arrived just as the doors were closing. They slipped in and rode with us to the 14th floor.

We walked down the hallway, and I knocked on the door to #1414.

A moment later, a woman's voice crackled through the speaker on the video doorbell. "Can I help you?"

I flashed my badge to the lens. "Deputy Wild with Coconut County."

11

Zephyr opened the door and had the usual deer-in-the-headlights look when she saw Brad and Logan standing behind us. Her face twisted with confusion, trying to figure out what they were doing at her doorstep.

Denise had already called with the unpleasant business of a death notification. Zephyr didn't look too broken up about it.

"We just have a few questions for you about your father," I said.

"I don't think I'll be of much help. I haven't spoken to him in a while."

"I spoke with the maid."

Zephyr rolled her eyes.

"She mentioned you two were... *estranged*."

She chuckled. "That's a polite way to put it."

"Do you mind if we come inside?"

Zephyr stepped aside and motioned us in.

We strolled down the foyer to the living room. It was a nice condo. Floor-to-ceiling window walls that opened to a large terrace. An open-concept design with sleek, modern furniture and coastal accents. There was a large flatscreen display and pastel works of abstract art on the walls.

"Not to be a fangirl, but I really liked you in *Rectifier*," she said to Logan.

Zephyr was a gorgeous young girl in her early 20s with pouty lips, sculpted cheekbones, and ice-blue eyes. She had short blonde hair that was spunky but not quite a pixie cut. She had a luscious figure to go with it.

Logan smiled. "Thank you. I really enjoyed the role. It's a great character. I look forward to filming several more."

"When is the next movie coming out?"

"Production starts in the fall."

Zephyr's gaze turned to Brad. "What about you?"

"After this project, I'm doing a serious dramatic work."

"About what?"

"The zombie apocalypse," he said dryly.

Zephyr laughed.

Brad smiled.

"When I woke up this morning, I never thought I'd have two movie stars standing in my apartment," Zephyr said. "But I'm glad you're here. Can I get you anything to drink? Coffee, tea, me?" she said, not even trying to hide her flirting.

I tried to steer the conversation back on track. "About your father..."

She rolled her eyes and groaned. "Right, I almost forgot," she snarked. "You have any idea who did this? To whom should I send my regards?"

"Usually, when I tell someone their parent is deceased, they're not quite as enthused."

"What can I say, deputies? Cornelius and I had a contentious relationship."

"Contentious enough for you to go to his house and put two bullets into him?"

She laughed. "That seems too good for him."

"You know, that seems to be a common theme among the people I've met that knew your father."

"I'm not surprised."

Zephyr looked at the movie stars. "Are you sure you don't want anything to drink?"

"We're fine, thank you," Logan said. "Don't pay any attention to us. We're just here to observe."

"Studying for a role?"

The two stars nodded.

I steered things back on course. "Can you tell me where you were between 8 PM and 10 PM last night?"

She lifted a sultry eyebrow. "You really think that I killed my father?"

"You're certainly making a case for it."

"I was here."

"Alone?"

"Sadly. I left about 10:30 PM, hit a few bars on Oyster Avenue, ended up at *Bumper*, then *Speakeasy*."

"Can anyone verify that?"

"My friend, Lauren. I'll give you her number, if you want?"

"Please."

"Do you know Vince Adler?"

Her eyes narrowed as she recalled the name. "Lives across the street from my father. Why?"

"Did you grow up in that house?"

"In my teen years. I left as soon as I could."

"Vince has levied some rather serious allegations against your father."

"That doesn't surprise me. What's he saying?"

I told her.

Zephyr didn't seem shocked.

"Do you think there's any truth to that?" I asked.

"Judging from personal experience, I'd say the girl's telling the truth."

I cringed. "Personal experience?"

"Do you need me to spell it out for you?"

"I know this may be uncomfortable, but we try to eliminate ambiguities."

Her posture stiffened. Then she stood tall. "My father abused me," she said, taking ownership of her past. She almost wore it like a badge of courage. "And by that, I don't mean he smacked me around. I mean, he..."

"I get the picture." It was hard to listen to something like that.

"So, when I hear a story about him abusing another young girl, I believe it."

"Did you ever tell anyone about the abuse?"

"I told my mother."

"How did she respond?"

"She didn't believe me." Her eyes filled. "No woman wants to hear that about her husband. She said I was making it up for attention. So I shut down. I held it all in, and the abuse continued. I didn't tell anyone. I was afraid no one would believe me." She broke down into sobs, unable to hold it back any longer. "You have no idea what that does to a young girl. This is a man that I was supposed to love and trust. A man that was supposed to take care of me, and yet he's doing these things. I can't tell you how confusing that was. And still is. Not only did he steal my childhood, he stole my ability to love him in a healthy way. He stole my ability to mourn his death. He stole everything. So, yeah, fuck that guy."

She grabbed a tissue from the coffee table and blotted her eyes. Her mascara was slightly smudged.

"Did your mother ever grow suspicious?" I asked.

Zephyr sniffled and composed herself. She was used to stuffing it all away and putting on a good front. "I think toward the end she began to realize that something wasn't right, but I don't think she ever wanted to admit it. Her whole world would fall apart. It's a big leap for someone to take. I remember things got tense between them toward the end."

"Of the marriage?"

"They went on a trip to Monaco. I never saw my mother again. She drowned in a boating accident."

Brad and Logan listened to the story, slack-jawed.

"You suspect foul play was involved," I said, reading her expression.

She nodded. "My mother was an excellent swimmer."

Zephyr blotted her eyes again. There was a long silence. The mood in the room was heavy.

She pulled herself together and stood tall. "But that's all behind me, and I'm determined not to let my past equal my future." She frowned. "But I can't even mourn that bastard."

I exchanged a look with JD.

"I know that makes me out to be a prime suspect," she said. "But I didn't kill my father. He stole my childhood. I certainly wouldn't let him steal the rest of my life by doing something stupid."

"Do you own a gun?" I asked.

"No. Even if I did, you think I'd be dumb enough to keep it around here after using it to shoot my father?"

"You mind if we look around?"

"Knock yourself out."

"Several paintings were missing at your father's house. If I showed you pictures of the interior, do you think you could tell me what's been taken?"

"I haven't been inside his house in years. My father was an astute collector, but he got bored easily. He'd acquire a piece, keep it for a few years, then sell it. Of course, he had his favorites that would stay in his collection forever. He had an eye for art. He just knew when something would appreciate in value. I never saw him lose money on a deal. He was charmed that way. Made a fortune in the stock market."

"And you're the sole heir, yes?"

She smiled. "Yes, I am. Though he could have written me out of the will. Who knows? Maybe he left it all to charity."

"You seem like you've done well for yourself."

"I made him give me a trust fund. I threatened to expose him to all his country club buddies. I told him how many zeros I wanted in my bank account, and he filled it up. That was the end of our relationship. I'm comfortable. I have more than enough. His money certainly wasn't a motive for murder."

We searched the apartment but didn't find any weapons.

I believed Zephyr. She wasn't stupid enough to keep a murder weapon around.

My phone buzzed with a call from Isabella.

12

"Cornelius left his house at 8:12 PM the night of his murder," Isabella said. "I should say, his phone left the residence. It traveled to the *VisionScape* gallery at 897 Mallard Lane. It was there for roughly half an hour, then returned to the house in Stingray Bay."

"So he was still alive at 8:45 PM," I said.

"One could reasonably assume. Before he left the house, there was a call between him and a woman named Astrid Blomqvist. She owns the gallery."

I cringed.

Isabella heard me sigh. "You know her?"

"You could say that."

"Intimately?"

"You could say that."

Isabella laughed. "This should be interesting. You want me to track her phone?"

"Please."

Her fingers danced across the keys. A moment later, she said, "Her phone left the gallery around 9 PM and headed to the museum. After that—"

"I know what happened after that."

She laughed.

I thanked her for the information, ended the call, and updated JD on the situation.

"Uh, oh," he said in an amused tone.

We rounded up the movie stars, left Zephyr's condo, and walked the hallway back toward the elevators.

"That was some story she told," Logan said.

"Heartbreaking."

"How do you deal with hearing that kind of tragic story on a regular basis?"

I shrugged. "It's never easy to hear something like that."

"I feel terrible about her situation. But she's also clearly a suspect."

"It's a balance. At the end of the day, we're searching for the truth."

We took the elevator down to the lobby. The concierge greeted us again with a bright smile. "Leaving so soon?"

The movie stars smiled.

"Maybe we'll be back," Logan said.

"Stop by anytime." She fluttered her eyelashes.

We stepped outside, and the valet hustled to pull the cars around. Brad hopped in with JD, and Logan rode with me. We drove to the gallery for an awkward conversation with Astrid.

It was in an upscale strip center with high-end boutiques.

The door chimed as we pushed inside. Large canvases hung on the wall. Colorful abstract paintings with vibrant swatches of color. Classic Impressionist works by notable artists. There were a few Renaissance masterworks, along with sculptures and contemporary installations. Works by Picasso, Matisse, Salvador Dali, Max Ernst, Campendonk, Julian Krause, Jackson Pollock, Kandinsky, Rothko, and even a Warhol.

The gallery had that hushed reverence that you'd find in church.

A patron drifted around, admiring the works.

Astrid spotted us right away and started toward us. She flashed a brilliant smile. "Good morning. To what do I owe the pleasure?"

"We're here in an official capacity," I said.

"Sounds serious," she said, mocking me. "Is something wrong?"

"I don't know if you're aware, but Cornelius Worthington is dead."

Her eyes rounded, and a look of surprise washed over her face, which was quickly followed by sadness. "That's terrible. I just spoke with him last night. What happened?"

She was asking the right questions.

A gorgeous young woman standing nearby couldn't help but overhear. She joined us. I think she was looking for an excuse to get close to the celebrities.

Astrid introduced her. "This is my assistant, Joyce."

We exchanged pleasantries.

She had smooth skin, raven hair, and crystal eyes. Full lips and alluring features.

I gave them limited details. "We know Cornelius visited the gallery last night between 8:15 PM and 8:45 PM," I said.

"Yes, he stopped by," Astrid replied.

"What did you two talk about?"

She looked at me with suspicious eyes. An uncomfortable realization came over her—I was looking at her as a suspect. "He brought in some pieces that he wanted me to sell on consignment. I told him I had potential buyers. I helped him unload the artwork, we chatted for a few minutes, then he left."

"Was that a regular occurrence?"

"I've done a lot of business with Mr. Worthington over the years. He was a valued client."

I asked Joyce if she was at the gallery last night.

She exchanged a glance with Astrid before answering. "No. I'm only part-time."

"It seems that someone broke into the house, and Cornelius startled the intruder. Perhaps he was ambushed. Hard to say."

Concern tensed Astrid's face. "This is just horrible. Do you have any leads?"

"Not at this time. We are pursuing all avenues. What did you do after your visit with Cornelius?"

"I closed up shop, then headed over to the museum, where I ran into you," she said in a sharp tone, growing annoyed by my implications.

"Can I see those paintings that Cornelius brought to you?"

She hesitated for a moment. "Sure." She addressed Joyce and pointed to the gallery patron. "Would you make sure he doesn't need any assistance?"

"Certainly." Joyce excused herself. "Gentlemen, it was a pleasure meeting you."

The movie stars smiled.

"The pleasure was ours," Brad said.

Astrid led us across the gallery and motioned to two paintings on the wall—one was a Picasso, the other was a painting by Max Ernst.

"Nice," Logan said.

The prices were eye-watering.

"Both are spoken for, but if you're looking for something in particular, let me know. I have connections around the world."

"Logan is quite the art collector," Brad said. "At least, that's what my ex-wife tells me."

Logan frowned and shot him a look.

"Just two paintings?" I said.

"Yes," Astrid replied.

"Interesting. A neighbor recalled seeing him load three into his truck."

Without missing a beat, "Maybe she's mistaken. What is it that they say about eyewitness testimony…?"

"It's often wrong." I knew the answer, but I asked anyway. "What did you do after you spoke with Cornelius?"

She gave me a salty stare. "Was it that unmemorable?"

I responded with a look. It was quite memorable.

"After Cornelius left, I gathered my things, closed up shop, and went to the museum, where I was promptly doused with paint. I think you know the rest. And for the record, I didn't kill Cornelius Worthington. As I said, he was a valued client." She glared at me. "Is there anything else?"

"I think that's all for now. Thanks for your cooperation."

"Anytime," she said with a bit of venom in her voice. She turned her attention to Logan. "If there's anything I can help you with, please get in touch."

She gave him a card.

We left the gallery and stepped outside.

"That was a bit awkward, wasn't it?" Logan said.

"Just a little bit," I replied in an understated tone.

"Does it create a conflict of interest? Shouldn't you recuse yourself from the case?"

"It's a small town. We're short on manpower. And I'm reasonably confident she wasn't involved."

"Still, there's a window of opportunity," Logan said. "She could have followed him home, shot him, then gone to the museum."

"She leaves her phone at the gallery when she commits the deed, then comes back and picks it up, then heads to the event," Brad said.

"The timing is tight," I said.

"But not impossible."

"I think you guys might make good deputies after all," I said.

They both smiled.

"Maybe we should just hand the case over to them," JD said.

"I'm down," Brad replied.

"Who knows, maybe the sheriff will deputize you," I snarked.

They seemed excited at the prospect.

"If it makes you feel better, I have no problem following this case through to conclusion, no matter where the evidence leads," I said.

Logan repeated the line in character with the same intensity.

JD and I gave him a look.

"What are you doing?" I asked.

"Rehearsing," he said as if it were a stupid question.

We climbed into the cars and drove across the island to the Platinum Dunes to catch up with Sabrina Adler. I wanted to hear her side of the story.

13

The mansions of the Platinum Dunes were similar to Stingray Bay. Of course, residents of either neighborhood could give you a list of reasons why one was better than the other.

We banged on the door to the McMansion at 679 Pine Court.

A soft voice crackled through the speaker in the video doorbell a moment later. "Can I help you?"

I flashed my badge to the lens and made introductions. "I'm looking for Sabrina Adler."

"She's not here right now."

"Do you know when she'll be back?"

"No."

The voice was young. I suspected I was talking to Sabrina.

The line crackled with static, then she gasped, "Is that Logan Chase and Brad Tyler!?"

The two leaned into the camera lens.

"In the flesh," Brad said with a smile.

"Oh, my God! No way!"

"Way," Logan said.

"Don't go anywhere! I'll be right there."

Footsteps rumbled inside, and Sabrina shrieked with joy. She pulled open the door with wide eyes and gasped again. She covered her mouth in shock and tried to scream, but no sound came out. The giddy girl bounced up and down excitedly.

Sabrina was a gorgeous young woman with raven hair, azure eyes, and the kind of clear skin you'd see on the cover of a teen magazine.

When she was finally able to speak, she said, "What are you doing here?"

Logan gave her the standard answer.

I tried to steer things back on course. "We just have a few questions for you about Cornelius Worthington."

She frowned. "I'm not really comfortable talking about him."

"I understand this is a difficult subject."

She ignored me and fixed her gaze on the movie stars. She pulled out her cell phone and snapped selfies with the two hunks. "Oh, my God. This is so awesome!"

"You heard that Cornelius is dead, right?" I asked.

"Yeah. Duh! It's all over the news. Do you know who killed him?"

She was hard to read. I couldn't tell if she was upset, happy, or putting on a front.

"Your father said—"

"I don't care what my father said. I'm not speaking to him. He's an asshole."

"Can you describe your relationship with Cornelius Worthington?"

The muscles in her jaw flexed. "I don't want to talk about it."

"It's my understanding that there was an assault," I said, putting it delicately.

Her face crinkled. "There was no assault."

"That's not what your father said."

She huffed. "Fuck him." She paused, curiosity getting the best of her. "What did he say?"

I told her.

She rolled her eyes. "I'm old enough to make my own decisions."

"Not in the eyes of the state."

"Fuck the state."

"So, there was something between you and Cornelius."

"Maybe there was. Maybe there wasn't. So, I like older men. Sue me."

She returned her gaze to the movie stars and smiled. "How long are you in town for?"

"A few weeks," Brad said.

"We should totally hang out. I can take you to all the cool clubs."

Brad gave her a suspicious look. "You're 16."

"17," she corrected. "And I have a fake ID."

Her face went long as she realized what she admitted.

I gave her a stern gaze. "Let's see the ID."

"I don't have it anymore. I lost it." She said in a flippant tone, then flashed a smug smile. Her eyes darted back to the movie stars. "You should ditch these two losers. They're a total buzz kill."

Brad and Logan laughed uncomfortably.

"Well, these *losers* are trying to solve a murder," Logan said.

Sabrina's mother appeared in the foyer. "What's going on here?"

"Mom, look who it is!"

Her eyes flicked to the movie stars. Her stern demeanor changed. She smiled and introduced herself. "I'm Stephanie Smith. Sabrina's mother." She batted her eyelashes, and her cheeks flushed. "This is such a pleasant surprise."

"I would have thought you two were sisters," Brad said, laying on the charm.

Mrs. Smith blushed.

"We're here with the deputies," Logan said.

I flashed my badge.

"What's this about?"

"Cornelius Worthington."

A look of disdain twitched her face. It told me exactly how she felt about the deceased.

"They think dad killed him," Sabrina said. Her eyes flicked to me. "I mean, that's why you're here, isn't it?"

Mrs. Smith's stern eyes found Sabrina. "You're grounded, young lady. That means no visitors. No matter who they are."

"Mom!"

"We just have a few questions," I said.

"Sabrina, get inside and go back up to your room."

"Mom!?"

"Now."

She huffed and sulked. "Bye, Brad. Bye, Logan."

Sabrina stepped into the foyer. As she stood behind her mother, she mouthed the words, "Call me," to Brad and Logan before trudging upstairs.

"Your ex-husband made several concerning allegations against Mr. Worthington," I said.

"And you think my ex-husband walked across the street and shot him?"

"He has motive, means, and opportunity. No alibi for last night. Do you believe that's something he's capable of?"

14

"I think anybody is capable of anything," Mrs. Smith said.

"What kind of guns does your husband own?" I asked.

"Former husband," Mrs. Smith corrected. "I don't really know. They all look the same to me. He had a few pistols, a few rifles, a shotgun, I believe."

"He seemed rather upset when we spoke with him."

"Rightfully so. Mr. Worthington had no business taking an interest in my daughter."

"So you believe the allegations to be true?"

She folded her arms and sighed. "I don't know what exactly transpired between Mr. Worthington and my daughter. But Vincent and I both agreed we didn't want her dragged through the mud. As you can see, she can be a bit... precocious. Now that Mr. Worthington is gone, I see no need to ever think of him again. If I were you, gentlemen, I would leave the matter alone. Somebody did the world a favor. Maybe you should be grateful."

Her response didn't totally surprise me. There were a lot of things in the Platinum Dunes and Stingray Bay that got swept under the rug. Things that nobody wanted to talk about. In a neighborhood where appearance and reputation were everything, people avoided scandal.

"Well, it sure has been a delight meeting you both," Mrs. Smith said, her eyes sparkling at the two movie stars. Her gaze flicked to us and turned serious again. "If there's nothing else, I really should be getting about my day."

I gave her a card and thanked her for her cooperation. We left the porch and headed back down the walkway to the vehicles.

Sabrina peered through an upstairs window and waved goodbye.

The celebrities waved back.

"What do you think?" Logan asked, smiling back at the girl.

"If that guy got hold of my daughter," JD said, "he wouldn't last as long as he did."

"You're just going to let this slide?" Logan asked.

"Nobody's letting anything slide," I assured. "Right now, Vince Adler is our best lead. We'll see what else turns up."

We hopped in the cars and drove back to Diver Down to grab lunch. We all took a seat at the bar, and Teagan fawned all over our guests.

We chowed down and shot the breeze. Customers gawked and whispered. A few came up and asked for autographs and selfies.

The movie stars obliged.

It was part of the package. They were used to it. The price of fame. You could never stay in your own head for long. Someone was always interrupting.

We were finishing the meal when my phone buzzed with a call from Sheriff Daniels.

"I need you two numbskulls to get over to 1214 Dolphin Park."

"What's going on?"

"Are those two tagalongs still with you?"

"Yep."

"Make sure they stay out of trouble and don't contaminate the crime scene."

15

Red and blue lights atop patrol cars flickered. A crowd of curious neighbors gathered outside the house. There were two black SUVs with tinted windows and government plates parked at the curb.

Paris Delaney and her crew were already on the scene.

Camera flashes spilled out of the open front door.

It was a nice home with pastel yellow siding, white shutters, and a red door. The yard was well groomed, and palms swayed overhead. The flower bed was full of colorful blooms and had recently been re-mulched. The smell of manure permeated the air.

JD and I walked across the lawn, and the movie stars followed. I cautioned them, "Remember, don't go traipsing through the house. Stay close to us. Observe. I have a feeling this one isn't going to be pretty."

"The last one wasn't pretty," Logan said.

Whispers of gossip rifled through the crowd when they spotted the celebrities. Some fans shouted their names and begged for autographs and pictures.

Logan and Brad just smiled and waved. We stepped into the foyer, and I told them to stay put. JD and I moved to the edge of the living room.

Dietrich snapped photos of the two bodies, and forensic investigators swarmed about. Brenda hovered over one of the corpses, wearing her usual pink nitrile gloves.

The interior was homey. Soft cushy cloth furniture, tan hardwood floors, pastel seascapes, and French doors that opened to a small patio and a pool. There was plenty of wrought iron patio furniture and a propane barbecue grill. The area was thick with foliage, and ivy climbed the walls, giving it a cozy, intimate vibe. A nice place to sit in the evening and sip a drink.

The gentlemen in navy suits with trimmed haircuts and black aviator sunglasses gave me concern. I figured they belonged to the government vehicles parked out front. There were five of them.

The victims lay on the hardwoods amid pools of blood. Crimson splattered the walls and the furniture. The husband and wife couple were in their early 40s. The man had light brown hair, average features, and a day's worth of stubble. The woman had short dark hair, brown eyes, and tan skin.

They were your normal suburban couple.

What the hell were the suits doing here? I figured they were with one of the three-letter agencies, and I was pretty sure I knew which one.

"What happened?" I asked the sheriff.

"I don't know, but the suits seem to have a theory," Daniels muttered in a doubtful voice. He didn't like the looks of this.

Neither did I.

The suits stepped toward us and made introductions. They flashed their credentials.

"Deputies Donovan and Wild," Daniels said. "They're a special crimes unit."

"I'm Officer Carter Nash." He pointed out his associates. "Officers Mason Maddox, Owen Wright, Alex Devlin, and Jonathan Pierce."

I doubted any of those names were real.

Nash's eyes flicked down the foyer to the movie stars.

They smiled and waved.

"Why are they here?" Nash asked.

I told him.

Unlike most of the people we had encountered, the suits seemed unimpressed. These guys were all business.

Carter Nash was late 30s. His brown hair was starting to recede, giving him a large forehead. He had narrow brown eyes and a serious face—one that defaulted to a scowl.

Mason Maddox was taller, with slick black hair, brown eyes, a square jaw, and a muscular physique. It looked like he could have been on a daytime soap opera.

Owen Wright was in his early 40s, with trimmed brown hair just starting to get hints of gray at the temples. He had blue eyes and a cocky smile. They all looked like they had secrets to keep, as did most in their profession.

Alex Devlin was mid-30s with wavy dark hair, a goatee, and narrow brown eyes.

Jonathan Pierce was the youngest of the bunch with a square face, deep blue eyes, and stylish coffee-colored hair. An arrogant, cocky look was a permanent feature.

"What brings you to our neck of the woods?" I asked.

"It seems we have a situation on our hands," Nash said.

"I see that. Care to go into detail?"

Nash took a breath, and his face tightened. He exchanged a glance with his colleagues, then said, "What I'm about to tell you has national security implications."

"I'm all ears," I said.

16

"We have reason to believe that a rogue officer is responsible," Nash said.

We all looked surprised by that information.

Nash continued, "We believe that Officer Penelope Cross entered the home under false pretenses, shot Mr. and Mrs. Nielsen, and abducted their daughter Haley."

"Why would she do that?" I asked.

"I'm afraid that information is classified at this time," Nash said.

My eyes narrowed at him.

"I wish I could say more. You understand." He paused. "Of course, we are not going to interfere with your investigation. By all means, do your thing. As far as the media is concerned, I would like to keep the details limited. Tell them Penelope Cross abducted Haley Nielsen. Give them no further information. I figure the more resources we can throw at this, the better."

"Have you tracked their cell phones?" I asked.

"Both are off the grid. I suspect Officer Cross will be using a burner phone from here on out. She's a professional. She knows her craft well. She'll be hard to find. She can go dark and stay dark." Nash paused. "I must warn you, she's extremely dangerous."

"I see that."

He displayed a picture of Penelope on his phone.

She was a stunning woman with light brown hair and smoldering blue eyes. There was certainly an air of mystery about her. He flipped the screen to display a picture of Haley. She was 14, with long, straight blonde hair, big blue eyes, and an innocent face.

"Send me those photos, along with any other information that you think might be helpful," I said.

Officer Nash nodded. "We've spoken with some of the neighbors, but I suggest you do your due diligence."

I excused myself and stepped to Mr. Nielsen's remains.

"Small caliber," Brenda said. "Probably 9mm. No shell casings. Somebody policed up their brass."

It made sense. A professional would try to remove as much evidence as possible.

"I'll know more once I get back to the lab," Brenda said.

"Time of death?"

"Maybe an hour ago, give or take. Allow for the usual two-hour window."

Dietrich continued to snap photos.

The forensic team analyzed the splatter patterns and would recreate the trajectory of the gunshots. They'd be able to pinpoint the approximate location of the shooter when both individuals were shot.

The analysis would take time to put together.

I stepped away from Mr. Nielsen's body and moved to Mrs. Nielsen's remains. She was on the other side of the living room. It looked like both had been shot from somewhere near the edge of the foyer.

I soaked in the scene, absorbing all the small details—the way they were positioned, the splatter patterns, etc. I tried to recreate the event in my mind.

JD followed me down the hallway to the bedrooms. We found Haley's room and took a look around. It was a typical teenage girl's room—light pink walls, a white four-post bed in the center, a desk, a bookshelf, and a few pictures of teen idols on the walls.

There were papers and pens on the desk. A journal, sticky notes, but no computer.

JD and I looked around the room and searched the closet but didn't find a laptop or a tablet.

It was unusual.

The window was ajar, and the breeze drifted through the room. The screen was off, and it looked like someone had made a quick exit.

I peered outside and surveyed the backyard—green grass, a small patio, Adirondack chairs, a barbecue grill. The yard was lined with flowers against the wooden fence. The blooms looked trampled in a spot where someone had gone over.

JD and I returned to the living room. I had a few more questions for Nash.

"Describe the scenario when you first discovered the bodies," I said.

"Sure," Nash said. "We tracked Officer Cross to this location. When we arrived, we saw her vehicle parked out front. We rushed inside."

"Was the door open, or did you force your way in?"

There were no signs of forced entry at the front door, but I wanted to hear his response.

"It was slightly ajar when we arrived," Nash said. "I entered the house first with my weapon drawn and quickly discovered the bodies in the living room. We believe the fugitive exited through the girl's bedroom window."

His story was consistent with my observations.

The other officers nodded in agreement.

"We're going to make an exit," Nash said. "I'll leave you to handle the press. If you need anything, don't hesitate to get in touch."

He had texted me his contact info, along with the photos of Penelope Cross and Haley Nielsen. He gave a nod to his crew, and they followed him out the front door, leaving a swirl of cologne in their wake.

They made a beeline for their SUV and ignored the questions and camera flashes of the reporters. Owen took Penelope's vehicle and followed Nash as he pulled away from the curb. He must have had a key fob to Penelope's vehicle.

The crowd parted, and the two vehicles sped away.

"That was weird," JD muttered. "There's more going on than what they're saying."

That was always the case with the three-letter agencies.

"What now?" Logan asked with eager eyes.

I texted Isabella and sent her the picture of Penelope Cross. "Tell me everything you can about this woman."

17

A bevy of reporters rushed to greet us as we stepped outside. Cameras flashed, and microphones hovered overhead. As soon as they caught a glimpse of the celebrities standing behind us, I figured they'd lose interest in the crime.

"Deputy Wild, what can you tell us?" Paris shouted.

I gave her limited details. "If anyone has any information as to the whereabouts of Penelope Cross or Haley Nielson, please contact the Coconut County Sheriff's Department."

"Are you working in conjunction with any federal agencies?"

"I can't discuss anything else at this time. Thank you."

I stepped away from the camera, and all lenses focused in on Brad and Logan.

"This is the second major crime scene you've visited. Did you expect to see such gruesome scenes when you came to Coconut Key?"

"We were mentally prepared for anything," Logan said. "We've seen some terrible things, no doubt. It's given us new insight, and we both have the utmost respect for law enforcement and the difficult job they have to do."

He flashed that winning smile, and so did Brad.

"Are you actively involved in the investigation?" another reporter shouted.

"We're just along for the ride," Brad said.

We canvassed the area, talking to neighbors on the street and knocking on doors. Mrs. Bowman lived directly across the street. She was in her late 80s with stark white hair that hung past her ears. Her thin skin, spotted with age, clung to her tiny frame. In a frail, shaky voice, she said, "I looked out the window and saw a black SUV pull to the curb. A woman got out, strolled the walkway, and knocked on the front door. If I recall, Mrs. Nielsen answered. They chatted for a few minutes before she invited her inside."

"Then what happened?" I asked.

"Well, I didn't want to be nosy," Mrs. Bowman said. She certainly had curious tendencies. "I thought it was odd. I didn't recognize the car or the woman. I stepped away from the window and went into the kitchen, and when I came back, there was another black SUV. The front door was slightly ajar."

"How much time had passed between the first vehicle and the second?"

She thought about it for a moment. "Oh, I don't know. Maybe 15 minutes. Maybe less."

"Did you hear any gunshots?"

"No. I don't remember hearing anything like that. But I did have the television on, and the dishwasher was running."

I gave her my card and told her to call me if she remembered any additional details.

Brad and Logan were still mugging for the cameras.

We rounded them up and climbed into the cars. Logan hopped into the Ferrari with me, and Brad rode with JD. They each wanted to get as much time with their characters as possible.

We drove around the crowd and headed back to the station to fill out after-action reports. Logan and Brad took the opportunity to mix and mingle with the other deputies.

By the time we finished typing, Logan and Brad were chatting up Denise. Brad sat on the edge of her desk, regaling her with stories of his time on various sets.

Denise ate it up.

She giggled, laughed, and flipped her hair, hanging on his every word.

I tried to hide my annoyance at the situation.

JD muttered, "You better watch out. He might steal her away from you."

"I think she's got more sense than that."

"Never underestimate the power of celebrity."

My relationship with Denise was complicated. The sheriff had a rule about interoffice romances.

I decided to break up the party, but Isabella called before I had a chance.

"What did you get yourself into this time?" she asked.

"Oh, the usual," I said, downplaying the situation.

"There's nothing *usual* about this. Penelope Cross... She's a ghost."

"What do you mean?"

"I can't find anything on her. You know what happens when I can't find out information about people? I get concerned."

"Somebody scrubbed her file."

"Somebody with connections. Usually, I can find breadcrumbs and piece something together. But she's been wiped from every database there is."

"Can you put any mobile devices at the Nielsen residence during the time of the attack?"

"The only cell phones that ping the tower from that residence belong to the Nielsens. There's nothing else. You're dealing with professionals."

"What about Haley Neilsen's cell phone?"

"That went off the grid just after they left the property."

"Can you tell where it went?"

"From the GPS data, it looks like they exited through the backyard and hopped the fence. Her phone was off by the time they hit the next street over."

"What time was that?"

She told me.

"Dig into a guy named Carter Nash." I gave her his associates' names as well.

"I'll let you know what, if anything, I find out."

I ended the call, slipped the phone back into my pocket, and made my way to Denise's desk. "I hate to break up the party, but we need to roll."

"Aw, you can't steal them away so soon," Denise said.

"Why don't you guys go on without us?" Brad said. "We'll catch up."

"Don't you want to meet the band?" I asked.

"We've got plenty of time for that."

I forced a smile. "Whatever you guys want to do."

"How about you leave the keys, and we'll meet you back at the marina?"

After a moment's pause, I dug into my pocket and handed them over.

Logan snatched them. "I'll drive." He winked. "Your car's in good hands."

18

I hopped into the Porsche with JD, and we headed across the island to the warehouse district.

"I told you," he said.

"I just don't want her to get hurt."

We pulled into the lot at the warehouse, and JD found a place to park near the entrance. The usual band of miscreants loitered around, drinking beer and smoking cigarettes, among other things.

We were greeted with high-fives as we entered the warehouse and made our way down the dim hallway to the practice room. The place rumbled with the sound of other bands rocking out. Bass drums thundered, and guitars howled.

The guys noodled around on their instruments when we stepped into the practice space. Styxx sat behind his candy apple red drum set, Dizzy ran through some scales, and Crash plucked a fat rhythm on bass.

They all looked at the door with eager eyes, but there was no one coming in behind us. JD closed the door, and the guys in the band looked confused and disappointed. They slumped.

"Where are Logan and Brad?" Crash asked.

"Change of plans," I said.

They'd all hung out the night of the museum adventure, and the guys had taken a liking to them. The movie stars weren't bad guys, but the sideshow got old quick.

The guys ran through their set. As usual, there were a few groupies in the practice space by the end of it. Afterward, JD took the guys out to dinner, then we hit our usual haunt for a few drinks. Of course, I had to live vicariously as the others indulged. I was counting the days until the procedure.

Tide Pool was packed, and pretty people frolicked in the outdoor pool. Taut fabric clung to perky peaks, and water beaded on supple skin. The smell of chlorine and fruity drinks filled the night air. Water splashed and sloshed. A beach ball got batted around, and chill music pumped through speakers.

It didn't take long for the guys to draw the attention of local groupies. Whatever local fame they had managed to garner evaporated when Logan and Brad joined us. They became the center of attention and soaked up all the lustful eyes of bikini-clad beauties. Everyone in the bar migrated onto the patio by the outdoor pool.

JD bought a round of shots for the movie stars. They toasted, downed the whiskey, then Jack ordered another round.

Logan didn't quite look like he'd swallowed gasoline this time. He was adapting, but this was still a little more than he was used to.

We stayed for a couple hours. The crowd seemed to get bigger and bigger with each passing moment as word of their appearance spread. The drinks kept flowing, and the crowd kept growing.

We invited a select number of people back to the boat for an after-party.

The paparazzi were waiting outside Tide Pool as we left.

Cameras flashed and flickered.

Logan weaved down the sidewalk. He spent the evening trying to keep up with Jack, drink for drink. But that wasn't a good idea for a rank amateur.

I cleared the way for him and kept the photographers from getting too aggressive.

I took my keys back and drove him to the marina. Logan was pretty lit up.

"This is fucking awesome," he slurred. "I'm having the best time. I'm so glad I'm doing this project."

I'm not sure he'd feel the same way in the morning.

At Diver Down, I parked the Ferrari, and I helped Logan down the dock. Somehow, I managed to keep him from falling into the water.

The paparazzi ate it up.

This was newsworthy footage for them.

I got aboard the boat, and our entourage followed.

It was a pretty typical after-party, just amped up a notch. We made our way up to the sky deck, and Jack dealt out drinks from behind the bar. It didn't take long for bikini tops to hit the deck and vivacious ladies to slip into the Jacuzzi.

"I gotta hand it to you boys," Brad said. "You party like rock stars."

JD smiled. "Work hard, play harder."

"Amen!" Brad said, lifting his glass.

They clinked and sipped the fine whiskey.

"Hell, this is tame," JD said. "You ain't seen nothing yet."

"I had a suspicion this project was going to be a good time. It has not disappointed so far."

My phone buzzed my pocket. I pulled it out and looked at the screen. It was from an unknown caller on the encrypted messaging app, *Memo*. I swiped the screen and took the call. "Hello?"

A woman's voice filtered through. "Is this Deputy Tyson Wild?"

"Who's asking?"

19

"My name is Penelope Cross. I think you're looking for me."

I lifted a surprised brow. "I am. Is Haley with you?"

"She is."

"Is she safe?"

"Yes. And I intend to keep her that way."

"How about you tell me where you are, and I'll come to you."

"No."

"Okay. Tell me how you see this working out. You're in a lot of trouble, and I want to make sure that Haley stays safe."

"I know this is going to be difficult for you to believe, but I'm not the bad guy."

"Killing two people and kidnapping their daughter would put you solidly in the bad guy category."

"I didn't kidnap Haley. I rescued her. I don't know what you've been told, but I would imagine it's along the lines of *I've gone rogue*. I'm sure you've been told this is a matter of national security. And that I'm dangerous."

"That's a good summary."

"All of those things are true, but not in the way that it's been portrayed. Carter Nash is the bad guy. Not me."

"Why am I not surprised that you said that?"

"Because you're perceptive. You've got good instincts, and you're good at what you do."

"You don't even know me."

"I know more about you than you think. I wouldn't have called otherwise. I've seen you on TV. I'm aware of your accomplishments. And you come with a high recommendation from Declan Cooper."

"You know Declan?"

"I reached out to him, and he suggested I call you. You're right. I'm in trouble. And I need your help to get me out of it."

"So, you're saying you didn't kill Haley's parents?"

"No. Of course not."

"Want to tell me what's going on? What's *really* going on?"

"That's classified."

"I think we're beyond that now, don't you?"

"I trust Declan, but I need to make sure I'm not making a mistake. I need to know that I can trust you. Let's meet. In person. I need a face-to-face."

"Tell me when and where, and I'm there."

"I'll call you in the morning. It will be a public place. Come alone and make sure you're not followed."

"Okay. But I want to talk to Haley. I want to make sure she's all right."

"She's in a secure location. I'll send you proof of life." Penelope paused. "We'll talk more tomorrow."

She ended the call, and I waited with anticipation for some indication that Haley was still alive.

My next call was to Declan. He was an old Navy buddy who'd done some time at one of the three-letter agencies after the Teams. He got into the private sector and started pulling the big dollars, then ended up lobbying in DC. He was pretty well-connected.

"I figured you'd be calling," he said when he answered.

"Tell me the story."

We were on a secure, encrypted call. Still, I got the sense that he didn't want to speak openly about it.

"She called me," Declan said. "I told her to call you. This kind of thing seems right up your alley."

"You know what she's accused of, don't you?"

"I'm aware of the narrative. But when was the last time the official narrative had a shred of truth?"

"I need details."

"I don't have details," Declan said. "But I'm willing to bet my life she's telling the truth."

"You feel that strongly about it?"

"I do."

"She's a ghost. How do you know her?"

"Let's just say we worked together on an operation that doesn't exist."

"Is there anything more there?"

"Wild, come on. What do you want, the full backstory?"

"Pretty much."

"No. I didn't sleep with her. It's not like that. But let's just say she's someone that I care about deeply. She's a good person. I'm not in a position to help her out, or I would."

"She's a wanted fugitive."

"Are you losing your edge, Wild? You can smell a setup, can't you?"

There was a long pause.

"Just hear her out. Listen to what she has to say. Make your own decision. I'll respect that either way."

"What about her hostage?"

"If she says she saved the kid's life, then she saved the kid's life."

I paused, taking it all in. "If what she's saying is true, this has the potential to get ugly."

"Yes, it does, my friend. Yes, it does." He paused. "Stay frosty."

I ended the call and updated JD on the situation.

The party raged on, and I noticed we'd lost Logan.

The sheriff buzzed my phone. At this hour, it couldn't be good.

20

It was heartbreaking.

I joined the sheriff and the other deputies on the athletic field under the bleachers. JD was with me, but Brad stayed behind. I'm not sure what happened to Logan. I figured he had crawled off to his stateroom and passed out.

The kid under the bleachers couldn't have been more than 17. His cold, lifeless body lay flat on the ground, his eyes open and fixed on the bleachers above. A glass pipe lay next to his hand, the inner bowl coated with residue.

Dietrich snapped photos.

Brenda hovered over the remains.

It didn't take a rocket scientist to figure out what caused the boy's demise. Brenda rummaged through the boy's pockets and pulled out a small baggie of red crystals. She handed it to me after I snapped on a pair of nitrile gloves.

"Looks like methamphetamine," I said.

The sheriff's face tightened. "I haven't seen anything quite like that around here before."

"Somebody's either bringing in new product, or there's a new cook in town," I said.

JD had downed quite a few drinks by this point. He teetered, his eyes bloodshot.

The sheriff scowled at him. "What's his problem? Never mind. I think he was just born that way."

Brenda found the kid's wallet. She thumbed through it and pulled out his ID. "Blake Butler. 17."

She handed the ID to the sheriff.

"Somebody run background on this kid." He handed the ID off to Deputy Halford.

He took the ID and hustled back to his patrol car in the parking lot.

"Who found the body?" I asked.

"Anonymous tip from a pay phone at the gas station near the edge of town."

"He must have been with a friend," I said. "They hopped the fence, looking for an isolated place."

"Blake ODs, and his friend freaks out and takes off," JD said, completing my thought.

"Some friend," the sheriff muttered.

"How long has he been dead?"

"An hour," Brenda said. "Maybe two."

Halford hustled back across the field to join us. He huffed, out of breath. "Kid's clean. No criminal history. Parents are William and Caroline. They live at 2212 Heron Hollow Lane."

"That's a nice neighborhood," Daniels said. He frowned and shook his head. "That shit will kill you. Doesn't matter where you come from. But these damn kids think they're invincible."

"I'll know more when I get him back to the lab," Brenda said.

Her crew bagged the remains.

"Who volunteers to notify the next of kin?" the sheriff asked.

Everyone remained silent.

"Wild. You look eager to take on the challenge," the sheriff said.

I forced a smile. "Thanks. We're on it."

"Leave him behind," Daniels said, pointing at JD.

Jack's face wrinkled. "I'm perfectly fine."

"Sit this one out."

"He'll stay in the car," I assured.

We marched across the football field, moved through the gate, and stepped into the parking lot. JD and I climbed into the Ferrari, and we headed over to the upscale neighborhood of *Whispering Heights.*

I parked at the curb in front of Blake's parent's home. It was a nice two-story French colonial with a large veranda, a white picket fence, and blooming flower gardens. Tall palms swayed overhead, and garden lighting lit up the front façade of the house.

I killed the engine.

Jack smelled like a distillery. It became more apparent now that the car had stopped and the wind wasn't swirling.

He pulled the lever and opened the door.

"You're sitting this one out, remember?"

He frowned at me but relented. "Fine. This isn't what I'd call the best part of the job, anyway."

I hopped out, passed through the gate, and strolled the red brick walkway to the front porch. I hesitated a moment before knocking. It broke my heart to do this kind of thing. Nobody liked to be woken in the middle of the night with this kind of news.

I put a heavy fist against the door and waited.

The house was dark and silent.

I banged again and rang the bell.

After a few moments, a light flicked on in the living room. A shadowy figure approached the door. The privacy glass blurred the man's form. He shouted, "Who is it?"

"Coconut County. Are you William Butler?"

He unlatched the deadbolt and pulled open the door with an annoyed face and sleepy eyes. He wore a flannel robe and pale blue pajamas underneath. He was a big guy in his early 40s with dark hair, just starting to gray on the sides. He had a square face and a pudgy nose. He had the same eyes as

Blake, but I figured Blake must have favored his mother. The kid had a narrow face and more angular features.

"I hate to be the bearer of bad news..."

Mr. Butler stiffened.

His wife appeared behind him at the end of the foyer with a concerned face.

She shrieked in horror as I broke the news.

It took a moment for William to process the information. Then he started swaying, unsteady on his feet.

I stood ready to catch him if he fainted.

21

The couple invited me in and offered me a seat on the sofa in the living room.

Caroline wept. She blotted her eyes with a tissue from a box on the glass coffee table. She had shoulder-length blond hair that curled at the ends and wore a white robe.

William looked stunned. They both tried to hold it all together.

"I know this is a difficult time," I said. "But I need to ask a few questions."

William nodded.

"Was there any indication that Blake was using drugs?"

The couple exchanged an uneasy glance.

William hesitated. "We caught him with weed before and some pills. But nothing like methamphetamine."

"What kind of pills?"

"He said they were herbal supplements. Perfectly legal. Got them at a smoke shop." He shook his head in frustration. "Hell, I didn't know what they were. We flushed everything. I told him not to bring that shit into my house again. He was almost 18. If he wanted to do that kind of thing, he could get his own place. He certainly wasn't going to do it here."

"You have any idea where he got the drugs from?"

William exchanged another glance with Caroline. Both of their faces tightened.

"I blame this all on Travis," William said. "You've got to understand, Blake was always a good kid. Ever since he started hanging around Travis, that's when the trouble began."

William tried to hold it together, but he broke down into sobs.

It was hard to watch. His chest jerked and heaved. He tried to stifle it, but that only made it worse.

"I should have made him go to rehab," William cried. "I didn't know he had that much of a problem."

"This could have been his first time," I said. "Or maybe he got hold of some low-grade stuff and didn't realize how powerful this was."

"Either way, my son is dead," he said, devastated.

"I'll need contact information for Travis. It's imperative that we find the source and get this stuff off the street before this happens again."

"I've got his number in my phone," Caroline said. "I can send it to you."

I gave them my card and offered my condolences once again. It didn't mean much. Nothing was going to bring their son back.

By the time I made it back to the Ferrari, JD was passed out. He woke up when I slammed the door. He popped up, trying to act alert. "I was just resting my eyes."

Travis lived a few blocks over on Bayview Street in the Pelican Place apartments with his parents. The complex was made up of several freestanding buildings with light gray siding and white trim. Tall palms shrouded the property.

I left JD in the car, hustled down a winding concrete path through the complex, and climbed the steps to unit C204. I banged on the door. That set off a dog barking that probably woke up the entire complex.

After a few minutes of beating on the door, a gruff voice shouted through. "What the hell do you want?"

"Coconut County. I need to speak with Travis for a moment."

An angry gentleman pulled open the door and scowled at me, holding a German Shepherd by the collar. The dog snarled, displaying its glistening teeth.

"What's this about?"

"Is your son here?" I asked.

He shouted into the apartment. "Travis! Get your ass out here!"

There was no response.

"Now!"

A door cracked open, and a sliver of light spilled into the living room. Travis poked his head out. In a worried voice, he asked. "What is it?"

"There's a cop here that wants to speak to you."

"Fuck that. I'm not talking to any cops."

"Travis!" his father said in a low growl. "Get your ass out here and talk to this gentleman, or you can get the hell out of my house."

Travis shuffled out of his room to the edge of the foyer and kept his distance. "What do you want?"

"Were you with Blake Butler earlier this evening?" I asked.

His face tightened, and he swallowed hard. "No."

"You sure about that?"

His mouth grew dry, and swallowing became more difficult.

"Your friend is dead. He died of an overdose. We know you called the department from the pay phone at the gas station near the Seahorse Shores."

Travis's face went pale as a ghost. "I didn't make any calls."

His dad looked like he was about to explode. He glared at his son, still holding the barking dog back.

Travis shrugged off his dad's look. "What!? I don't know what he's talking about." Then he addressed me. "I haven't talked to Blake all night."

"Shut that fucking dog up!" a neighbor yelled from below.

"Hogan, settle down," Mr. Hall said.

The dog hushed for a moment, but he clearly picked up on the tension.

I asked Travis, "Did you leave your friend to die, or was he dead when you left the football field?"

He shifted uncomfortably.

"What the hell have you gotten yourself into?" his dad said.

"Nothing. I don't know what he's talking about."

"I need to know where the meth came from," I said.

"I don't know anything about meth," Travis said.

His dad glared at him.

"Let me tell you how this is gonna work out," I said. "We're going to subpoena your phone records. I'm guessing the GPS data on your phone is going to put you at the football field under the bleachers where we found your best friend. I bet we'll also be able to put that phone at the gas station when you made the call from the pay phone."

"Why would I make a call from a pay phone when I've got a cell phone in my pocket?"

I gave him a flat look. "I don't really care about you. I care about who sold you the meth."

He hesitated for a moment, his eyes darting between his father and me. "I don't know anything about it."

"Tell the man what he wants to know before your ass gets in real trouble," his father commanded.

Travis fidgeted.

22

"I don't know anything." Travis hesitated. "I mean, look. Blake told me he had scored some drugs. But I don't do drugs. So, I didn't want anything to do with it."

It was total and complete bullshit.

"Where were you tonight?" his father asked.

"I was hanging out with friends."

"Who?"

"What, am I on trial here!?"

"I need to know where the drugs came from," I said.

"I'm telling you, I don't know. Some connection that Blake had."

My face tightened, and I exhaled a frustrated sigh. "You don't seem terribly upset or surprised about your friend's death."

His eyes narrowed at me. "It's fresh. I haven't processed it yet."

Travis was with Blake when he OD'd. No doubt in my mind.

I gave his father my card. "All I want is a name. Nobody's going to get in trouble. Just tell me where the meth came from. If you make me do this the hard way, there's no telling how things could turn out. Leaving your friend to die could result in criminal charges."

Travis's eyes bugged out. "I didn't do anything."

I looked at his father. "Talk some sense into him."

He scoffed. "He doesn't listen to me."

I left the apartment and hustled back to the Ferrari. Jack was passed out again. I texted Isabella Travis's number and asked her to track his location data.

I drove back to the marina at Diver Down. By the time we got back aboard the boat, the party was winding down. JD stumbled to his stateroom, and I settled into mine.

Hell of a way to end the evening.

It took a while to fall asleep, my mind racing, wondering how long it would be before more turned up dead from the lethal concoction. When I slept, I dreamt of red meth, but I could never find the source. I hoped it wasn't an omen.

Morning rays of sun spilled around the edges of the blinds, painting slashes of light on the deck. All was calm aboard the boat at the ass-crack of dawn.

I peeled open sleepy eyes, yawned, stretched, and pulled myself out of bed. I looked over the aft deck at the marina as the warm morning rays filtered across the boats. There were no paparazzi on the dock. No lingering fans hoping for a glimpse of their favorite movie star.

The day was starting out normal—as normal as any day could be around here.

Isabella had texted back. *[Travis Hall's phone was at the football field at the same time as Blake Butler's phone.]*

It didn't come as a surprise. I couldn't use the information, and I didn't have enough to get a warrant to compel the provider to hand over the cellular data. I wanted to lean on the punk and get him to come clean about the source, but I didn't have any leverage at the moment. Nothing solid to scare him with.

After I showered and dressed, I headed down to the galley and started grilling breakfast. I didn't think I'd have many early risers today. The party had raged into the wee hours of the morning. The boat was quiet.

Fluffy tip-toed into the kitchen. In a rare display of affection, the aloof white cat brushed against my shins and meowed before moving on.

Bacon sizzled in a pan, and the smell of brewing coffee filled the galley.

To my surprise, Brad stumbled in just as I was finishing the eggs. Despite the amount of alcohol consumed the night before, he looked bright-eyed and bushy-tailed.

"Smells good," he said.

"Help yourself."

"Don't mind if I do."

I dished up a plate, and so did he. We took our food up to the sky deck and enjoyed the morning.

"So this is pretty much it? Solve crimes, chase tail, drink copious amounts of liquor."

"Pretty much."

"Where do I sign up?"

I laughed. "It gets a little challenging at times."

"By challenging, you mean dangerous?"

I nodded.

"But you're doing something meaningful. You don't lie awake at night wondering what you're doing with your life. It has purpose. There's something to be said for that." Brad paused, contemplating his own existence. "I like to think I'm bringing entertainment to the masses. Enriching people's lives. Giving them an escape from reality. I'm not minimizing that, but that seems less tangible than what you do."

"Sometimes what we do doesn't seem very tangible. We take out one bad guy, and another one pops up. We can take down a drug operation and confiscate 140 kg of cocaine. The next day, there will be another shipment that's even bigger, and we never know about it."

"That's kind of depressing. How do you stay motivated?"

"One case at a time. Helping one person at a time." I paused and thought about it for a moment. "You do what you can. You give it your best. Sometimes your best is good enough, sometimes it isn't. But, at least, we try."

"Amen."

My phone buzzed my pocket. I pulled it out, swiped the screen, and took the call that came through on the encrypted app, *Memo*. "Good morning."

"Good morning, Deputy Wild," Penelope said.

"Are you ready to meet?"

"I am. Go to Taffy Beach. Rent a SeaCycle™. Take it out on the water, and I'll meet you."

"Time?"

"One hour. Come alone. Make sure you're not followed. If I sense a setup, I'm gone."

"No setup. I promise."

She ended the call.

"Was that the fugitive?" Brad asked.

I nodded.

"Need backup?"

I chuckled. "No. I can handle this on my own."

"You sure about that? Aren't partners always supposed to stick together?"

"I don't want to spook her."

"Fair enough."

"Tell Jack I'll be back shortly."

"You got it." He paused. "You sure you don't want me to go with you? I'm pretty handy with a pistol. I've had a lot of onset weapons training."

I smirked. "You ever been shot at with real bullets?"

"No."

"It's a different ballgame."

"I'm sure it is."

I finished breakfast, changed into board shorts, and grabbed my helmet and gloves. I hustled down to the dock, hopped on my sportbike, and cranked up the engine. The exhaust growled, and the high-strung engine hummed. I eased out the clutch and rolled out of the parking lot.

The bike attacked the road. I hugged the tank and twisted the throttle. The 1000cc crotch rocket launched forward, and the front wheel lifted from the ground slightly. This thing was pure adrenaline. It felt like being shot out of a cannon.

The wind whistled through my helmet, and my clothes flapped in the breeze. I hit triple digits in no time. There weren't many cars out on the road at this time of the morning.

For an instant, everything else faded away. The bike demanded total focus and attention. One mistake, and you'd pay for it in blood. It was sex and death in a sleek, overpowered package. Smooth surfaces and angular lines. Race-worthy aerodynamics. The latest performance gadgets. It was a thrill machine.

I made it to Taffy Beach in no time, despite taking the long way. I doubled back a few times to make sure I wasn't followed. Every destination on the bike came too soon. Every journey not long enough.

The momentary escape was over.

I pulled into the lot, found a place to park, and killed the engine. I stowed my helmet and gloves and scanned the area for threats.

The parking lot was fairly empty.

I trudged through the soft, white sand toward the rental shack. Teal waves crashed against the shore, and gulls hung on the breeze, squawking. A few tourists were already sunning themselves, laying out on colorful beach towels. Some looked like they hadn't seen the sunshine all winter—blinding pale slabs of exposed flesh that required sunglasses. Even then, you were risking retinal damage if you stared too long.

There was a young kid behind the counter at the rental hut. The thatched roof was just a decoration. The whole thing was built from plywood and two-by-fours, the exterior painted in festive tropical colors. The skinny clerk with dark hair wore a royal blue shirt with the company logo in white above the left breast pocket.

He looked bored.

A summer job. Probably home from college.

I flashed my badge for good measure. "I need to rent a SeaCycle."

He told me the price per hour and gave me the laundry list of requirements. "I'll need a driver's license, a major credit card, and you'll need to sign an indemnity waiver. Liability insurance is mandatory, and you can purchase an additional damage policy that covers the bike in case of an accident."

I plunked down my credit card and filled out the mountain of paperwork. "Has anyone else rented a cycle today?"

The clerk shook his head. "You're the first, bro."

Once everything was squared away, he tossed me the key fob and told me which cycle.

I hustled across the sand, pushed the watercraft into the surf, and hopped on. I cranked up the engine, twisted the throttle, and crashed through the swells.

The morning sun glistened the water, and a gentle breeze tousled my hair. Mists of salt water sprayed, and the briny smell filled my nostrils. I rode out beyond the break and floated around for a while, waiting for Penelope Cross to magically appear.

23

I kept scanning the shoreline and the horizon but didn't see anything.

I was out there for 30 minutes, and still nothing. I called Penelope on the encrypted messaging app, but she didn't answer.

Kids played in the shallow surf. A few sailboats dotted the horizon. I even saw a pair of dolphins.

I waited another 15 minutes, then rode back to shore. I tried to have a little fun along the way, riding in on the swells. They weren't much, but it was better than nothing. I slid the cycle onto the sand and cut the engine, then climbed off. I trudged back to the rental hut, granules of sand clinging to my wet feet. I returned the key fob to the clerk, and he gave me a receipt—proof that I had returned the vehicle.

"Looks like you had fun," he snarked.

I shot him a look, and he returned my shoes and socks that I had left with him.

I carried them to a shower station, rinsed my feet, then let them dry in the beaming sun before putting my footwear back on. I kept scanning the area, my head on a swivel.

I didn't see anyone or anything suspicious.

The beach was starting to fill up with tourists. As I strode back to the parking lot, I noticed a few skimpy bikinis that warranted further investigation. Another time, perhaps.

I climbed on my sport bike, pulled on my helmet and gloves, and cranked up the engine. I glanced around one last time before pulling out of the parking lot and heading back to the marina at Diver Down.

By the time I got back to the boat, Jack was in the galley grilling up breakfast.

Brad sat at the breakfast nook. "Just in time for a second breakfast," he said. "How did it go?"

"It didn't."

I gave them the details, then asked, "Where's Logan?"

Brad laughed. "I think last night was a little too much for him. I banged on his stateroom and told him breakfast was ready, but the only thing I got in response was an indecipherable groan."

Logan staggered into the galley from the below-deck quarters a moment later.

"Well, speak of the devil," Brad said.

Logan looked like reheated death. His eyes were bloodshot and puffy, his hair tousled, his stride uneasy.

"Morning, sunshine," Brad said with a cheery smile.

Logan glared at him and slid onto the bench seat at the breakfast nook across from him.

"How are you feeling, buddy?" Brad snarked.

"Never better."

Brad laughed.

Logan tried to suck it up, but he was hurting. The veins in his temples throbbed. We'd all been there before—the elephant standing on your skull, the world a little wobbly, the stomach twisting.

Jack fixed him a plate.

Logan took small, cautious bites at first. That stayed down, so he gradually began to scoop more into his mouth.

My phone buzzed with another call. I hoped it was Penelope with some kind of explanation, but it was another unknown number. I swiped the screen and held the phone to my ear. "This is Deputy Wild."

"I got your number from the department. I'm told you're the lead investigator on the Worthington case."

"What can I do for you?"

"My name is Simon Sinclair. I don't know if this is relevant to the case, but I thought I'd reach out. I'm an art historian and appraiser. A client recently brought a piece to my attention that he was looking at acquiring. The seller agreed to allow me to evaluate its authenticity. It was a piece by Julian Krause from a lost part of his catalog. There are no pictures of the artwork in any of the books. Only preliminary sketches and notes. Paintings that fall into these lost categories can often have great investment potential. A new discovery. On the downside, it is hard to establish their provenance. My client was sure this painting was legit. It had been authenticated before, but he wanted to do his due diligence. Measure twice, cut once. I can appreciate clients like that. I found something unusual about the painting."

"Unusual?"

"In the late 1800s, you couldn't go to the local art supply and buy pigments. Many of the artists of the day made their own or had them specially crafted. This particular painting used titanium white, which wasn't widely available until the 1920s. Before that time, zinc white was prominent. In my estimation, the painting is a forgery. A good forgery, but a fake nonetheless."

I started putting all the pieces together. "Let me guess, the seller of this painting was Cornelius Worthington."

"The nature of my business requires discretion and confidentiality. It is not uncommon for me to sign a nondisclosure agreement with both my client and the seller. As such, I cannot disclose the name of either party. But I wouldn't disagree with your assumption."

"What was the name of the painting?"

"Again, I can't disclose that information. But it's the opposite of noon."

His answer was a bit cryptic, and I had no idea what he was referencing. But it was something to go on. "Thank you. I appreciate the information."

"I hope it helps."

"Do you think the seller forged the painting himself?" I asked.

"If he did, he's one talented artist. I would have authenticated the piece had I not discovered traces of the pigment."

"Off the top of your head, do you know anyone who is producing forgeries of that caliber?"

"I don't. I don't run in those circles. Whoever is responsible would be wise to keep their identity to themselves. The market potential is astronomical. After seeing something like this, I have no doubt there are forgeries hanging in major galleries and in esteemed collections."

"Do you still have the painting?"

"No. It was returned."

"Thanks for the heads up."

"Anytime."

He ended the call, and I updated JD.

"We need to have another talk with your girlfriend," Jack said.

"She's not my girlfriend."

"She was the other night."

Brad chuckled.

Logan was still too hungover to laugh.

After the gang ate breakfast, we made another trip to the gallery to speak with Astrid.

24

"Are you bored?" Astrid asked. "Here to harass me again?"

The gallery was empty at the moment. If tourists happened to stumble in, they stumbled out quickly after a look at the prices. This wasn't the place to pick up that beach pastel for the bathroom.

"Just a few more questions," I said.

"What if I don't feel like answering your questions?"

"I'd be disappointed."

"Get used to disappointment." She was still salty.

"Were you aware of any paintings by Julian Krause in Cornelius Worthington's collection?"

"It wasn't my business to know his full inventory."

"What about a painting with midnight in the title?"

She hesitated for a moment. "The Garden of Midnight?"

"Yes," I said, rolling with it.

"I believe that was in his collection at one point in time. I'm not aware of the current status of that painting."

"Did you have any involvement in that transaction?"

Her eyes narrowed at me. "I'm not sure where you're going with this?"

"It's a simple yes or no question."

"That came into our possession from a known collector. Cornelius purchased it, and I would suspect it's still in his collection."

I showed her photos of the interior of Mr. Worthington's house. "Do you see the painting on the walls?"

She thumbed through the images on my phone. After going over the pictures, she shook her head. "I don't see it. But many clients store their works in climate-controlled facilities. People don't always buy art to display it."

"Seems a shame to hide something like that away, unseen by the world."

"People do lots of strange things. It's none of my business once the check clears."

"I have it on good authority that the painting in Worthington's collection is a forgery."

Her brow lifted with surprise, and she scoffed. "A forgery?"

"So I'm told."

"Who told you that?"

"Is that relevant?"

"Yes, it most certainly is. I would like to know this person's history, experience, and credibility."

"What do you do to authenticate the pieces that come to you?" I asked.

"Most of the people that I deal with are accredited buyers and sellers. People that have a reputation and have been in the game for a while. Not everyone can afford to drop $50 million on a canvas. It's a select group of people, and we all know each other."

"You didn't answer my question."

"You didn't answer mine."

"I can't disclose that information at this time," I said.

She squinted again, staring deep into my eyes, looking for clues. "A few people come to mind. There are not many in this line of work. I'm going to go out on a limb and say it's not somebody that I regularly work with." She paused in thought. "Simon Sinclair."

"I can neither confirm nor deny."

She laughed. "I would take everything that Simon says with a grain of salt. He's known to go against consensus. And he's been wrong before." She paused, stood tall, and lifted her nose with pride. "I can assure you that every piece that comes through this gallery has either been authenticated by an expert or comes from a reputable source. I don't take these types of allegations lightly. The kind of thing you're suggesting could ruin my career."

"I'm not suggesting anything. I'm merely saying—"

"You're saying you believe one of the paintings that I sold Mr. Worthington is a forgery. But you're not taking into account other possibilities."

"Such as?"

"The first, and most obvious, is that Simon is wrong. The second is that Mr. Worthington had commissioned a forgery and was trying to pass it off, selling it to a third party."

"I thought you said you only dealt with reputable clients."

The muscles in her jaw flexed. "I can't possibly know the intentions or actions of all of my clients. I can assure you, if a forgery passed through this gallery, I was unaware of it."

"So, you acknowledge that's a possibility."

"Anything is possible, deputy." A frustrated sigh escaped her lips. "If there's nothing else, I have business to attend to."

"Sorry to disturb you."

She glared at me.

"I do have one more question. Do you know anyone in the game who is capable of this type of high-end forgery?"

"I do not." She forced a smile. "Good day, gentlemen."

"Who does your appraisals for the gallery?"

Her annoyed eyes burned into me. "Augustus Huntington. Feel free to talk to him. He'll say the same thing I have."

"Do you happen to have his contact information handy?"

"I do. I'll text it to you."

We left the gallery and regrouped on the sidewalk outside.

JD muttered, "I don't think she likes you anymore."

"I don't think so either." I frowned.

"That's a shame," Brad said. "She has... qualities."

My phone buzzed with a text from Astrid. As promised, she sent Augustus Huntington's contact information.

I texted her back. [Sorry. Just doing my job.]

She didn't respond.

I dialed Augustus. It rang a few times, then went to voicemail. I left a message, then contacted Denise.

She looked up his physical address, and we headed across town to the *Coral Palms*. It was a luxury mid-rise complex—a step above most of the hive-like apartments on the island.

There was a visitor parking lot in front and a circular drive with a large fountain of dolphins spitting water. A 24-hour valet and concierge attended to guests and residents. It was six stories of opulence.

I pulled to the valet, and Jack was right behind me. The white stucco exterior reflected the brilliant Florida sun. Towering palms stood guard, and the flower beds were well-maintained with a variety of colorful blooms.

The valet rushed to get my door.

I hopped out and slipped him a few bills, and told him to keep the car up front. He gave me a ticket, then hustled to JD's Porsche.

We gathered at the entrance, and I flashed my badge. The doorman greeted us with a smile and pulled open the door.

The interior was opulent—soaring ceilings and marble floors. Shafts of light filtered through the skylights. The concierge sat at a desk to the left, dressed in a suit with a gold nameplate above his suit pocket. He smiled as he greeted us. "Good afternoon, gentlemen. How can I help you?"

He did a double-take when he saw Logan and Brad, but he maintained his composure. He didn't get giddy like a fan. His job was to maintain his composure at all times. Still, the questions behind his eyes were apparent. *What the hell were these two doing here with two cops?*

I kept my badge on display and smiled. "We're here to see Augustus."

"Should I let him know you're here?"

"That won't be necessary."

We proceeded to the elevators, and I pressed the call button. It lit up, and we waited for the carriage to arrive. The doors slid open, and we stepped aboard and vaulted up to the sixth floor. The entourage ambled down the hallway, and I put a heavy fist against the door to unit #617.

Footsteps shuffled down the foyer a moment later. The peephole flickered as someone inside peered through.

I held my badge to the fish-eye lens and said, "Coconut County."

The deadbolt unlatched with a thunk, and the door pulled open. Augustus surveyed us with narrow blue eyes that were a little puffy. He was in his early 60s with silver hair, a distinguished amount of wrinkles, and a snooty air. He wore a black designer suit and shirt—a little overdressed for lounging around his apartment, but Augustus struck me as the type of man who always dressed to impress, even if there was no one around.

"What can I do for you?"

His eyes flicked to Logan and Brad, but like the concierge, he maintained his cool. I figured his line of work put him in contact with celebrities, tech moguls, business tycoons, and the like. Still, it must have been confusing.

"I hope we're not disturbing you," I said. "I left a message but didn't hear back. We figured we'd just stop by and have a quick chat."

"I don't suppose this is about those parking tickets?"

I laughed. "No."

"I'm not under arrest, am I?"

"Have you done anything worthy of an arrest?"

Augustus stood tall and looked down his nose. "I should think not."

"I want to get your opinion on a painting."

"Then you've come to the right place." He stepped aside and motioned us in. "Please, come in."

We stepped inside, and the movie stars followed.

Augustus closed the door behind us and latched the deadbolt. It made a clunk that echoed down the hallway.

We stepped from the foyer into the living room. It was a nice place and had an open-concept floor plan. The kitchen was modern and stylish with marble countertops. There were light hardwood floors in the living room and skylights with adjustable shades that allowed copious amounts of light into the elegant space. A large terrace with a barbecue grill and lounge chairs provided a relaxing view. The apartment was filled with high-end artwork and sculptures. The paintings were lit with track lighting. Whimsical sculptures sat atop pedestals, each meticulously positioned and lit.

Augustus wasn't short on style.

He finally spoke to the movie stars. "I hear you're in town doing research for your next project."

They both smiled and nodded.

"I hope you're finding our fair city enjoyable."

Brad grinned. "Most definitely."

Augustus's eyes flicked to Logan, who still looked like he'd been through the ringer. "Seems like the island might not have been so kind to you."

I think Logan was a little stunned that someone actually told him he looked like crap. On his worst day, he still looked better than most men. His face tightened initially, then softened as he came to respect the directness of the comment. "Perhaps the island treated me too well last night." Logan finished with that charming smile of his. It was infectious, and Augustus couldn't help but smile back.

We gathered in the living room but remained standing.

"Please, have a seat," Augustus said. "Or stand if you prefer. What do you need my opinion on?"

There was no doubt in my mind that Astrid had called him the minute we left the gallery. But he played dumb.

"The Garden of Midnight."

His face remained stoic. "Ah, yes. Fascinating piece by Krause."

25

"Many factors go into determining the authenticity of a work of art," Augustus said. "I look at the style. If it is something that is not previously known to be part of the catalog, I look at the piece in the context of the other works by the artist. Most people attempting to pass off forgeries are lazy and make obvious mistakes. Often, the age of the canvas doesn't match the age of the supposed painting. You can't just go to your local art supply store, get paint, and use it to create a forged masterpiece."

"How do you determine if the materials used were authentic?" I asked.

"Years of experience. I know how different materials and pigments change over time. I know how well they hold their color, the conditions under which they crack or break apart. Of course, we have all kinds of modern advances that can analyze materials. In some cases, when it's warranted, we will use spectroscopy. We take minute samples of paint to be evaluated."

"You actually scrape off part of the paint?" I asked.

In a soothing, assured voice, he said, "Very minuscule. Imperceptible amounts. I'm talking particles thinner than the width of a hair. It's perfectly safe. But I can tell you, in the wrong hands, priceless works of art can be damaged beyond repair."

"So that's not something you do for every painting," I said.

"It's not necessary for every painting."

"When you evaluated the *Garden of Midnight*, did you use spectroscopy?"

His face stiffened. "No. I didn't."

"Why not?"

"There were enough indicators that the painting was authentic. I stand behind that declaration, and nothing is going to change my mind."

"Not even the opinion of other historians and analysts?"

He frowned, and his eyes narrowed at me. "I can assure you, there is no one else on this island with the same level of expertise as myself. I would treat all other opinions as suspect."

"So, you're infallible," I snarked.

That earned me a subtle scowl.

"I am human, deputy. I am flawed and prone to error like everyone, but when it comes to artwork, I don't make mistakes. You're talking about a piece of art that was sold to Cornelius Worthington. I'm aware of the current drama surrounding his demise. Apparently, he was trying to sell that piece outside of the gallery on his own. Perhaps you should consider the fact that he was trying to pass off a forgery and kept the original for himself."

"That was mentioned to me by Astrid."

"Not surprising. Astrid is an astute gallery owner. She is wise to the ways of the many scams in this business."

"We've not been able to find the painting in question, and Astrid claimed it was not among the paintings that Cornelius returned to the gallery for her to sell on commission."

"You asked for my opinion on a piece of artwork," Augustus said. "Unless you present that work to me, I can't give you a fully informed opinion. I can only speak to my personal experience with the *Garden of Midnight*. The painting that I saw in Astrid's gallery was authentic. Beyond that, I have no opinion."

"Let's say Cornelius commissioned a forgery. Who would he hire for something like that?"

"I would imagine that's a short list. But I wouldn't know who to contact about something like that."

"You only deal with legitimate collectors," I snarked.

He sneered at me. "One must be very careful with one's reputation in this business."

I thanked Augustus for his cooperation, then we left his apartment.

"Think he's full of it?" Brad asked as we walked the hallway toward the elevators.

"I think everybody's full of it till proven otherwise," JD said.

We climbed into the cars and drove back to Diver Down. We took a seat at the bar, and Teagan dealt out menus.

Harlan sat at the end of the bar, staring at Logan with a curious look. The salty old Marine sipped his beer, then spoke his mind.

26

Logan couldn't help but notice that Harlan was staring at him. The movie star was used to that kind of thing, but Harlan's gaze was intense and unsettling.

"You was in that movie, wasn't ya?"

Logan smiled graciously.

"Dog shit."

Logan's face went long, stunned. "Excuse me?"

"You heard me. Dog shit."

Flustered, Logan responded, "What movie are you referring to?"

"You know. That one where you get stuck in those catacombs with that backwards ass son-of-a-bitch and..."

Logan knew instantly what he was referring to. "Oh, well, they can't all be gems."

"Have you been to a movie theater lately?" Harlan asked. "Do you know how much a ticket and a bag of popcorn costs for two people? For that price, every movie ought to be a diamond."

Logan was a good sport. "I'm sorry you didn't enjoy it."

"Sorry doesn't get my money or my time back."

Logan's face tightened, but he forced a smile. "Teagan, give my friend another round on me."

"Make that two," Harlan said. "I deserve something for pain and suffering."

Logan laughed. "Put whatever he wants on my tab for the rest of the day."

Harlan nodded and took another sip of his long neck.

Brad seemed amused by the whole exchange.

"I don't know what you're laughing at, pretty boy," Harlan said. "You had some stinkers, too."

Brad shrugged and smiled.

Logan took comfort in the fact that he wasn't alone.

We chowed down and shot the breeze about the cases. In the afternoon, we took the movie stars to the practice space for rehearsal with the band.

The miscreants loitered out front as usual. Those guys didn't get excited about much, but their eyes filled with awe when they saw the celebrities. There were high-fives all around.

"*Rectifier* rocked," one of them said.

Brad rolled his eyes.

"How many more are you going to make?" another asked.

"There are two more in my contract with the studio," Logan said.

"Right on!"

They chatted for a bit and signed autographs before stepping inside. We spilled into the practice room. Dizzy and Crash noodled around. Styxx hadn't arrived yet.

"You mind if I play drums?" Brad asked.

Dizzy and Crash shrugged.

"I don't think Styxx will mind," Dizzy said.

Brad grinned and climbed behind the candy apple red drum set. He grabbed a pair of sticks, twirled them around, and clicked off a beat. Dizzy strummed a few chords, and Crash joined in on bass.

Brad wasn't half bad, and the improvised jam sounded good.

Styxx showed up a few moments later, looking surprised. Playing another man's instrument was like pawing on his girlfriend.

"Watch out," JD said. "You might get replaced."

Styxx sneered at him. "Never."

Brad was good, but he wasn't as good as Styxx. And Styxx didn't seem to mind the movie star banging on his kit.

After the little jam, Brad gave up his seat, and Styxx took the throne. The band ran through their set, and Brad and Logan soaked it all up, storing it in their memory banks for character development.

By the end of the jam, groupies packed the room, eager to meet Logan and Brad. Word had spread.

There were lots of short skirts and low-cut tops. Bright eyes and long lashes. Silky smooth legs and pert assets.

Logan and Brad signed autographs in sharpie on various body parts.

After practice, we grabbed dinner at the *Bluewater Bistro*, then the entourage of fans met us at *Tide Pool*. The drinks flowed, and it didn't take long for a bevy of beauties to surround Logan and Brad. The guys were both single at this point in time, and there was no shortage of options.

"How long are these guys going to be here?" Crash asked me.

I shrugged. "A couple of weeks."

"I mean, this is cool and all. But I'll be glad when they leave."

I chuckled.

"Dude, they're seriously drawing all the hotties."

The band was used to being the center of the universe when we went out. Now they were playing second fiddle.

"There's plenty to go around," I said.

"I thought you hated each other," a beautiful blonde said to Brad and Logan.

Brad slung his arm around Logan and flashed a smile. "Where'd you hear that? We're best buddies."

Logan played along and smiled back. "Water under the bridge."

"Didn't Logan sleep with your wife?" the girl asked, picking at the scab. She was a little tipsy and not the most tactful individual in the world.

Brad forced another smile. "It doesn't really bother me. My ex-wife said he's got a really little…" He gestured an infinitesimally small distance between his thumb and index finger.

Logan didn't appreciate that.

He stepped back and squared off. His intense eyes blazed. "I didn't sleep with your wife. Okay!?"

"Oh, you didn't. It was just all over the tabloids."

"Do you believe everything you read?"

The crowd looked on with eager eyes. Two celebrities airing their dirty laundry in public was prime entertainment.

"I'd like to see your dick," the girl said with a naughty glimmer in her eyes. "I'll tell you if it's big or small."

"Anybody got an electron microscope to help the lady out?" Brad quipped.

Logan's face reddened. His jaw clenched, and his hands balled into fists. The veins in his forehead bulged. "We're above this, aren't we? Stop being childish."

"What's childish is putting your hands on another man's wife."

"Nothing happened between us while we were on set."

Brad scoffed.

"We didn't connect until after the divorce."

"The bro code, dude."

"We aren't *bros*, and we never were," Logan said. "We did one film together a decade ago."

"It's shady. That's all I'm saying."

Logan took a deep breath. "Look. I'm sorry. Perhaps it was poor judgment on my part. She left me for Ryan Knight, anyway. What does any of it matter now?"

I stood close by in case this got out of hand. The last thing I needed was these two brawling in public. They were both a bit tipsy.

"It matters to me," Brad said.

"Then I apologize. Can we just put this aside and move on?" Logan asked, extending his hand.

Brad eyed Logan's hand with curiosity for a moment.

27

The crowd waited with bated breath.

After a long moment, Brad finally extended his hand and shook Logan's.

The crowd cheered.

"Just one more thing," Logan said.

He cocked his fist back and swung with all his might. His knuckles careened through the air.

The crowd looked on with shock and awe. Like ancient Romans at the coliseum, they awaited the spectacle with morbid glee.

It happened too fast for me to stop it.

I thought the tension had been diffused, but apparently, Logan wanted to get even for that first sucker punch.

Logan's fist rocketed toward Brad's face.

Brad dodged.

Logan's fist whiffed, missing Brad's cheek by millimeters.

Logan had put his shoulder into the punch. The momentum carried him forward, and his fist smacked a girl standing near Brad.

The impact echoed across the patio.

Blood spewed from her nose, and the blow staggered her back. Someone caught her before she fell into the pool. She was dazed for a moment, then a horrible screeching sound spilled from her mouth. Blood poured from her nose, dripping over her lips and down her chin. She shrieked with terror, and tears flowed from her eyes.

Logan's eyes rounded, and his jaw dropped. "Oh, my God! I'm so sorry."

POW!

The girl's boyfriend didn't care who Logan was. He responded with a quick shot to the jaw, dropping Logan to the ground in an instant.

I stepped in and flashed my badge.

The big guy was ready to go after the movie star, but I held him back.

The crowd gasped and gawked.

The girl clutched her nose, blood seeping through her fingers. Tears streamed from her eyes, and she howled and squealed.

This was a fiasco.

People had their cell phones out, recording video and snapping photos.

JD called for an ambulance, and a cocktail waitress brought a few napkins to help the girl stem the tide of blood. Dark circles had already formed under her eyes.

Her boyfriend fumed with anger.

Jack attended to Logan and helped him stand. The movie star was still a little wobbly. He was unsteady before he threw the punch, and even more so now. You could almost see the stars swirling around his head.

"That fucker needs to go to jail," the girl's big boyfriend said.

"I'm so sorry," Logan said. "It was an accident. I'll cover all of your medical expenses."

"Oh, you're gonna cover a lot more than that," the boyfriend said. "Look at her nose. It's all jacked up."

The girl's eyes rounded. "Is it broken?"

It was a little crooked. Maybe a lot.

She used her phone's camera as a mirror to see the damage.

Her eyes rounded at the sight, and she freaked out even more.

"Ma'am, do you want to press charges?" I asked.

She thought about it for a moment.

Her boyfriend said, "Hell yes, she does!"

"Keep in mind, you assaulted Logan Chase as well."

"Self-defense, bro!"

"Well, your girlfriend can press charges against him, and he can press charges against you. You can make up your mind if you want to go down that route."

"Why are you defending him?"

"I'm not defending him. I'm just telling you how things might play out."

The EMTs arrived and evaluated the girl. They took her to the emergency room to have her nose set and evaluate her for any other trauma.

I had no doubt a lawsuit was inbound.

We rounded up the gang and left Tide Pool. By the time we hit the sidewalk, there were dozens of paparazzi snapping photos and recording video. Paris Delaney and her crew were on the scene filming as well.

Logan was distraught. He hung his head low and tried to avoid the cameras.

I escorted him through the crowd, keeping the onlookers at bay.

"Why did you hit the girl?"

"What started the fight?"

"Are you taking Logan to jail?"

I got him back to the Ferrari, then climbed behind the wheel and drove to Diver Down. We hustled down the dock and boarded the boat, trying to avoid the horde of media that chased us home.

There would be no after-party on the boat tonight.

"I totally screwed up," Logan said, taking a seat on the settee, his head falling into his hands. He looked tortured by the event.

Brad and JD entered behind us, followed by the rest of the band. They'd brought a few girls with them.

Paparazzi and news crews gathered on the dock at the stern.

"That's what you get for trying to sucker punch me," Brad said.

Logan glared at him. "Just trying to get you back."

"You need to learn to let go of your anger," Brad taunted with a grin.

"Fuck you."

Somehow I don't think the feud between the two was going to end anytime soon.

Logan got on the phone with his agent and his PR person. He left the salon and moved below deck to his guest stateroom. We didn't see him for the rest of the night.

My phone buzzed with a call from my agent in Hollywood. I knew I was about to get an earful.

28

"What the hell is going on?" Joel asked. "You're supposed to be keeping them out of trouble."

"No, we're supposed to be letting them shadow us. I never signed on to be their babysitter. Besides, nobody told me they hated each other."

"Have you seen the tabloids?"

"No."

"This isn't good. I'm already fielding calls from the studio. Susan wants to know what's going on."

"What do you want me to do about it?" I asked, exasperated.

"I want you to keep them out of trouble so that this project moves forward as scheduled."

"They're adults. They should be able to handle themselves in public."

"No. They are not adults," Joel said. "They are movie stars, which means they are infants. Their development stops the moment they achieve fame. From then on, everything is handed to them."

"Not around here."

Joel sighed.

"I'm sure Logan's PR team will get ahead of this."

"There's no getting ahead of this," Joel said. "It's going to be *full damage control mode* now. Video clips of the incident are all over the internet. They're already making memes about it."

"I'll do my best to keep them out of trouble."

"Try harder."

Joel ended the call, and I slipped the phone back into my pocket.

I didn't even want to look, but I searched the internet and found some of the gossip blogs.

It wasn't pretty.

Paris Delaney called.

"No," I said before she even spoke.

"You don't even know what I'm going to ask."

"Yes, I do, and the answer is no."

"He needs the PR opportunity. This would be a chance for him to get out in front of things and tell his side of the story. An exclusive interview. That's all I'm asking for."

"You're asking a lot."

"I'm doing you a favor."

"Me?"

"It's your show." She paused. "C'mon, you owe me."

"I owe you?" I said, incredulous.

"Ok, I'll owe you. How's that?"

"I'll talk to him. No promises."

"Thank you."

The next morning, we ate breakfast on the sky deck, soaking up the morning sun. Logan freaked out when he read the headlines.

"*Logan Chase punches fan after she insults latest movie.*" His face twisted with a scowl. "That's total bullshit!"

"Take it with a grain of salt," Brad said, still amused. "Like you said, the tabloids always lie."

Logan glared at him.

"Maybe you shouldn't throw random punches at friends."

"You're not my friend," Logan said.

Brad clutched his heart in a mocking fashion. "Aw, that hurts my feelings."

"You'll get over it."

"Can you guys put your bullshit aside?" I snapped. "I'm tired of it. You two can either get along or you can go home."

They both look stunned. I don't think anybody ever spoke to them that way before.

"This isn't a game. We're dealing with real victims of real crimes. There's a young girl out there that's been kidnapped, we have a few unsolved homicides, and someone is selling potent meth that is killing kids. All this nonsense is just a distraction." I paused, still glaring at the two of them. "How about you both take some time to figure this out? Think about whether or not you really want to do this project. If you do, you better get your act together. Like it or not, I have casting approval, and I will fire both your asses."

JD's eyes rounded, surprised by my outburst.

I took my plate, pushed away from the table, and plunged down to the galley.

As I was cleaning up the mess, my phone buzzed with a call from Sheriff Daniels. "This is getting a little out of hand."

"I know. It all happened before I could do anything about it."

"About what?"

"Last night. That's what you're talking about, isn't it?"

"No. I'm talking about the fire at the Montana."

My brow lifted with surprise. "What!?"

"You heard me. You and numbnuts need to get over there. Figure out what's going on. Maybe somebody left the stove on. Maybe there's something more to it."

29

After I finished the call with the sheriff, I updated JD. I grabbed my pistol, press-checked it, and holstered it for an appendix carry. As we hustled through the salon, Brad and Logan caught up with us.

"Can we ride along?" Logan asked.

"Why don't you guys sit this one out?" I said, still annoyed.

"We won't cause any trouble," Logan said.

"Yeah. We squashed it," Brad added.

I regarded them with a healthy dose of skepticism.

"I swear," Brad continued. "We're here to do the work. We want to make this project a success."

After a pause, I nodded.

The two actors grinned and followed us across the aft deck.

There were a few paparazzi and reporters on the dock, waiting to catch a glimpse of Logan and ask him questions about the night before.

We hustled across the passerelle and were greeted by a barrage of questions.

"Logan, do you have any comments about your actions last night?"

"Is the girl pressing charges?"

"I hear she plans to file a lawsuit. Do you have any comment?"

Logan said nothing.

One of the reporters addressed me. "Are you giving Logan special treatment because of his celebrity status?"

"To my knowledge, no formal complaint has been filed."

They shouted a few more questions, but we ignored them.

I climbed into the Ferrari, and Logan took the passenger seat. I twisted the ignition, cranked up the V8, and put the car into gear. The engine roared as I launched out of the parking lot.

Jack followed us across the island to the warehouse district. A few blocks down from the practice space, one of the old warehouses had been converted into lofts. What used to be a dilapidated old building was now a hip and trendy residential spot for artists and young professionals. The *Montana* wasn't cheap by any stretch of the imagination, and you wouldn't find many starving artists here.

Red and blue lights atop patrol cars flickered in front of the four-story brick building. Smoke still billowed into the sky.

Soot and ash drifted about, and the acrid smell filled the air—toxic fumes containing plastics, polymers, fire retardants, and other nasty stuff you don't want to breathe.

Several red fire trucks were on the scene. They had gotten the blaze under control, but smoke still wafted from open windows in the building. Firefighters in full gear scurried about. EMTs and paramedics attended to victims of smoke inhalation.

The residents had been evacuated. They stood on the street, staring at the building with mortified eyes. This was their home. All of their worldly possessions were at risk.

I found a place to park beside the loading dock, killed the engine, and hopped out. The sheriff gazed up at the structure, standing near a fire engine. We joined him as first responders darted about.

"Anybody injured?" I asked.

"Don't know yet."

"Do we know how the blaze started?"

"Talk to arson, but looks like it started on the fourth floor in that unit," he said, pointing.

I told Logan and Brad, "You guys should probably wait outside."

They frowned.

"Where's the fun in that?" Brad asked.

"It could be dangerous in there. Structural integrity may be compromised. Not to mention, there's some nasty stuff in there you don't want to breathe."

"That's what respirators are for," Brad said.

I figured the movie studio would have a fit if they knew about this. They had a lot of money tied up in the project and typically went to great lengths to keep movie stars out of real danger. If your lead actor dies during the middle of your $200 million blockbuster, that's not good for business.

Brad begged. "Come on. We'll stay right in your footsteps. We won't wander off, and if you tell us it's not safe, we'll leave."

"I'm telling you, it's probably not safe."

"You said *probably*. That's not an absolute."

I hesitated with a tight face. "Stay close. Don't wander off."

We waited for the firefighters to finish up, grabbed respirators, and followed the arson investigators inside.

A firefighter said to me, "There's one casualty so far. Unit #403."

30

The first floor was untouched by the blaze.

The property manager's office was to the left. The large lobby was lined with sleek furniture, fine art on the walls, and a bar area with a self-serve coffeemaker. The space was often used for small art shows, Christmas parties, and other resident-focused events.

We followed the investigators up the metal staircase, footsteps echoing off the walls. The elevator wasn't working at this point. Even with a respirator, the sharp smell of the charred building filtered through.

We opened the steel fire door and stepped into the hallway. There was no mistaking that the blaze had started in unit #403. The flames had spread out from there. It had been pretty well contained to that unit and the ones on either side.

Firefighters had broken through the door, and the inside of the apartment was soaked. What was left of the walls was blackened and scorched. Studs were cracked and shriveled from the flames. It looked like a hellish landscape from a nightmare.

The loft had an open-concept floor plan. There was a bathroom to the right of the foyer. The living area was about 1,600 square feet and flowed seamlessly into the kitchen. There were a couple charred chairs and the framework of a sofa. The cushions and fabric had melted away. Only the springs remained.

The fire had decimated the loft and burned away part of the hardwood floor. The large joists remained, and a few items that started out in this apartment ended up in the one below.

Fires typically burn upward. I figured an accelerant had been used. It likely seeped through the floorboards and facilitated the destruction.

Burned fragments of several large canvases were stacked against the walls. Most of them were scorched beyond recognition, but there were some that remained. Stacked behind others, they'd been spared from direct contact with the flames. In the corner of the room, there was a metal easel that survived. Tubes of oil paint melted from the heat.

The body on the floor rested close to the section of hardwoods that had been burned away. The flooring was brittle and probably not structurally sound.

An arson investigator put a cautious foot into the apartment and tested out the flooring. It creaked and groaned but didn't give way. He inched forward, taking another step. The dry boards popped and cracked.

This probably wasn't a good idea.

The Montana was an old building, built the old-fashioned way. It had received a modern renovation, partitioning what was once cavernous warehouse space into luxury lofts.

I told Logan and Brad to stay put. They didn't seem too eager to step into the seared and blistered apartment.

Brenda and her crew joined us.

Arson investigators made their way deeper into the apartment, creeping across the floor.

The firefighters had already been in this room, making sure the blaze was extinguished. That's when they found the deceased. It was illegal to move a body until the medical examiner had a chance to evaluate the scene.

The body still smoldered, blackened and charred, looking like a log that had been on the fire. There was no need to check vitals, but it was a matter of protocol. The resident of this apartment was now a lump of coal.

"You know who the victim is?" Brenda asked.

I shook my head. "Shouldn't be too hard to find out."

We cautiously followed the arson investigators inside. Brenda snapped on a pair of nitrile gloves and trailed in. The floorboards made noise, protesting, perhaps warning. I began to wonder how much weight this floor could actually hold. Were we standing on a ticking time bomb?

Brenda knelt down beside the body.

At first, the cause of death seemed obvious. Smoke inhalation is usually the primary culprit, asphyxiating the victim before the fire engulfs them. Sometimes the flames get them first. Either way, it's not a pleasant way to go.

After a few minutes, a curious look tensed Brenda's face. She pointed to the remains. "Here's the problem."

JD and I hovered close.

By this time, Brad and Logan had inched into the room.

"Looks like the victim was shot twice," Brenda said. "Small caliber. Probably a 9mm. I'll know more when I get him back to the lab."

I exchanged a curious glance with JD.

Logan and Brad crept up beside us to get a closer look.

"Didn't I tell you guys to stay in the hallway?"

"Nobody's fallen through the floor yet."

"Get back outside. I don't need you two getting hurt on my watch."

They both raised their hands innocently and backed away from the corpse.

Logan stopped and examined some of the canvases stacked against the wall near the foyer. These weren't as badly damaged, but still, there wasn't much left of them—just charred fragments. The painting leaning directly against the wall, underneath the others, suffered the least amount of destruction. Logan tilted the other two frames away to get a better look at it. Fragments crumbled and fluttered, and the wood creaked.

"Holy shit!"

I glared at him. "What are you doing? This is a crime scene. Don't touch anything."

He leaned the other frames back against the wall and raised his hands innocently. "Sorry."

Logan had piqued my curiosity. "What did you find?"

31

"The apartment belongs to a guy named Marcel DeLeon," the sheriff said when we spoke to him in the hallway. His voice was muffled by his respirator. "I don't know about you, but the fact that this guy was an artist and was shot to death in his loft makes me think this might have something to do with Cornelius Worthington."

I didn't disagree. "Arson says an accelerant was used. Probably gasoline. They soaked the place and torched it on the way out."

"I want a look at building security footage, if there is any," Daniels said.

I nodded, then addressed Logan. "Are you sure about the painting?"

"I'm not an expert," Logan said. "But I have a couple works by Julian Krause in my home. I recognized the style."

"You recognized the style from a fragment of a painting?" Daniels said with a healthy dose of skepticism.

"Look, I'm just telling you what I saw."

"What's the value of that painting?"

"Again, I'm no expert, but I paid $20 million for mine."

The sheriff's brow lifted. "$20 million? For paint on canvas?"

"I've had offers for twice that much. It's been a good investment."

"Shit. I'm in the wrong business," Daniels grumbled.

There were dozens of burned paintings in the loft. No telling what their value was, if any.

JD said, "Are you thinking what I'm thinking?"

"We may have found our art forger," I said. "It would make sense. Somebody wanted to shut him up."

"I want what's left of those paintings evaluated by an expert," the sheriff said. "Let's find out what we're dealing with."

"Why kill an art forger?" Logan asked.

"Because he's probably the only one that can identify the forgeries that are hanging in galleries, museums, and private collections," I said. "We could be talking about hundreds of millions of dollars' worth of paintings."

"That's all speculation at this point," Brad said.

"True. But it's a place to start. And it pays to be suspicious."

"Dig into this guy," Daniels said. "See what you can find out."

Brenda and her crew bagged the remains and removed the body on a gurney.

We left the building and stepped into the Florida sunshine. I peeled off the face mask and took a breath of the fresh air. Well, somewhat fresh. It was still tainted with traces of smoke and ash.

I called Denise to give her an update on the situation and to ask her to run a background check on Marcel DeLeon.

"I suppose you want me to notify the next of kin?" Denise asked with a hint of annoyance in her voice.

"I'd appreciate that," I said.

She stifled a groan.

"I'll do it. Give me the contact information."

Her fingers danced across the keyboard. "Looks like you're off the hook. Both parents are deceased. Died in a boating accident 10 years ago. Marcel DeLeon. 32. No criminal history. Sole heir."

"You say that like his parents had money."

"Looks like they did." Denise's fingers clattered against the keyboard. "They were partners in a prominent law firm in New York and won several big settlements. They had a second home in the Keys."

"So, Marcel's a trust fund baby," I said.

"Could be," she replied, her fingers clacking the keyboard once again. "This is interesting and maybe a bit ironic. They died in a fire on board. It was ruled an accident. There was a brief investigation, but nothing much came of it. The fuel line ruptured, supposedly."

"Was Marcel a person of interest?"

"For a time. According to this news article, there was a little speculation," Denise replied.

"Interesting," I murmured. "What about friends, associates, a girlfriend?"

Her fingers danced again. "From his social media profile, it says he's in a relationship with Stacey Allen. I'll send you her contact information."

"You're the best," I said.

"I know," Denise replied dryly. "How are your shadows?"

"Staying out of trouble for the moment," I said, giving them a glance.

A small crowd had gathered around them. The movie stars smiled and signed autographs.

"Brad asked me out," she said, almost taunting me.

I tried to stifle my annoyance. "Did he?"

"Eh, I figure he's just being a flirt."

"Where are you two lovebirds going to go?" I asked, pretending to be unaffected.

"I don't know. We haven't settled on the details yet."

"I'm sure you two will have fun," I said, being a good sport about it. "Just be careful."

"Are you telling me to use protection?" she said with a sassy grin in her voice. She was just trying to get under my skin, and she was doing a damn good job of it.

"I wouldn't want to see you get heartbroken," I replied.

"I'm a big girl. I think I can take care of myself."

"I have no doubt," I said, the muscles in my jaw flexing.

"I gotta go. I'll talk to you later," she said, ending the call.

I slipped the phone back into my pocket.

"What's the matter?" JD asked, noticing my displeasure.

"I'll tell you about it later."

I searched the crowd for the property manager.

Debbie looked frazzled when I found her. There was no telling how long it would be before residents could return to their apartments. The smell permeated the entire building. The damage was relatively limited, but there were at least a dozen units that suffered severe water damage. It would take extensive remediation and repair. Mold would grow in no time. Drywall, insulation, and furniture would need to be removed. People's lives had been upended.

"I'm hearing rumors that someone didn't make it. Do you know who?" she asked.

Debbie had short dark hair with frosted highlights and a plump figure. Every waking hour outside the office was spent in the sun, and she had a deep tan and weathered skin to show for it.

I broke the bad news.

Her face tightened with sadness, and her eyes misted.

She told me the only security cameras were in the main lobby and at the rear exit of the building. That was it. There was nothing in the hallways. "I'll check the files and send over the footage when the power gets restored." Then she added, "No telling when that will be."

"Did you ever have any problems with Marcel as a tenant?"

"Oh, Lord, no! I wish they were all like Marcel. He paid his rent on time, and I never got any noise complaints. He didn't live in the building. This was his studio. Sometimes he'd be in there painting all day and all night." She paused. "Do you know how the fire started? I know some of those art supplies can be flammable."

"We haven't determined the definitive cause of the blaze just yet," I said, not wanting to put out too many details at this time. "Have you seen anyone unusual in the building?"

She looked at me like it was a ridiculous question. "We have an eclectic mix of residents. *Unusual* is pretty normal around here."

"Did Marcel mention any problems he had with anyone?"

Her eyes narrowed with curiosity. "This was an accidental fire, wasn't it?"

"We're just being thorough." I flashed a disarming smile.

She knew I was holding something back. Debbie's sharp eyes didn't miss much, and she wasn't going to let me get away with a brush-off. "What are you not telling me?"

I finally admitted, "We believe the fire was set deliberately."

"By Marcel?" she asked, astonished.

"By the person who killed him."

Debbie gasped. "What!? Who would do something like that? Was this a robbery?"

I shrugged. "If anything comes to mind, get in touch."

I gave her a card and thanked her for her cooperation.

We started canvasing the crowd, asking anyone if they had seen or heard anything unusual. I shouted, "Does anyone know Marcel DeLeon?"

A few people raised their hands.

We spoke to a woman who lived across the hall from him. She didn't remember seeing or hearing anything strange.

Half the residents were at work during the time of the blaze. Some were just now arriving to see what damage had been done.

We talked to a few more residents, but nobody remembered hearing gunshots.

I figured whoever shot Marcel was the same person that shot Cornelius. A suppressor had probably been used. His neighbors to the sides and below were all at work.

Paris Delaney and her news crew approached. "Deputy Wild, what can you share with us?"

I gave my usual reply. "I can't share any specifics at this time. If anyone has seen anything suspicious leading up to the fire, please contact the Coconut County Sheriff's department."

"Is it true that the fire claimed the life of one victim?"

"I don't think the fire was responsible."

"Can you tell us more?"

"Not at this time."

She gave me a disappointed look.

We wrapped up at the scene and headed back to the station to fill out after-action reports. We sat in the conference room, typing away on iPads while Logan and Brad mingled in the office. They weren't terribly interested in the tedious, boring part of the job. I can't say that I was much interested in it either, but it was a necessary part of the deal.

Brad poked his head into the conference room as we were finishing up. "Denise says Marcel has no next of kin, but she searched his social media profile. It looks like he's got a girlfriend. Stacy Allen. Should we pay her a visit?"

"Way ahead of you," I said, my eyes blazing.

32

After she stopped crying, I started asking questions. Death notifications were never easy. We caught up with Stacy Allen at the Delphine. It was a luxury mid-rise with stylish floor plans, hardwood floors, and exorbitant rents. Pretty much par for the course.

She had invited us in, and we sat on the sofa in the living room. Stacy sat in a chair catty-corner, blotting her eyes with a tissue from a box on the glass coffee table. Her mascara streaked her cheeks. She was an adorable young girl in her mid-20s. Soft skin, caramel eyes, elegant cheekbones, and a slender figure. She had a gentle, nurturing voice. Wholesome. The kind of girl you wanted to keep around for a while. Perhaps a lifetime.

We left Logan and Brad behind. Now was not the time to overwhelm Stacy with their presence.

The apartment was light and airy, with teal coastal accents. A large watercolor of a conch shell in a soft pink frame hung on the wall above the sofa. There was a nice flatscreen display, surround sound speakers, and a gaming console. A shelf housed various knickknacks and shells. Verdant plants lined the corners.

"I talked to him last night," Stacy said. "I just don't understand." Her face wrinkled with sorrow, and she tried to stem the tide of tears. "Who would do something like this?"

"Tell me about his artwork," I said.

"He was a really good painter. So expressive. He could paint anything."

I exchanged a glance with JD.

"What kind of things did he like to paint?" I asked.

"He did a lot of abstract Impressionist stuff."

"Did he ever copy the great masterworks?"

She gave me a curious look. "All artists copy. It's part of the learning process. You take a work that you admire, and you try to recreate it. It helps you to get into the mindset of the original painter."

"Did he ever sell any of these copies?" It was a delicate way to put it.

Stacy's brow knitted. "I'm not sure what you mean. He sold his artwork. As I said, he was quite good."

"Was that his sole source of income?"

"No, Marcel had a trust fund," Stacy said. "Don't get me wrong, he made a good living from his art. He'd have been just fine if that was all he had. Marcel was all about passion."

She broke down into sobs again, the tears flowing. Her chest heaved and jerked, and she blotted her eyes.

We gave her a moment to collect herself.

"Did he ever sell the copies?" I asked again.

She dried her eyes and regarded me with caution. "What are you getting at?"

"Did he ever sell the copies as originals?"

That hung there for a moment.

"That would be highly unethical," she said, almost offended.

"It would. But that's not what I asked."

Stacy hesitated for a moment. "Why are you asking me these questions?"

"As I mentioned, Marcel was shot twice with a 9mm. His studio was burned, presumably to cover up any evidence."

"Evidence of what?"

"A forgery," I said.

Her face stiffened.

"We think there may be some connection to the death of Cornelius Worthington," I said.

Curiosity filled her eyes.

"Do you know if Marcel had any dealings with him?"

"The art world is a small community. Everybody knows everybody. Cornelius had a vast collection, and if I'm not mistaken, he did purchase a few pieces from Marcel. Originals, I might add," she said in a sharp tone.

"Any forgeries?"

The muscles in her jaw flexed. "I don't think I like the implication."

"We're just trying to understand what's going on and why two people involved in the art world are dead. It's clear to me that you cared deeply about Marcel. You want us to find out who killed him, don't you?"

"Of course." She broke down into sobs again. "I loved him. We were going to get married."

"Can you think of anybody who may have wanted to harm Marcel?" I asked.

She blotted her eyes and shook her head.

"Was he into anything illegal? Drugs?"

Stacy hesitated a moment. "I mean, he was an artist. He liked to smoke a little weed here and there. Every now and then, he'd take something to expand his mind. But it's not like he had a problem with the stuff."

"LSD? Mushrooms?

She nodded.

"Cocaine?"

She hesitated. "Not on a regular basis."

"Did he owe anybody any money? Did he have any gambling debts?"

"Marcel didn't owe anybody anything. He was loaded. I mean, he wasn't a billionaire. But he had more than enough."

I paused and exchanged a glance with JD.

He shrugged.

"Once again, I'm sorry for your loss," I said. "We won't take any more of your time. If you think of anything else, please get in touch."

I set my card on the glass coffee table.

"So what happens now?" she asked with concerned eyes.

"We try to find out who killed your boyfriend."

33

"Your doppelgängers left a little while ago," Teagan said as we took a seat at the bar.

I had noticed my car wasn't in the lot anymore when we arrived. "Hopefully, they're not getting into too much trouble."

"It's been pretty quiet around here since they left," Teagan said. "There were a ton of paparazzi earlier."

"I think we should enjoy this moment of normalcy," JD said.

I didn't disagree.

"You boys hungry?"

We nodded with eager eyes and growling bellies.

Teagan dealt out menus, and we perused the items. Jack ordered a lobster roll, and I went with the jerk chicken.

"Where do you think they disappeared to?" JD asked.

"One way to find out." I pulled out my phone and called Logan.

He answered after a few rings. "What's up, deputy?"

"Should I be worried about you two?"

He laughed. "No. We're just getting a taste of the local flavor. Brad and I are having lunch at the Coconut Grill. It's pretty good." He paused. "Did you talk to Stacy?"

"We did." I updated him on the situation.

"We stopped by the gallery and talked to Astrid."

"You did what?"

"We wanted to get her reaction to Marcel's death. See if we could suss out any connection between them."

I tried to stifle my annoyance. "How about you leave the investigative work to us?"

"Sure. No problem. Sorry. We just figured we'd try to help out a little. I mean, you guys only have so much time in the day. There's only two of you. Why not share the caseload? Plus, it will give us good insight into the process."

"While I appreciate your enthusiasm—"

"I know, I know. Leave it to the professionals. You got it, boss."

My face tightened. I paused for a moment and began to realize why Daniels hated it so much when I called him boss.

The damage was done. Hopefully, they learned something. "What did you find out?"

"It's probably not important," he said, taunting me.

"Spill it."

I think he sensed I wasn't in the mood to play games.

"She knew Marcel. Said he was a great artist. Apparently, he had a showing at her gallery, and she helped sell a few of his paintings. All originals, she added. I asked her if she knew of any Julian Krause paintings that Marcel had in his possession. Astrid said she wasn't familiar with the details of Marcel's private collection."

"What else did you get from her?" I asked.

"She was a little cagey, if you ask me."

"I'm surprised she talked to you at all," I said.

"Well, she likes us better than she likes you. Don't feel bad about that. I don't know why, but people tend to open up to us. They see us all the time in movies and TV. They feel like they have a personal connection and are more comfortable with us. Also, I didn't sleep with her and accuse her of a crime the next day."

I stifled a response.

"No judgment. You gotta do what you gotta do."

"When are you guys coming back to the marina?"

"I figure we'll chow down, then see the sights. Don't worry—I'll keep your car safe."

"You two are getting along?" I asked, doubtful.

Logan took a deep breath. "We both realized that we need to put the past aside and move forward. It's the best thing for us and the best thing for the project."

"Keep in touch. I'm responsible for you guys while you're here."

"Yes, *Dad*."

I ended the call, and we finished our meal. Afterward, we headed back to the *Avventura*, and I took Buddy out for a walk.

We decided now was a good time to go looking for meth. We were less conspicuous without the celebrities in tow. There was one sure-fire place in town where drugs were an easy score—Dowling Street. JD and I headed down to the seedy part of town in the Porsche.

For the right price, you could find just about anything you wanted and some things you didn't. We cruised the boulevard and pulled to the curb at the corner of Dowling and Clinton. A lovely young lady approached the car wearing fishnets with runs in them, a tight hot pink tube top, and a black miniskirt. The bottle blonde looked like she'd been working this strip for a long time—thin and weathered. It wasn't an easy life. She leaned against the car, doing her best to display some nonexistent cleavage. "What can I do for you, sugar?"

I showed her a picture of the red crystal meth on my phone. "You wouldn't happen to know where we could find something like this, would you?"

She lifted an eyebrow, and a flash of recognition flickered in her eyes. "If you want to get high, honey, I'll take you to the moon."

I laughed. "I bet you could."

"And I bet you got a rocket ship that could take us both there."

I smiled.

Her breath reeked of cigarettes and beer.

"Smile for me, would you?"

She did, exposing a considerable amount of tooth decay.

I figured she was no stranger to meth use. "Now, I know you can tell me where to find what I'm looking for."

"You two cops?"

"What would make you think something like that?" I asked.

"I thought I smelled bacon." Her eyes darted between JD and me. "I've seen you two down here before."

"Regular customers," I said.

"Shit," she said, drawing the word out, balking at the notion.

"It's new stuff. Really good. I know word travels fast on the street. Don't try to tell me you've never seen it before."

"I just say no to drugs," she said flatly.

I gave her an incredulous look.

"I ain't no snitch. And I don't need to get my ass beat."

"Fair enough. But I'm looking in the right place, aren't I?"

She hesitated for a long moment. "You're a little cold right now. You keep driving a few blocks, you might get hotter."

I smiled. "Thanks for the help."

She backed away from the car, pulled a cigarette from her purse, and lit it as we drove away.

We kept cruising down the block, but I had no doubt word would travel fast that we were out looking.

It didn't matter what time of day or night you came down here. There was always somebody willing to sell you something. All you had to do was pull to the curb, and somebody would approach.

We pulled over at the corner of Jefferson.

An upstanding young gentleman wearing baggy jeans, brand-new white sneakers that looked like they just came out of the box, and a hoodie approached the vehicle. It was summertime. The shoes were untied—a fashion statement. "What do you need?"

34

"Looking for a little glass," I said. "The red kind."

The dealer hovered by the window and glanced from me to JD. Then he thought better of it. "I don't know what you're talking about."

He backed away from the car.

I'm not sure what tipped him off. Maybe he had good gut instincts.

"Maybe you could point me in the right direction," I said.

"I'm just waiting on the bus."

This wasn't a stop on the route.

We cruised a few blocks down and found another street-corner dealer. He had long, greasy hair and a narrow face. A concert T and baggy jeans covered his thin frame. Plenty of pockets to stash goods or a gun. When we pulled to the curb, he approached with caution. "What you looking for?"

I told him.

"Man, you don't want that. I got something way better."

"Better?"

"Yeah, you don't want to be up for three days tweaking. Yo, I got pure Molly. You'll have a great time, and the comedown is easy."

"Pure, huh?"

"Nothing but the best," he assured.

"I really had my heart set on red ice."

"Sometimes you gotta roll with what life gives you. Be willing to adapt, improvise, and overcome."

I stifled a response. He didn't strike me as the motivational type, but he was giving it a good go. "Sorry. I got this thing about getting exactly what I want."

"I hear you, bro. We all want what we want. Come back in 20 minutes. I'll have it for you."

"Alright. How far do you have to go to get it?"

"Shit, that's *need to know*. And only I need to know."

"20 minutes," I said.

JD pulled away from the curb, and he watched us go.

Another customer pulled up behind us and took his attention. We took a left at the next intersection, circled around, and JD pulled over. I hopped out, hustled down a side street, and held up on the corner of Jackson and Dowling. I peered around the building and got eyes on the dealer. He'd already made the exchange with the other client. He got on his phone, made a call, then slipped the device back into his pocket. He loitered around for 15 minutes.

Then another car pulled up.

The dealer leaned into the passenger window, and there was a brief exchange. They shook hands, then the black Monte Carlo with red interior pulled away.

The dealer went back to holding up the wall.

I noted the plates on the car. The way the transaction went down made me think Mr. Monte Carlo was the street dealer's supplier.

I waited for JD to pull around and hopped in the car. We circled around and drove back to the dealer.

He approached the car as we pulled to the curb.

"You get the goods?" I asked.

He smiled. "I always come through."

With a wad of cash in my hand, I shook his. He dropped a baggie of crystal meth into the car. It fell between the seat and the door. I fished it out as he stepped away.

My face tightened with a frown. "Hey! This isn't what I asked for."

"That's red... *ish*."

"It's not what I asked for."

"Beggars can't be choosers. It's good stuff."

"I want my money back."

"Sorry. No refunds."

I glared at the little punk.

A lot of thoughts ran through my head. I wanted to hop out, slam the kid to the ground, and put him in cuffs. But this was his lucky day. He obviously didn't have the connection that we needed. I didn't want to make a scene and spook every other dealer down here.

Today, he got a pass.

I nodded to JD, and he pulled away from the curb. We headed back to the station, logged the drugs in as evidence, and we filled out after-action reports. We could always pick up the dealer later if need be.

Denise ran the plates on the Monte Carlo. Darius Johnson. A real upstanding member of the community. Priors for possession and assault. A small-time player. Not who we were looking for.

In the afternoon, JD and I headed across the island to the practice studio. We met up with the band and ran through the set one more time before the show. They were scheduled to play at *Sonic Temple* the next day.

Afterward, we hit Red November. The submarine-themed bar was full of long legs and short skirts. Not a bad place to be.

JD ordered a round of drinks, and we took in the sights and sounds. The guys in the band were glad to be the center of attention for an evening.

"Where are Logan and Brad?" Crash asked.

I shrugged.

"Good. Let's keep it that way."

My phone buzzed with a call from Stacy. She was the last person I expected to hear from.

"Can you come over?" she asked, panic in her voice.

"What's going on?"

"Two guys just banged on my door."

"What did they want?"

She hesitated a moment. "They said they wanted to talk. I've never seen them before in my life. They wanted to know what I told the cops."

"What did you tell them?"

"I told them I didn't say anything and that they needed to leave or I was going to call the cops. So I'm calling you."

"Are they still there?"

"I don't think so. I didn't open the door. I told them I had a gun, and I knew how to use it."

"Do you have a gun?"

"No."

I'm not sure I believed her. "I think it's time you tell me what's going on."

She was silent for a long moment. "Are you going to come over?"

"Yes. We'll be right there. But how about you go ahead and tell me? I'm pretty sure I already know."

"Stop wasting time and get over here."

35

I stayed on the phone with Stacy as we drove back to her apartment. JD parked in the visitor lot out front, and we hustled into the lobby. We took the elevator up to her floor, and I palmed the grip of my pistol as we stepped into the hallway. I gave a cautious glance around but didn't see anyone.

We hurried down the corridor, and I banged on Stacy's door. Footsteps padded across the foyer. The peephole flickered. "Is there anybody else out there?"

"The hallway is clear," I said.

She unlatched the deadbolt and pulled open the door with worried eyes. Stacy poked her head into the hallway just to make certain.

She hurried us inside and latched the door behind us.

"You sure you don't recognize the men that were at your door earlier?"

"I swear, I've never seen them before in my life. How did they know I talked to you?"

"Maybe they saw us earlier."

"You mean they've got me under surveillance?" Stacy paced around nervously, her brow furrowed, her tawny eyes distraught.

"I think it's time you came clean," I said.

"I'm not gonna get in trouble, am I? I mean, I didn't do anything."

An exasperated sigh slipped from my mouth. "You're not going to get in trouble."

"You promise?"

I gave her a stern gaze.

"Okay." She paused and took a deep breath. "You were right. Marcel may have painted a few *replicas*."

"Replicas?"

"Homages."

"Forgeries," I clarified.

"If you want to put it that way."

"And he sold them to Astrid," I speculated.

She nodded. "Among other places."

"If Marcel had a trust fund, why would he do that?"

Stacy shrugged. "He wanted to see if he could. I mean, it was kind of fun. He was just going to do it once, just to see if he could pass off his work as one of the greats," she said with admiration in her eyes. "It was so much fun. The thrill of it. I mean, we knew we were doing something wrong, but it really wasn't wrong. He was just making a painting. Putting another piece of art into the world. Something that people would enjoy. Collectors were desperate for these things. The paintings were amazing."

"Apparently."

"I mean, he really captured the spirit of these artists. He channeled their energy, and they came to life through him. Reborn."

I stifled an eye roll.

She was passionate. "I really believe that. We held a séance and summoned the departed. Marcel offered himself as a vessel so that they could paint once again through him. In his mind, it wasn't really a forgery. Marcel was allowing the artist to do what they loved once again. It really was kind of noble."

JD and I regarded her with skepticism. It never ceased to amaze me the mental hoops people would jump through to justify their nefarious actions.

"Did Astrid know the artworks were forgeries?"

"I don't know what she knew, and I didn't ask. We went to great lengths to make them seem authentic. She had them all appraised. She made a ton of money. We made a ton of money. Well, Marcel did."

"And you didn't get anything out of the deal?" I snarked, full of doubt.

"Like I said, we were going to get married. I wasn't concerned with money. Marcel took care of me."

"Why were these guys at your door asking questions?"

Stacy shrugged. "I don't know."

"Did Marcel have any partners in this enterprise that you didn't know about?"

She shook her head. "It was just me and him. We created elaborate backstories about how we came into possession of the artwork. Inherited from his parents' collection. That's what he told Astrid. And that's what Astrid told the clients."

"So, she knew?"

"I don't know."

I regarded her with doubt and thought for a moment. "Do you think you could pick out all of the forgeries that Marcel painted?"

36

Astrid didn't look pleased to see us when we stormed into the gallery. It was full of patrons, wine glasses dangling from tipsy hands. The guests mixed and mingled, looking at the large canvases of art on display. Astrid had taken her paint-splattered dress, affixed it to a canvas, and called it art.

People loved it. *"So avant garde."*

We caught the tail end of the showing. It was another stuffy event for Coconut Key's elite. Vera Voss was there. So was Joyce.

Paris Delaney and her news crew mingled, soaking up footage of the event. I may or may not have tipped her off that something was about to go down at the gallery. She had arrived before us on the pretense of covering Coconut Key's social scene. Under normal circumstances, it would be good PR. Tonight, however, it would prove disastrous.

Astrid spoke with a couple and excused herself when her eyes locked onto me. The murmur of conversation drifted through the air. Astrid strutted across the gallery, a devil behind her eyes. "This is an invitation-only event."

"You know Stacy, don't you?" I said in a patronizing voice, re-introducing the two. "Marcel's girlfriend."

Stacy shifted uncomfortably, her eyes darting toward the floor.

Astrid forced a smile. "Yes, it's good to see you. I'm so terribly sorry about your loss. Marcel was such a talented man."

Stacy forced a grim smile.

Astrid sucked in a deep breath. "So, what is it that I can do for you?"

"It's my understanding that Marcel may have passed forgeries to your gallery," I said. I didn't shout it, but I didn't lower my voice either.

A few people standing by craned their necks and stared with wide eyes upon hearing my words.

Rage flourished under Astrid's skin, but she forced a pleasant face. "Not possible. As I mentioned before, I only deal in artwork with known provenance, or that has been thoroughly vetted."

Stacy muttered in my ear, then pointed to one of the paintings on the wall.

"Are you sure?" I asked.

She nodded, then her nervous eyes flicked to Astrid.

The gallery owner's eyes threw daggers.

Paris and her cameraman closed in.

"That's one of Marcel's," Stacy said, her voice carrying across the crowd.

"You're saying that painting is a forgery?" I said a little louder.

There were gasps among the patrons standing nearby.

"It's time for you all to leave," Astrid said. "I don't appreciate the disruption." Her laser eyes focused on Stacy. "I don't know what you're up to, but these defamatory statements are without merit."

"That's one of Marcel's paintings," Stacy declared. She looked around the gallery. "That's not the only one I see."

"So, you are admitting to fraud? Marcel represented those paintings to me as authentic. They've been verified. I'm not sure if this is an attempt to ruin my reputation or if you're playing some game to adjust the valuation of the paintings. Either way, I don't find it amusing."

"I'm not lying," Stacy said.

Gossip rifled through the crowd, and it wasn't long before the entire gallery was talking about it.

I was pretty sure the revelation would put a damper on sales for the rest of the evening.

The camera hovered close.

Astrid composed herself, then spoke in a tone loud enough for everyone to hear. "I can assure you, every work in this gallery is authentic. I challenge anyone to prove otherwise." She hedged her bets. "At the end of the day, I have to rely on what the experts tell me and the declarations made by the sellers." Astrid took a breath. "I welcome this opportunity to once again verify the authenticity of the works in question. The art world needs to be held accountable. Only through transparency can we build trust." Her eyes blazed into Stacy's. "Go ahead, pick out the so-called forgeries," she said in a snooty voice. "We will have an independent evaluator come in and authenticate them. We will put this notion to rest, and you will have to answer to my lawyers."

Stacy swallowed hard.

I hoped she was telling the truth.

Stacy walked through the gallery and picked out three more paintings that she claimed Marcel forged.

Paris ate it up. Her face was filled with glee. This story would be the talk of the town by morning.

"Deputy Wild, how did you first become aware of the potential forgeries?" Paris asked.

"Thanks to Logan Chase. He recognized a painting at an earlier crime scene that was suspicious. I reiterate, at this time, we don't know if the painting is a forgery or not."

"Do you know how many forgeries could be in circulation?"

"I'm afraid I can't say at this time."

We left the gallery and caught a rideshare to the station. The three of us couldn't fit in the Porsche. Stacy filled out a sworn affidavit, and we recorded her statement on video. Then we took her to the Seven Seas. I made the driver double around a few times to make sure we weren't followed.

Stacy didn't feel comfortable staying in her apartment, so we put her up in the hotel. I gave her the usual speech.

"Don't use your cell phone. Don't call your friends. Don't tell anyone where you are. You've clearly ruffled a lot of feathers."

Stacy frowned. "I know. You have to believe me. I'm not lying. Marcel painted those works."

"I believe you," I said.

"You said I'm not going to get in trouble, right?"

"As long as you keep cooperating and testify, if need be."

She nodded.

We left and caught a rideshare back to her apartment and picked up the Porsche. Then we headed back to the marina at Diver Down. It was early, and the band was still out carousing around. I had no doubt they'd show up later on with an entourage, looking to extend the festivities.

My Ferrari wasn't in the lot, and the movie stars weren't on the boat. I resisted the urge to check in on them. They were big boys. They could handle themselves.

JD slipped behind the bar and poured two glasses of whiskey out of habit. "If what Stacy says is true, there's gonna be a lot of pissed-off people in this town."

He handed a drink to me, but I declined.

"Oh, yeah. Right." He went back to his rant and two-fisted it. "Can you imagine holding the bag on a worthless painting that you paid millions for?" JD shook his head. "I think I'd be inclined to do everything possible to prove it was real, even if I knew it was fake."

There was no incentive to discover forgeries. Everybody in the system made money on the paintings. They were incentivized to keep up the charade.

The sheriff buzzed my phone. "This is your responsibility."

"What is my responsibility?"

"You and numbnuts need to get over to the corner of Redfin and Gobi Drive."

"What happened now?"

"You'll see." There was almost a grin in the sheriff's voice. A tone that almost made me sick to my stomach. I knew what we were going to find before we got to the scene.

37

Red and blue lights swirled atop patrol cars. A small crowd of pedestrians gathered on the sidewalk.

I saw it right away, and I closed my eyes. I couldn't bear to look.

JD pulled to the curb at the intersection, and I had to confront the reality. We hopped out of the Porsche and ambled to the scene.

The white Ferrari had plowed into a telephone pole that was now at a slanted angle. The wires sagged above, and the hood was crumpled like an accordion. Both doors were open, and the vehicle was empty. An ambulance was on the scene, and red and white LEDs flickered.

Traffic crawled by—a sea of headlights and taillights. Rubberneckers taking in the spectacle.

I looked around for the culprits but didn't see them anywhere.

Daniels was on the scene with folded arms, almost delighting in my misfortune. "Care to explain why your car is wrapped around a telephone pole?"

"I loaned it out."

"Well, those two idiots fled the scene. I don't know who's worse, them or you?"

"Any witnesses?"

"Not so far." Daniels gave me a stern gaze. "Rein those two in. This isn't Hollywood. I'll be damned if those guys are gonna come to my town and act like a bunch of assholes. They might be able to get away with this in Los Angeles. Not here."

"I'll sort it out."

"You better."

I called Logan. The phone rang several times and went to voicemail. "You'll never guess what I'm looking at right now—my car wrapped around a telephone pole. It would be wise for you to call me back as soon as possible," I said in as calm a voice as I could manage.

I had to admit, I was maintaining pretty well. I was mad. So mad that I didn't react.

There were bits of plastic and glass sprinkled around the wreckage, glittering from the mercury vapor light overhead.

JD and I surveyed the damage.

He cringed. "Yeah, that's gonna take a little bit more than a new coat of paint."

"I'd say."

He shook his head. "Damn shame. It was a nice car."

"It was growing on me."

We canvassed the area, talking to pedestrians, but nobody saw anything. Or they weren't saying.

Paris Delaney showed up, and the cameraman started gathering footage. The ambitious blonde approached me. "Isn't that your car?"

"It is."

"What happened? Did you get into an accident?"

"No. It seems the car did it all on its own."

It didn't take much for her to put the pieces together. "Was someone else driving?"

"It didn't drive itself into the pole, now did it?"

She sneered at me. "Who was driving?"

I shrugged. "I didn't see it happen. So I don't know who was driving."

"You must have some idea," she said, knowingly.

She waved her cameraman over.

"I have no comment at this time."

It didn't take long for a wrecker to show up. I had the car towed to Jack's body shop guy, but with the amount of damage that the car had, I doubted it would ever be the same.

DOT showed up and cleaned up the street, and we headed back to the *Avventura*. I thought about how I would handle the situation on the way back.

38

"I don't know what happened," Logan slurred when he returned to the boat. "We came out to the car and it was gone."

His sheepish gaze found Brad.

Brad hesitated. "Yeah. Gone."

"Really?" I said in a doubtful voice. "You're telling me the car was stolen?"

They both nodded.

I didn't buy it for a second. They were three sheets to the wind and could barely stand. Their hair was tousled, and their cheeks red. Bloodshot eyes. They both looked a little roughed up, and Logan had a welt across his forehead where it hit the steering wheel. The car was too old for airbags.

"You expect me to believe that?" I scoffed. "There was no damage to the steering column. The car wasn't hot-wired."

"I must have lost the keys," Logan said. "Look, I'll buy you a new one. It's not a big deal."

"It's a big deal."

"I get it. I know how passionate you are about that car."

"It's not about the car," I growled. "Let me see your collarbone."

"What?"

"Take your shirt off."

His brow crinkled. "Why?"

"Because I said so."

"Look, I don't really swing that way, but..."

"Take it off!" I commanded.

Logan complied.

A red rash and purple bruising ran from his collarbone across his chest. It was the width of a seatbelt.

"Lie to me one more time," I said, staring him down. "I dare you."

There was a long pause.

"You guys got in the car, blitzed out of your mind, and put it into a telephone pole," I said.

Logan sighed. "Look, we were getting chased by paparazzi. We had to ditch them. Shit happens. I'm really sorry, man. I'll totally make it up to you. Like I said, I'll buy you another car."

"You could have killed somebody. You fled the scene of a crime. That's a felony."

"You're not gonna arrest me, are you?"

I glared at him.

"If this gets out to the press, I'm screwed. It could jeopardize the entire project."

He was just trying to save his ass.

I exchanged a glance with JD. This was a problem.

My phone buzzed with a call from the sheriff. "Did you find the idiots that were driving your car?"

"I think so," I said in an annoyed voice. Dealing with these two was like herding cats.

"I run this town based on law and order. I'm not gonna turn a blind eye to their shenanigans. Paparazzi are claiming to have seen Logan behind the wheel."

"Did anybody see the accident?"

The sheriff sighed. "No. But I'm sending two deputies to take Logan into custody."

I stepped onto the aft deck for some privacy and slid the glass door shut behind me.

A patrol car pulled into the parking lot. Deputies Halford and Matheson stepped out and headed down the dock toward the *Avventura*.

I cringed. "Nobody can definitively put Logan behind the wheel at the time of the accident."

I wasn't going to jump on board and defend Logan's actions, but I knew this was going to be a shit show.

"I have a handful of witnesses and paparazzi that saw the two of them leaving Oyster Avenue in an inebriated state," Daniels said. "They got into the car, caused a ruckus when they left, and tore off like a bat out of hell. Doesn't take a rocket scientist to put two and two together. If that little punk keeps his mouth shut, he might walk away from this. But he's not gonna beat the ride. He's gonna spend the night in jail. Maybe it will teach him a lesson."

A gaggle of paparazzi and reporters flooded into the parking lot and hustled down the dock.

Halford and Matheson crossed the passerelle to the aft deck.

"Evening, Wild," Halford said with a slight grin. He was going to arrest a celebrity and get his 15 minutes of fame.

Logan freaked out inside the salon when he saw the cops.

"Logan Chase," Halford said when he stepped inside. "You're under arrest for driving under the influence, reckless driving, and fleeing the scene of an accident."

Logan's face drained of color, and his eyes rounded.

"Turn around. Put your hands behind your back."

"You can't arrest me! I didn't do anything."

Halford wasn't putting up with his nonsense. "Turn around and put your hands behind your back, or the situation is going to get a whole lot worse."

Logan frowned but complied.

Halford ratcheted the cuffs around his wrists.

Brad looked on with amusement.

Halford took Logan by the arm and escorted him out of the salon.

Cameras flashed, and the news crew soaked up the footage. The media had swarmed the dock.

"You have the right to remain silent..." Halford began.

"I suggest you keep your mouth shut," I muttered to Logan as he passed.

He hung his head low as they escorted him across the gangway. The horde of paparazzi shouted questions.

"How much have you had to drink tonight?"

"Were you behind the wheel?"

"Will you be going to rehab?"

The deputies escorted Logan down the dock and stuffed him into the back of a patrol car while the swarm followed, video cameras rolling, camera flashes flickering.

JD and Brad joined me on the aft deck to watch the sideshow.

"It's a damn shame," Brad said. "I told him we should take a cab home."

Paris Delaney texted. *[Care to comment?]*

[Nope.]

[LOL. Didn't think so.]

Every gossip blog sensationalized the story in no time. It was all over the internet.

My phone buzzed with a call from Joel. In as calm a voice as he could muster, he said, "Care to tell me what happened?"

39

In the morning, my phone buzzed with a call from the sheriff. JD, Brad, and I were finishing up breakfast.

"Your boy just got arraigned. Prosecution decided not to bring charges at this time. Go figure."

"I told you. Without a witness putting him behind the wheel, it's all speculation."

"He should be processed out soon. Keep him on a short leash from here on out."

"You got it."

I ended the call, and we chowed down.

"It's my fault," Brad said. "I should never have let him get behind the wheel like that."

"I need you both to get it together. Enough of this nonsense."

Brad raised his hands innocently. "No more shenanigans. We are totally focused from here on out."

I'd believe it when I saw it.

Daniels gave me another call just before Logan got processed out. I took the Devastator to the jail and waited. As usual, a horde of paparazzi crowded around. They went into a frenzy when Logan stepped out of the jail. He looked like he'd been through the wringer—tousled hair, bloodshot eyes, and the welt on his forehead had turned into a nasty bruise. I would imagine he was pretty sore this morning from the impact.

He wasn't moving too fast.

I escorted him through the crowd as they shouted more questions.

Again, Logan kept his head hung low as I escorted him to the passenger seat. I hustled around, climbed behind the wheel, and cranked up the HEMI.

The media surrounded us, taking pictures, videos, and screaming questions.

I blew the horn a few times to get them to move out of the way. Logan shielded his eyes with his hand, slinking low in the seat. We pulled away from the curb, and a caravan of reporters followed us back to the marina.

"Have fun last night?" I asked.

Logan gave me a look, and I grew concerned he might not make it back to the boat without hurling. His skin had that pale, sickly green color.

"I fucked up. I know."

We pulled into the lot at Diver Down, and I parked by the dock. We hustled out of the car and made our way back to the *Avventura*, trying to stay ahead of the media. We crossed the passerelle to the aft deck and into the salon.

A gorgeous blonde in a fashionable gray pantsuit greeted us with a friendly smile.

Logan looked relieved to see her.

"I don't want you to worry," she said to Logan. "My team has been working on this all night. I just got in a few minutes ago. We have a game plan. We're going to get ahead of the story, and with any luck, it'll be gone by the next news cycle."

Logan nodded.

"I don't know what's worse. This, or the fact you punched a girl. But we're working on both." She looked him up and down. "You look like shit. Get showered and changed."

He ambled out of the salon like a scolded child and made his way to the below-deck guest quarters.

The blonde extended her hand, and we shook.

"I'm Heather. His publicist. I'll be handling the fallout from this event."

She looked past me at the mob of media on the dock.

She studied the crowd, formulating a game plan. "I think the best course of action is to ignore and deny. Hopefully, somebody else will do something stupid to draw attention away from this." Her eyes gazed at Brad.

He raised his hands innocently. "Don't look at me. I'm all out of stupid."

"We need a good political scandal. That will take eyes off the situation. I'll make a few phone calls."

I exchanged a curious look with JD. The girl was ruthless. She dialed a number. "Hey, I need a favor."

I don't know what she was about to cook up, and I didn't want to know. She moved out of the salon and into the galley for some privacy.

"The girl's good at what she does," Brad said. "She's with the best PR firm in Los Angeles. She's a miracle worker. You get in a bind, call Heather. She'll clean it up."

"Will she hide the bodies too?" JD asked.

"Yes, and you'll get a bill for it at the end of the month."

I think he was joking. But I'm not entirely sure.

I flipped on the TV in the salon just to see what they were saying. Paris Delaney was on the dock doing a live shot at the stern of the *Avventura*. A long lens let the camera see into the salon. It was a little surreal watching ourselves watch the television.

I dimmed the glass to eliminate their view. The perks of a luxury yacht with all the latest technology.

After 20 minutes of phone calls, Heather returned to the salon. "Okay, gentlemen. I have a solution. But this is going to take a joint effort. I will need all of your cooperation. Can I count on your support?"

40

I shouldn't have been shocked by her solution. After all, she was a Hollywood publicist with deep connections.

Heather strode across the aft deck and crossed the passerelle with a confident smile.

The reporters crowded around her as she hit the dock.

"As you all know, Logan is in town doing character research for an upcoming project. Authenticity has always been a key component of Logan's performances. Unfortunately, last night, Logan was carjacked while driving a friend's car. We've obtained traffic cam footage of the event, and I will be releasing that to media outlets after I make this statement. It's clear to me these carjackers went on a joyride and crashed the vehicle."

"Why was Logan arrested?" a reporter shouted, interrupting.

"Let me speak," she said, her eyes blazing into the reporter.

Heather was not a girl to be messed with.

She continued, "The facts of the situation were not known at the time. The deputies were just doing their duty to protect the local community. No one is above the law. Once the situation was explained, this matter was cleared up. Still, as a matter of experience, Logan decided he wanted to spend the night in jail to see what it was like. Thanks to the Coconut County Sheriff's Department, that lifelong dream was made a reality. Logan can take that experience now and utilize it in future performances." Heather smiled. "This whole event has been understandably traumatic, and we ask that you respect Logan's privacy in this matter. Thank you."

It was total BS.

"Why was he arraigned this morning if he was in jail of his own volition?"

The reporters clamored, shouting more questions.

Heather spun around and strutted across the gangway to the aft deck, ignoring them. She stepped into the lounge.

"Let's see this video," I said.

Heather grinned, pulled out her phone, and displayed the clip. Sure enough, what looked like grainy Department of Transportation footage appeared on her screen.

A white Ferrari 308 pulled to a traffic light.

A masked thug exited from the vehicle that pulled up behind them. He ran to the driver's side of the Ferrari, brandishing a pistol, and pulled the driver from behind the wheel.

This was low-resolution footage at night from a distance, but it looked convincing.

With the occupants out of the vehicle, the carjacker hopped into the Ferrari and took off.

The footage wasn't real.

A special effect like this was child's play for a Hollywood visual effects studio.

Brad muttered into my ear. "I told you she was good."

"You think people are going to believe that?" I asked.

"I know they will," Heather said with confidence.

Paris Delaney buzzed my phone. "Here's where I call in that favor."

My brow knitted with confusion. "I don't recall owing you a favor."

"Well, let's just pretend that you do. I'll find a way to make it up to you," she said in a sultry voice.

I knew what she wanted.

"You give me that sit down with Logan, and I help disseminate this BS story. He gets to talk about his traumatic experience at gunpoint, and I get a scoop. Everybody's happy."

I handed the phone to Heather. She gave me a confused look.

"The local news," I said.

Heather took the phone. "Hi, this is Heather. How can I help you?"

The ladies chatted and worked out some kind of deal. Afterward, Heather gave me the phone back and smiled. "See, it's all working according to plan."

"Provided nobody comes forward that actually saw the accident," I said.

Heather shrugged it off. "Deny till death. And who are they going to believe? A beloved movie star, or someone off the street trying to cash in on a quick money-grab by making a false accusation?"

Heather was one girl you didn't want to get on the wrong side of. She was ruthless.

Logan stayed in his stateroom for most of the day, hiding out, avoiding us and the paparazzi.

He decided to take the evening off, but Brad rode with us over to Jack's house. He barely fit in the back of the Devastator. We grabbed the Wild Fury van and drove to the practice studio.

The '70s era matte black van was a full-on resto-mod with a souped-up engine, chrome exhausts, Cragar S/S rims, and a custom cut grill that looked like shark's teeth. The band's logo was emblazoned on the sides. There was no mistaking the van.

We pulled into the lot, and the usual band of miscreants loitered out front. There was a little chit-chat with Brad on the way in, then we met up with the guys in the band. Pinky and Floyd loaded the gear into the Wild Fury van. We drove to Sonic Temple, and the roadies loaded in the gear. The guys got on stage for a quick soundcheck. After a few songs, Brad got on stage with the band and sang *High Octane Love*.

He wasn't half bad.

He didn't quite have the howling vocals of *Thrash*, JD's stage name. But his performance was good enough that the band decided to pull him on stage during the actual show.

Sonic Temple was packed, as usual. Girls in tight miniskirts. Long legs and stiletto heels. Low-cut tops, teased hair, and plenty of eyeliner. It was a retro explosion of the '80s.

I think many were hoping to catch a glimpse of the movie stars.

The band was nearing the end of the show when JD shouted into the microphone, "We have a special guest for you tonight. All the way from Los Angeles, California, please welcome to the stage, Brad Tyler!!!"

The crowd went wild, screaming and howling.

Brad stepped into the spotlight and soaked up the adulation of the crowd. He was truly the movie star version of JD, dressed as an '80s rocker with leather pants and a cut-up concert T.

Girls threw bras and panties on stage and flashed their perky peaks.

Brad took the microphone, bowed humbly before JD, and said, "I just want to thank these guys for welcoming me into their circle, and letting me tag along. I'm really excited about the upcoming project and I hope to do it justice."

Styxx clicked off the beat, and the band broke into *High Octane Love*. Dizzy's guitar cut like a chainsaw, and Crash's bass boomed. A wall of sound slammed the audience, and Brad did his best impression of Jack. He flung his hair and pranced around the stage like a rockstar, having the time of his life. He howled into the microphone and belted out the lyrics even better than he had done during soundcheck.

The crowd ate it up.

He wouldn't put JD out of a job anytime soon, but it was a spectacle. And people loved a spectacle.

I stood stage-left, taking it all in.

The security guard tapped me on the shoulder and shouted into my ear. "There's a girl here that says she knows you."

He pointed her out. She hovered by the barrier next to the stage.

I didn't recognize her at first.

"Says her name's Penelope."

41

Penelope wore a raven wig that dangled at her shoulders. She was dressed like a regular groupie. She didn't look bad in that short skirt and low-cut top, the girls pushed together.

I moved to the barrier and ushered her inside the security area. I took her by the arm and escorted her down the hallway toward the green room.

She jerked her arm away as we reached the door.

"Where were you the other day?" I asked.

"You were followed," she said.

I rolled my eyes. "I wasn't followed."

"There were people there waiting. Whether they followed you or not is irrelevant. It wasn't safe."

My eyes narrowed at her, full of skepticism. "Where's Haley?"

"She's safe."

"Take me to her, now!"

"No."

We stared at each other for a long moment.

I escorted her into the green room and pulled the door shut behind us. The rumble of Wild Fury seeped through the walls, but at least it was a little easier to have a conversation.

Beer bottles on countertops vibrated with each stomp of the kick drum.

"Tell me your side of the story," I said.

"I told you. I'm not the bad guy here."

"Right," I said, my voice thick with sarcasm. "Nash is."

"Isn't it obvious?"

"Start talking."

She surveyed me for a long moment. "They want Haley."

"Yeah, they want to see that she's safe and sound."

"No. They don't. They don't give a shit about her. They want what she can do for them."

"What's that?"

"What she's created can change the world. If it falls into the wrong hands, that change is going to be for the worse."

I gave her an exasperated look.

"The kid is a genius. She wrote a program that can crack any encryption. And I mean *any* encryption. No data is safe. I'm talking access to DoD servers. Foreign intelligence could get access to troop movements, contingency plans, weapons capabilities, nuclear codes."

That hung there for a moment.

"Are you starting to get the picture?" Penelope asked.

I nodded.

"This thing doesn't need a supercomputer to run. It's unlike anything else out there. A foreign government or terrorist organization with this technology could render our systems useless, wreak havoc on our domestic infrastructure, and turn our weapons against us. Everybody wants this technology—foreign governments, terrorist groups, non-state actors, the CIA, the Department of Defense."

"How does Nash play into all of this?"

"I've had my suspicions about him for a long time. I tried to bring my concerns to my superior, and they were ignored. It's no wonder I was set up. Nash killed Haley's parents. They're framing me. I had to get her out of there, and I had to keep this technology safe."

"You think Nash is selling secrets?"

"I can all but prove it."

"That's the kind of thing you need to prove."

"I get shut down at every turn. I think my whole division is corrupt."

"Those are pretty big allegations."

"Doesn't make them any less true."

"Where's the software?" I asked.

"It's safe."

"I want you to take me to Haley."

She hesitated.

"You need to trust me," I said.

"I don't trust anybody," Penelope replied.

There was another long silence as we stared deep into each other's eyes. Her eyes weren't bad to look at.

"Declan says you're a good man. But I'm not sure what we can do against someone like Nash. He's got a lot of power."

"How many copies are there of the program?"

"One, on an encrypted drive. It can't be copied."

"So destroy the drive."

"I considered that," Penelope said.

"What stopped you?"

"At this point, it's the only leverage I have. Sure, someone could force Haley to write the program again, but that would take months. There's no telling if she would cooperate."

"Why did she write it in the first place?"

"To see if she could," Penelope said. "She's 14. She's not jaded and cynical like the rest of us. At least she wasn't. She's getting that way fast. She thought it could be used for good. In the wrong hands, it's the end of the world."

"How do you see this playing out?" I asked.

"I want her safe. I want the software in the right hands. I want my life back."

I stifled a chuckle. "Good luck. You're burned. There's no going back. You don't exist. Neither do Nash or his associates."

"What can I say? We are all high-level operators." She paused. "Declan tells me you have resources. Cobra Company."

"Declan tells you a lot."

"We go way back."

"Were you followed here?"

"No," she said.

"Are you sure about that?"

"I spotted the tails at the beach, didn't I?"

"I didn't have any tails at the beach," I said, adamant.

"Maybe you're slipping," she said, lifting a salty eyebrow.

"I don't slip."

"I hope you're as good as you think you are."

My face tightened with annoyance.

"Sensitive," she teased.

I ignored her. "Take me to Haley. Now."

42

We slipped out the back door of the club and stepped into the parking lot. The rumble of the band thumped the building and shook the ground.

It was loud.

Even in the lot, through a foot of concrete.

Penelope planted her plump lips on mine and gave me a passionate kiss out of the blue.

I didn't mind. I didn't mind at all.

I figured I might as well take advantage of the situation. I pulled her close with my hand in the small of her back and pressed her body against mine. She radiated warmth. A little hot rock of desire. She went for broke. If I didn't know better, I'd think she meant it.

Her lips were like heaven, and the fruity scent of her shampoo filled my nostrils. Her cherry lip gloss added to her lustful flavor.

I could get used to this kind of thing.

She parted with a hungry gaze in her eyes. She whispered, "Don't get excited. That's just for show, in case somebody is watching. I'm just another groupie you're taking home."

She clung onto my hand and played the part well, pulling me toward the street to catch a cab.

Drunk revelers listed up and down the avenue. Fans loitered around the entrance to Sonic Temple. The moon glowed overhead, and the stars flickered. Lights from signage bathed the boulevard in a kaleidoscope of colors. Cars whizzed by.

I glanced around, looking for anything suspicious. So did Penelope as she clung to my arm, pretending to be a drunk groupie.

We didn't have to wait long. Penelope flagged down a passing cab. I'm sure the driver spotted those long legs from a mile away. We hopped into the backseat, and Penelope gave the driver our destination.

We sped away from the curb, and she let go of my hand. There was no need to keep up the charade, but I tried to think of excuses.

My suspicious nature forced me to look over the driver's ID by the meter and compare the image to his features.

He watched me in the rearview.

"Busy night?" I asked.

"It's okay."

I gave him an extra tip and told him to backtrack a few times. He took us around in circles, and we both kept a watchful eye, making sure we weren't followed.

I leaned in and whispered in Penelope's ear. "I think you should kiss me again."

That sassy eyebrow lifted. "Is that what you think?"

"Just in case someone is following us."

"No one is following us."

"Are you sure?"

"I'm positive," she said in a definitive voice.

"How can you be certain?"

That earned me another sassy look.

I chuckled. It was worth a try.

The driver took us to the Seahorse Shores. It was a cheap motel on the edge of town, not far from the Pussycat Palace. It was one of those roadside fleabags that didn't ask a lot of questions. You could rent by the hour if need be. It had an old deco-style marquee out front, aglow with neon.

The driver pulled into the lot and dropped us off. We hopped out, and Penelope took my hand, leading me to unit #7. The two-story motel had been built in the late '50s. The last time it was remodeled was in the '70s—It had taken on a retro-chic quality.

She slipped the key into the slot and pushed into the room. I gave a glance around the parking lot, then followed.

The green shag carpet had its fair share of stains. Orange comforters lined the beds. They were rumpled from a few days of occupancy. Wood paneling lined the walls, and a 45-inch flatscreen display sat atop the dresser.

There was nobody in the room.

"Haley?" Penelope called out in a concerned voice.

A sinking feeling twisted in my gut.

Penelope darted to the bathroom and knocked on the door. "Haley, are you in there?"

There was no response.

Penelope pushed open the door to find an empty bathroom. She stepped inside and ripped the shower curtain back to make sure. The hooks rattled against the bar.

She stormed back into the bedroom, her eyes filled with terror. "She's not here."

"Maybe she left to get a snack."

"No. I told her not to leave the room."

"Since when do teenagers listen?" I regarded the whole situation with a healthy dose of skepticism. *Was Haley ever here?*

I grabbed Penelope's arm and held it tight as she moved toward the door. "If you're lying to me..."

"I'm not lying to you. She was here?"

She pulled her phone from her clutch and launched an app. After studying the screen for a moment, she murmured, "Shit!"

"Where is she?"

She dialed a number before answering me. Penelope held the device to her ear. After a few rings, Haley's voice crackled through the speaker. "Hello?"

"What are you doing?"

I could barely make out what Haley said. "I wanted to go home. I needed to get some things."

"I told you to stay in the hotel room."

"I've been in that hotel room for days."

"Stay put. We're coming to get you."

"Who is we?"

"I'm with Deputy Wild."

"Can we trust him?"

Penelope's eyes found mine. "Yes."

"I'm tired of this," she said, her voice breaking down into sobs of fear and sorrow. "I just want my life back."

"I'm sorry, but you can't go back to that life. It doesn't exist anymore."

Haley sniffled and cried.

"Just stay where you are. We're on our way. Stay on the phone with me till I get there."

"My battery is about to die."

"How is your battery about to die? I told you to stay off the phone. Who've you been talking to?"

"Nobody."

"Haley!"

"I called a few friends."

Penelope groaned in frustration. "What did I tell you about phone calls?"

"Not to make any. But I can't just not talk to anybody for the rest of my life. Besides, you said this phone was secure."

"It is secure. But if they're monitoring your friend's phone calls, they'll figure out you called and will be able to track your location."

I called a rideshare, and Penelope kept talking to Haley while we waited.

Before long, we were in the back of another car, heading to Haley's house. The driver wouldn't go fast enough for my taste.

Penelope stayed on the line until the call dropped. She tried to call Haley back, but the phone went straight to voicemail.

43

We turned the corner onto Haley's street. My body instantly tensed.

Two of Nash's thugs dragged Haley down the walkway and shoved her into the back of a black SUV with no plates and slammed the door shut. With her secured in the back, they hopped in up front.

The tires barked as they launched from the curb.

"Follow that SUV!" I shouted.

"It's not on the route," the driver said.

I dug into my pocket and pulled off a crisp C-note from my money clip and handed it to him.

He snatched the bill, stuffed it in his pocket, and stomped the pedal. The little four-banger did its best impression of a howl as we chased after the SUV.

Almost instantly, alerts from the rideshare company buzzed my phone. The driver got them too. The company knew that we hadn't stopped at our destination and were still in the car. The text message read: *[Is something wrong? We noticed you're still in the vehicle and have not reached your destination.]*

I texted back. [Everything's fine. Change of plans.]

[Please select a new destination within the app. Please note, we may not be able to accommodate all requests. It may be necessary for you to request a new ride. Thank you for choosing Zoomber.]

I stopped corresponding.

Tires squealed as the SUV turned right at the next intersection.

Our driver followed, albeit a little hesitant to keep up with their speed.

"Drive faster!" I growled.

"I don't want to get a ticket."

I flashed my badge. "Don't worry about it."

"If you say so." His foot stomped the gas, and the car accelerated, flinging Penelope and me against the seatbacks.

The SUV barreled down the residential street, whizzing past cars parked on gravel shoulders, zipping by white picket fences and towering palms.

The SUV took a hard left at the next intersection, and we followed.

It didn't take them long to figure out they had a tail. The SUV started pulling away, and I told the driver to go even faster. "Do not lose them! There's an extra hundred in it for you if we catch them."

"Make it two hundred."

"Deal."

The SUV took a hard right onto Harbor Heights. It threaded the needle into traffic.

We had to stop at the intersection and wait on a few cars before turning.

The SUV had opened up a large gap.

Our driver mashed the gas and weaved in and out of traffic. The car rolled from side to side with each change of direction. It didn't have the tightest suspension in the world.

We raced past shops and storefronts, trying to catch up. There were two lanes in either direction, split by the median.

For a moment, I thought they were going to get away, but the SUV got caught behind traffic at a light. Cars in front of the vehicle kept them from blasting through the intersection.

Two more black SUVs blew past us like we were standing still. The little four-cylinder of the rideshare only had so much get up and go.

A vehicle on the cross street pulled into the intersection, blocking the flow of traffic. It kept Nash's goons from advancing even after the light turned green.

Horns honked, and drivers shouted through open windows.

The two additional black SUVs pulled behind them. More goons hopped out, shouldering assault rifles. Decked out in black tactical gear, their faces covered with black balaclavas, they advanced toward Nash's men and opened fire.

My heart sank.

The clatter of gunfire echoed through the night air, and muzzle flash lit up the roadway like a string of firecrackers. The assailants peppered the driver and passenger with bullets. Glass shattered, and metal popped and pinged.

With the CIA agents neutralized, one of the assailants hammered the stock of his rifle against the back seat window, shattering it.

Shards of glass fell away.

He reached his arm inside, unlocked the door, and pulled it open. The goon yanked out a terrified Haley and ushered her toward one of the assailant's SUVs.

By this time, we had caught up to the traffic jam.

I drew my weapon and hopped out of the rideshare. I crept along the side of the car and angled my pistol over the hood at the goons.

One of the assailants saw me and opened fire.

Bullets snapped through the air, and I took cover behind the fender.

The thugs stuffed Haley into the vehicle, climbed in, and banked a U-turn, mowing down the shrubs in the median. The SUV bounced and bobbled, making its way into the opposite lane of traffic, racing away.

The two vehicles disappeared into the night.

I hopped back into the rideshare. "Follow those two SUVs."

"Fuck that!" the driver exclaimed, fear bathing his eyes. The left front of his car had been riddled with bullets.

"Then get out. I'm taking the car."

He scowled at me. "Fuck you. You can't do that."

"Get out. Now!"

I hopped out of the backseat, hustled around to the driver's side, and tried to yank open the door, but it was locked.

By this time, Penelope had her pistol pointed at the back of his head.

The driver had an abrupt change of mind. He unlocked the door and hopped out.

I slid behind the wheel.

Penelope joined me in the front seat

"Fuck you both!" the driver shouted.

I turned the wheel and hit the gas, barreling over the median. The car bounced and rattled.

The driver looked on in horror as we totally demolished the suspension.

I turned into the opposite lane and gave chase, but the SUVs were long gone.

To complicate matters, the left front tire was flat. The rim ground against the concrete, sending sparks into the night.

I don't know if the tire burst when we hit the curb or if it had taken a bullet. Either way, we didn't get far.

I pulled over, killed the engine, and we hopped out.

The driver jogged to catch up with us. "That's what you get for trying to steal my car, motherfucker. I'm going to report you both."

I called dispatch and had them send a patrol unit.

The driver kept bitching up a storm. "Who's going to pay for this?"

"It will be taken care of," I assured.

"It better be!"

I asked Penelope, "Do you have another way to track Haley?"

44

The distant sound of sirens warbled, drawing closer. Penelope was still technically a fugitive, and I had assisted her. We took off on foot before the patrol unit arrived. We didn't want to be anywhere near the scene. There would be a lot of explaining to do, and that would only slow us down. Time was of the essence now.

The driver shouted obscenities at us as we sprinted away.

We rounded the corner on Sable Palm Drive.

"I gave Haley another tracking device to activate in case of emergency," she said, huffing and puffing. "Let's hope it's still operational."

We slowed up after a distance when I spotted a cell phone on the ground. I scooped the battered device up. The screen was cracked, and the case scuffed.

"That's the burner I gave Haley," Penelope said. "They must have tossed it out."

Penelope checked the tracking app on her phone.

There was no indication of Haley's current location.

I called the sheriff. He wasn't too pleased about the late-night call. "This better be good, Wild."

"We have a little situation."

I gave him a brief update.

"And you buy her story?"

"I watched Nash's men abduct Haley with my own eyes."

"Maybe they were just recovering her."

"She didn't look too cooperative."

"Maybe the girl's head is messed up, and she doesn't know who to trust."

"That's possible," I admitted.

"Bring Penelope in. Let's sit down and have a debrief and get to the bottom of this. I want the full story. Everything. And I don't want to hear the word *classified*."

"No time," I said.

The sheriff exhaled a frustrated breath. "Why is it always difficult with you?"

"I don't make things difficult. They get that way all on their own."

"You'll find Nash's men in an SUV at the corner of Harbor Heights and Marlin Avenue."

"Any idea who the attackers were?"

"No."

"The minute you hear anything about the girl, you call me. I'm gonna get down to the scene and see what I can sort out. In the meantime, I'm going to pretend we never had this phone call. I hope you're making the right decision by trusting her."

"Me too."

Penelope eyed me.

I ended the call and tried to arrange another rideshare, but our previous driver had left a major complaint with the service, and they declined to accommodate my request.

I called Jack, but it went to voicemail. I figured the guys in the band were knee-deep in extracurricular activities by now.

"I've got her," Penelope exclaimed with excitement as she studied the tracking app on her phone.

She showed me the device. The signal emanated from Salt Point Harbor.

Now we just needed a way to get there.

Penelope glanced around, saw what she wanted, and marched to a nearby lawn. She grabbed a stone from a border that lined a flower bed. She hefted it down the street and smashed it through the back window of a red four-door sedan.

Glass shattered, and nearby dogs barked.

I cringed.

She reached her hand in through the broken window and unlocked the front door. The minute she opened the door, the lights flashed, and the alarm honked.

Penelope slipped behind the wheel and took a seat. She fiddled under the dash.

This wasn't her first rodeo.

She knew to break out the rear window so she wouldn't be sitting in glass as she hotwired the car.

Within a few seconds, the alarm stopped honking, and the lights stopped flashing. A few more moments, and she had the car running. She poked her head out the window. "Are you coming?"

I shook my head as I jogged around to the passenger seat and climbed in.

Not only was I aiding and abetting a known fugitive, we just stole a car.

Penelope dropped it into gear and stomped the gas. The tires barked as we launched away from the curb just as the owner opened the front door and shouted, "Hey! That's my car!"

We raced down the lane and took a left on Mangrove Court.

Penelope had two speeds. Fast and faster. I liked the way she drove. We hauled ass to Salt Point, and she killed the lights as we pulled into the parking lot of the marina.

We hopped out, and Penelope studied the tracking app. We looked around, trying to pinpoint Haley's exact location. After examining the screen, I pointed to an abandoned tug at the far end of the harbor. It had been there for years. Rust bubbled through the exterior paint, and the boat was worn from years of sun, salt, and wind.

We drew our pistols and hustled down the dock toward the vessel.

There were no signs of life aboard.

The moon hung high overhead, and the marina was still. It was mostly commercial fishing boats, dive charters, and a few liveaboards.

We crept across the gangway and boarded the tug. The boat creaked and groaned as it swayed and mooring lines stretched. We hustled across the foredeck that was lined with debris, old barrels, and rusted chains. We held up at the entrance to the wheelhouse.

The faint traces of Russian voices filtered through the bulkheads from below deck.

I reached a cautious hand to the hatch, twisted the handle, and inched the door open. It creaked and groaned slightly, and I winced at the sound.

Penelope shot me an annoyed look.

45

We crept into the wheelhouse and held up at the top of the stairs that led down to the engine room. It was a deep, black abyss. The vessel was without power.

Voices filtered up from the bowels of the ship.

Haley sobbed, "Let me go!"

A deep voice asked in a thick Russian accent, "Where is the program?"

"I don't know."

I put a cautious foot on the step below and descended into the darkness.

The voices continued to spill from a storage locker at the stern.

Quiet as ninja cats, we dropped below deck and took cover behind one of the two massive CAT diesel engines. Once a vibrant yellow, they were now rusted and dulled with age and dust. The dank space smelled of oil, grease, and diesel.

It was almost pitch black down here. The only light seeped from a goon's flashlight in the aft compartment. It spilled down through the open hatch and down the hallway, barely silhouetting the massive engines. It fluctuated with the goon's movements, casting ever changing shadows.

I peered around the starboard engine and looked down the aft central corridor. I had a clear line of sight. With eyes on Haley, I felt slightly relieved, but dread still filled my gut. My heart thumped with adrenaline.

Two thugs menaced Haley, continuing to question her about the program.

I figured they were probably Russian SVR—members of the foreign intelligence service. It didn't really matter who they were. We were going to put a wrench in their plans.

Penelope and I crept along the starboard side passage to the aft bulkhead of the engine compartment. We held up near the hatch.

"I'm going to ask you one more time," a goon threatened. "Where's the program?"

"I don't have it," Haley said. "Penelope took it."

The two thugs grumbled to each other in Russian.

They had Haley cuffed to a center post in the storage locker. Tears streamed down her tormented face.

Anger swelled within me. I wanted to take these scumbags down.

Footsteps pinged against the metal stairs as someone else descended into the engine room.

Penelope and I took cover at the aft end of the starboard diesel engine.

A third thug plummeted down the steps and marched across the compartment.

We crouched in the darkness, keeping still and silent. Not a breath. My pulse pounding in my ears. I worried the thud of my heart might give us away.

The sound of his footsteps clanked across the deck.

The goon walked right past us. He stepped into the corridor, strolled past the tanks, one on either side, and stepped into the aft compartment.

There was another exchange in Russian.

They wanted to track down Penelope. The lead goon bitched at the other two for tossing out Haley's cell phone. He figured the device would have Penelope's contact information in the recent call list.

The thugs weren't too concerned about concealing their identity. They didn't wear masks, and they tossed about each other's names without a second thought. Ivan, Anatoly, and Oleg.

It told me they never planned on releasing the hostage.

I was fluent in Russian and recently had the opportunity to practice with Katerina.

"Stay with the girl," the leader of the pack said. I gathered his name was Anatoly.

He left with Oleg and marched back down the hallway. They moved through the engine room and climbed the steps to the main deck.

I figured now was the best opportunity to strike. I crept through the darkness to the edge of the hatch and peered down the hallway.

Ivan was a big guy with broad shoulders and a trapezoidal head that disappeared into his mountainous shoulders. His sandy-blond hair was buzzed close, and he had a wide, stubby face that resembled a pug.

"Looks like it is just you and me," he said to Haley with despicable intent.

He pulled out a pack of cigarettes, grabbed a stogie, and stuffed it between his thin lips. He took a lighter from his pocket, sparked the flame, and lit the cigarette. The cherry glowed, and he inhaled a deep breath.

He clicked his silver zippo shut and stuffed it back into his pocket.

The flashlight dangled from his hand, pointing at the floor, bouncing reflected light around the compartment, giving them both an eerie, ominous look.

Ivan offered Haley a cigarette.

She declined with an angry face. "No, thank you."

Ivan chuckled. "How old are you?"

"It's none of your business," Haley said.

"Old enough, I suppose," Ivan said with a lecherous grin.

My blood boiled. This guy was a creep.

With his back to me as he ogled Haley, I advanced down the compartment, moving without a sound.

Haley's eyes rounded when she saw me approach.

I was almost to the goon when her gaze alerted Ivan. I planned to put him in a choke hold, but he spun around and reached for his weapon holstered in his waistband. I grabbed his forearm before he could take aim.

I came across with a hard right, cracking him in the face with the grip of my pistol.

Blood spewed from his nose, and he wrenched his head aside.

By the time he regained his wits, I had my pistol in his face. "Drop the weapon, or you are going to get a lot uglier."

He snarled at me but complied. With Penelope right behind me, her weapon drawn, he realized this was a losing battle.

He let go of the pistol, and it clattered to the deck.

I kicked it away and hissed, "Face down. On the ground. Now!"

Blood trickled from Ivan's nose, flowing over his lips and down his chin, staining his suit. He reluctantly ate the deck.

Penelope covered him while I released the handcuffs from Haley's wrists, then used them to secure Ivan to the pole.

"Haley, this is Deputy Wild. He's here to help. You can trust him like you trust me."

Haley nodded.

Footsteps clattered down the main stairs, and we scampered toward the bulkhead, holding up on either side of the hatch.

Ivan shouted, "We have intruders!"

Penelope grabbed the flashlight and aimed it down the hall, trying to blind the intruders.

"Coconut County!" I shouted. "On the ground. Now!"

That was met with a barrage of gunfire.

I took cover behind the bulkhead as bullets snapped toward me.

After a beat, I angled my pistol through the hatch and opened fire at the goons. Muzzle flash flickered from the barrel, and the deafening bangs echoed off the bulkhead.

Haley plugged her ears and crouched in a far corner away from the action.

Bullets rocketed through the narrow passageway, pelting the aft bulkhead as the goons kept firing.

"We have you cornered," Anatoly shouted, taking cover behind one of the diesel engines. "There's no way out."

46

I tried to call the sheriff for backup but couldn't get a signal.

Bullets kept streaking down the corridor into the storage locker.

There was a pause in the action.

I angled my pistol around the corner and took aim down the passageway.

Penelope had set the flashlight on the deck, and the beam illuminated the pathway between the engines.

There was an eerie moment of silence that seemed to go on for an eternity. The goons had taken cover at the forward end of the massive diesels and crouched low, out of sight.

Then Oleg angled his pistol around the engine and opened fire again. With the flashlight in their eyes, they couldn't see much. It gave us a slight advantage.

Slight.

I fired a few rounds in Oleg's direction, then Anatoly swung his pistol around the port side engine and blasted a few rounds. Muzzle flash flickered, and bullets clattered into the bulkhead before me.

I ducked for cover.

We exchanged a few more volleys.

Penelope tagged Oleg in the shoulder. Her bullet spun him around and splattered the forward bulkhead of the engine compartment with crimson. He writhed and groaned on the ground, taking cover behind the engine.

"One down, one to go," I shouted.

"Fuck you!" Anatoly shouted back.

He angled his pistol around the engine and blasted off a few more rounds. His finger squeezed the trigger with furious anger.

The slide locked, the weapon empty.

He ducked behind the engine, pressed the mag release, and dropped the magazine. He jammed another one in, the sound echoing off the bulkheads.

I took the opportunity to advance down the hallway into the engine compartment. I took cover behind the aft end of the starboard engine as Anatoly reloaded.

He angled the pistol around and opened fire.

Bullets snapped through the air, pelting the bulkhead behind me.

Penelope fired in his direction and kept up the onslaught while I advanced along the starboard side of the engine. I held up as I reached the forward end.

Anatoly was no dummy. He knew I was attempting to flank him. By the time I angled my pistol around the engine, he had disappeared into the port side passageway behind the port engine.

Penelope advanced down the corridor and held up at the hatch. She swung her pistol into the engine room, angling it to port.

We were gonna box the son-of-a-bitch in.

I advanced across the centerline to the port engine and held up for a moment. Then I swung the barrel of my pistol around the corner and opened fire at Anatoly in the passageway.

He got a few shots off in my direction as he scampered aft.

One of my bullets caught him in the throat, and a geyser of blood spewed. He fell to the deck, clutching his throat, gasping and gurgling. Blood spewed through his fingers, and his body twisted and convulsed until he bled out.

It didn't take long.

Soon he was a lifeless sack of bones.

"Target down," I shouted.

I advanced down the narrow passage, kicked his weapon aside, and knelt down beside the body to assess the damage.

Anatoly was gone.

By that time, Penelope hovered over him as well.

"Get Haley," I said. "Let's get out of here and call the sheriff."

She hustled back into the storage locker, collected Haley, and joined me in the engine compartment. We hustled out and climbed the steps to the main deck.

Penelope led the way, with Haley in between us. I pulled my phone from my pocket, hoping to get a better signal when I stepped outside.

Haley opened the hatch and put a foot onto the side deck. As she did, she was greeted by two assault rifles.

Nash's familiar voice filtered into the wheelhouse. "Penelope. So good to see you."

I drew my weapon as they disarmed her.

"Drop the weapon and surrender, Deputy Wild, or your companion dies," Nash shouted.

Haley went pale, and tears streamed from her eyes.

I had no choice but to comply.

Nash and his goons marched Penelope back into the wheelhouse and disarmed me.

Nash smiled. "I'm so glad we could all be reunited."

47

We found ourselves back in the storage compartment again, only this time, we were the captives. My wrists were cuffed to Penelope's, and the support beam was in between us. We weren't going anywhere.

They separated us from Haley. I assumed they had her in the wheelhouse.

Ivan had taken a stray bullet during the firefight and was no longer breathing. His body lay on the deck, oozing blood.

Nash surveyed the dead guy. "I see you met our Russian friends. I owe you my gratitude. They killed two of my men. Thank you."

I glared at him.

"Let's get down to business, shall we? First, I must say I really hate all of this. It's so terrible that Haley had to witness such violence. My heart goes out to her. It really does." He couldn't have sounded more insincere. "So let's make this easy on everyone and bring this to a swift resolution. Then we can all go home happy."

He had no intention of letting us go home.

"Haley tells me that Penelope knows where the program is." He stared into Penelope's eyes. "All you have to do is take me to it. Once I verify its authenticity, we can wrap up this operation."

Penelope glared at him as he circled the two of us like a vulture.

"Now, I could have Haley write the program again, and I will, if need be. But that could take weeks or months. I'm impatient. There's no telling if she could recreate it under such immense pressure. You don't want her to go through that, do you? Sequestered away from friends and family." He clutched his heart, then feigned empathy. "Oh, I almost forgot. She has no family."

Penelope seethed, her eyes blazing into him. She looked like a rabid dog. If she could, she'd take a bite out of his jugular. "You killed them."

Nash laughed. "I didn't kill anybody. You did."

"You think anyone's going to believe that?"

"They're believing it, honey. Have you seen the news reports lately? You are a monster."

He taunted her with glee.

There was a long moment of silence as we both stared the bastard down.

"I figured you might not be so cooperative. But that's okay. I have a Plan B. Now, I can't march Haley in here and put a gun to her head and threaten to kill her. You know I'm not going to do that until I have what I want. I don't see that as an effective means to get you to talk. I mean, I could torture her in front of you. Pull out her fingernails one by one. Break small bones. But I really hate to do that kind of thing. She's so young and innocent. I really do abhor violence. But it's a necessary evil in this line of work. You know that."

Penelope swallowed hard, and anger swelled inside both of us.

Nash put his pistol to my temple. "Now, I realize you two don't have much of a connection. You hardly know each other. I mean, maybe you slept together. I don't know. But I suspect, out of your sense of duty and honor, you're not going to let me pull the trigger and splatter his brains across the bulkhead."

Penelope and I exchanged a look. I had to admit, I hoped she would be amenable to the idea. I didn't particularly want a bullet racing through my skull at high speed.

Nash warned Penelope, "Of course, if that doesn't work, I will resort to pulling out *your* fingernails. Breaking *your* fingers. Cutting them off, burning out your eyes with a cigarette, hooking up an electrical current to your sensitive parts. Whatever it takes. Eventually, you will tell me what I want to know. It might be today. It might be in three weeks or three months. I will waterboard you, keep you sleep deprived and locked up. By the end of it, you'll beg me for mercy and be willing to do anything. You know the drill. And I can certainly think of a few things I'd like to do to you."

A look of repulsion twisted on Penelope's face.

"One way or another, I will get what I want."

"You're such a nice guy," I muttered.

Nash smiled. "I know. Sometimes my compassion knows no bounds."

His finger tightened around the trigger, the barrel pressed against my skin.

I gave Penelope a look, imploring her to give up the goods.

She hesitated for a long moment.

"Tick-tock," Nash said. "I'm getting impatient."

48

Nash and his thugs drove us to the Seahorse Shores. We were both handcuffed and stuffed into the cargo area of the SUV.

Goons in the backseat kept an eye on us. I searched around, looking for anything to pick the handcuffs with, but there was nothing in the back. We bounced up and down as the vehicle rambled down the highway.

The SUV pulled into the lot, and the goons hopped out. They lifted the back hatch and marched us out of the vehicle at gunpoint.

At this time of night, nobody was up at the motel, and if they happened to look out the window and see three feds with prisoners, I don't think they'd get involved.

They'd taken our keys, phones, and anything else that was in our pockets.

Nash unlocked the door to room #7 and marched us inside. The thugs piled in and closed the door behind us.

"Where is it?" Nash asked.

"You want to take these cuffs off so I can get it?" Penelope asked with a sassy gaze.

"Not particularly."

"In the bathroom. Taped to the underside of the lid of the toilet tank."

"That's a risky place to keep it."

"What can I say? I like to live on the edge."

Nash chortled.

He nodded to Owen, who marched into the bathroom. The sound of ceramic on ceramic filtered out as the goons lifted the lid. "Got it!"

Owen emerged a moment later with a triumphant grin and handed the USB drive to Nash.

He regarded it with skepticism. "This is it?"

"That's it," Penelope assured.

"I hate disappointment," Nash said. "If this isn't it, I'm going to make your life miserable."

"Too late," Penelope quipped.

Nash handed it to Mason, who took a seat on the bed, opened a laptop, and stuck the drive into the USB port. He tapped on the keys and studied the screen. He launched the application and fiddled with it for a moment. Satisfied, he gave Nash a nod.

Nash grinned. "Sometimes you impress me, Penelope. You're not as dumb as you look."

The muscles in her jaw flexed.

Nash commanded Mason, "Do it. Make the transfer."

The goon nodded, and his fingers danced across the keyboard. He focused intensely for a moment.

"Transfer?" Penelope asked.

Nash smiled. "At first, I was going to sell this technology to the Russians for a pretty penny. Then I thought better of it. That was small thinking. I started thinking big. That program is a key. A key that can unlock any door. With the help of that program, we are transferring funds into a numbered account in the Cayman Islands. From there, it will be transferred into several crypto accounts and disseminated. It will be untraceable. Except for the IP address, which leads back to this motel. A room in your name." He smiled, proud of his accomplishment. "The world already thinks you're a wanted fugitive that kidnapped Haley. Now they'll know the motive. Meanwhile, me and what's left of my associates will find unique and interesting ways to spend $1 billion." He grinned again.

"This is all about money?" she asked.

"Newsflash. Everything is always about money. Or sex," he admitted.

"Sounds like pretty small thinking to me," Penelope said.

"So you're going to keep the program for yourself?" I asked.

"Oh no," Nash replied. "This technology is far too dangerous for any one person to control. If it should fall into the wrong hands, the consequences could be disastrous. It must be destroyed."

"Haley could just create another program."

"I know. And as much as I like her, she has to die. It's the way it must be. For the good of society, of course," Nash said. "We can't have people running around, doing what we're doing here tonight."

Penelope glared at him.

Mason nodded. The transfer was complete. He couldn't help but grin. "It's done."

"It's time to get out of here," Nash said.

"Who did you steal from?" Penelope asked.

"It doesn't matter."

The thugs marched us out of the motel room and back into the SUV. Once again, we were curled up in the fetal position in the cargo area.

Owen in the backseat lorded over us with a pistol, leaning over the seat back.

I figured we were on our way to die.

49

The SUV spiraled up to the top of the parking garage. The rumble of the engine, and the squeal of the tires, echoed off of the concrete walls.

We reached the top. Doors opened, goons climbed out, and doors clambered shut. They hustled around and opened the rear hatch. Owen waved us out with his pistol, and we awkwardly climbed out of the vehicle, our hands cuffed behind our backs.

The moon loomed overhead, and the faint sound of rotor blades pattered in the distance, drawing near.

"You really think you're gonna get away with this?" Penelope asked.

Nash smirked. "Without a doubt. The world will be looking for you, but you've disappeared, along with a substantial amount of money."

"Is Ronan in on this?"

"What do you think?"

"I think this whole division is corrupt."

"You always were a good officer," Nash said.

A sleek black helicopter drew close. The rotor wash blasted across the top of the parking garage like a hurricane.

The skids touched down, and Nash shouted over the engine, "Take them far enough out so they won't wash ashore."

The goons marched us under the rotor blades and into the helicopter. We climbed into the back seat, and Owen joined us in the front, keeping his pistol aimed at us.

Nash smiled and waved as I looked out the window. Mason stayed behind with him.

The pilot adjusted the collective and lifted it from the structure. The rotor blades thumped, and we pulled away from the garage. Nash and the SUV grew small as we slipped away into the night.

It wasn't long before we were racing over the inky water, heading out to sea.

"I'm sorry I got you mixed up in all of this," Penelope said.

"It's all Declan's fault, really," I teased.

She mustered a thin smile.

"Who's Ronan?"

"Group Chief."

The full moon reflected on the midnight water. Soon the island behind us was a tiny speck, the lights of the city flickering.

The stars looked on as we flew to our doom, impartial observers to our demise.

Owen looked over his shoulder at us and grinned. "I hope you two can swim."

I figured they were going to dump us out over the water and let us die the hard way. We'd spend the night trying to keep our heads above the surface, cuffed behind our backs, as the inky swells rolled.

I had other plans.

I dug a pen out of my back pocket that I had taken from the motel room. It was sitting atop the dresser next to a pad of paper. I'd snagged it while Nash and his thugs were patting themselves on the back.

I wedged my fingertips between the clip and the pen and broke the thin piece of aluminum. It flicked away and hit the seat.

I stuffed the pen back into my pocket, then fumbled for the metal clip. I almost had it but ended up pushing it into one of the crevices in the seat. I spent the next few minutes trying to dig it out without drawing attention to myself.

Finally, I had the damn thing in my grasp. I used it to shim the locking pawl open. It took a little doing, but the cuffs swung free. I quickly released the other cuff, then slipped the clip to Penelope when Owen wasn't looking.

She worked on her cuffs while I kept my hands behind my back, waiting for the opportune moment to strike.

When Penelope had released her cuffs, I lurched forward, reached my arm around the seat, and did my best to choke out Owen.

He clawed at my arm, trying to angle his pistol toward me.

Penelope lunged forward, grabbing his gun and his forearm.

I kept choking the bastard, but he squeezed off a round that blasted the pilot's skull. Blood and brain splattered against the bulkhead, and the craft instantly began to rotate without inputs on the pedals or cyclic.

Penelope stripped the pistol, then put two bullets into Owen.

The deafening bangs filled the tiny compartment.

The helicopter spiraled out of control, swirling toward the black water below.

"I hope you know how to fly one of these things," she said in as casual a voice as she could muster.

I opened the door and pushed the pilot out. His lifeless body tumbled through the air and smacked the surface of the water after a considerable drop.

I climbed into the seat and took the controls as the helicopter swirled out of control.

50

I stabilized the rotation with the pedals and leveled us out with the cyclic before we plowed into the onyx water.

"Find his phone," I shouted to Penelope.

She dug through Owen's pockets and pulled out his phone, keys, and wallet.

I banked the craft around and headed us back toward Coconut Key.

Penelope's face tensed with concern. "We need to stop Nash before..."

"I know."

We may have been too late to save Haley, but we were going to try our best.

"Look through his recent call list," I said.

Penelope held the device in front of Owen's face and unlocked the security screen. She thumbed through his recent calls.

"Let me see his phone," I said.

She handed the device to me. I noted the calls, then dialed Isabella. I wasn't sure she would answer from an unknown number, but she picked up after a few rings. "Hey, it's me."

"What kind of trouble are you in this time?"

"How do you know I'm in trouble?"

"You're always in trouble when you call me from an unknown number."

"I need you to track Carter Nash." I took a screenshot of the recent calls and sent the image to Isabella.

"Where are you now?"

"In a helicopter on my way back to Coconut Key."

Penelope shoved Owen out and took his seat. He tumbled through the air and slapped the water below. I'm sure he'd wash ashore in a few days, if the toothy critters didn't make a meal of him.

Isabella's fingers tapped the keys. A moment later, she said, "That phone is at 712 Tiki Terrace. Another phone on that list is also at that location."

"That's Nash, and Mason is with him." I thanked her for the info, then dialed the sheriff. I gave him the address and told him to put a tac team together.

"What the hell is going on?"

I filled him in on the details.

"How did you acquire your intel?" Daniels asked.

"You know how," I said.

"So, you have no legitimate reason to believe Nash is at that location?"

"Definitely legitimate," I said, knowing damn good and well I couldn't use the intel Isabella had acquired.

"Echols is never going to sign off on a warrant."

"I don't care if he does or doesn't. I'm gonna breach that house."

"Is there another way we can put Nash at that location?"

"He kidnapped us and he's going to kill Haley. I don't care about procedure at this point. All I care about is Haley. Time is of the essence. Nash is going to get suspicious if he doesn't hear from Owen soon."

Daniels grumbled.

After I spoke with the sheriff, I called Jack.

He didn't answer.

It didn't take long to reach Coconut Key. I piloted the craft to the Sheriff's Department and touched down on the helipad.

I powered down the craft, and we hustled into the station and joined the sheriff. I made a brief introduction to Penelope.

"Where's that nitwit partner of yours?" Daniels asked.

"I'm not sure."

I tried to call Jack again from the perp's phone, but he didn't answer. The sun wasn't up yet, and I was pretty sure they had a wild night, as usual.

Owen's phone buzzed with a text from Nash. *[Where are you?]*

[On the way back.]

[Is it done?]

[All taken care of.]

[Meet us back at the safe house for debrief.]

[Will do.]

"He's about to get a big surprise," I said to the sheriff.

We rode with Daniels in his patrol car to Tiki Terrace. Erickson, Faulkner, Halford, and Robinson followed.

The sun would be cresting the horizon soon.

The neighborhood was calm and quiet in the early morning hours. We parked a few houses down, hopped out, and had a quick huddle.

I took a bulletproof vest and grabbed an AR-15 from the trunk of the sheriff's patrol car. With a whack, I jammed in a magazine, pulled the charging handle, and chambered a round. I flicked the weapon on safe.

"She stays put," Daniels said, pointing at Penelope.

Her brow knitted. "I want a little payback."

"You're still technically a fugitive until this thing gets sorted out."

She huffed.

"I don't need the bad press if anything goes wrong."

"Did you see that?" I said, pointing to the house. "I just saw Nash in the window."

The sheriff's eyes narrowed at me, knowing I was full of it.

I raised an innocent hand. "I swear."

Penelope waited by the patrol car as we advanced onto the property. I took the front door with Erickson and Faulkner. Halford and Robinson took the rear. Daniels and I huddled on either side of the entrance.

I wasn't about to give the scumbag a heads-up. I nodded to Erickson and Faulkner. They heaved the battering ram. It smashed into the door, splintering the jamb. It flung wide and slammed against the wall. The door handle put a hole in the sheetrock.

We stormed down the foyer, weapons shouldered.

I finally shouted, "Coconut County!"

Halford and Robinson breached the back door, flooded into the kitchen, and joined us in the living room.

We surrounded Mason.

He had his pistol drawn but quickly realized he was outnumbered.

"Drop it! Now," I shouted.

He tossed the weapon to the ground and raised his hands in surrender.

"Where are Nash and the girl?" I demanded.

He nodded down the hallway to the master bedroom.

Halford and Robinson secured Mason, slapping the cuffs around his wrist.

I advanced down the hallway with the rest of the tac team, my heart thumping, the AR-15 pressed tight against my shoulder.

I kicked open the bathroom door and cleared the space. We moved down the hall to the guest bedroom and did the same.

Both were empty.

We continued down the hallway and held up at the door to the master bedroom. When the team was in position, I kicked the door down and angled my weapon into the room.

Nash stood in the corner by the window with his pistol to Haley's head. He crouched behind her, using her as a shield.

Pure scumbag.

For the first time, the normally cool and collected officer looked unnerved. His hair was disheveled, and a thin mist sprouted on his forehead. Fear and uncertainty filled his eyes. He looked pretty damn surprised to see me.

He warned, "Come any closer, and she dies."

51

"Back out of the room. Now!" Nash demanded.

Nobody moved, which enraged him further. "Don't fucking test me!" His face was red, and the veins bulged. His frantic eyes darted about.

I motioned to the team to fall back.

They did.

I hovered in the doorway, keeping my weapon shouldered, aimed at the side of him. I didn't have a clear shot, and I wasn't about to risk Haley.

She stood as stiff as a board, tears flowing down her cheeks.

"Haley, everything's going to be okay," I assured. "I'm not going to let anything happen to you."

She nodded.

"Don't lie to her," Nash said. "This is a precarious situation. She's not stupid."

"How do you see this working out?" I asked Nash.

"I see you backing off and complying with my demands."

"What are those demands?"

"I want transportation. Bring the helicopter. Fully fueled. Set it down in the street. I'm gonna walk out of here with Haley, get in, and fly away."

"Where will you go?"

"That's for me to know and you to find out."

"You can't hide. Wherever you go, we'll find you."

"I know how to disappear."

"Good for you. I'd love for you to disappear."

He sneered at me.

"How about you let Haley go as a gesture of good faith, and I'll get the helicopter here?"

Nash laughed.

"It was worth a shot. Can you blame me?"

There was a long, tense moment as we stared at each other.

"What are you waiting for?" Nash griped. "Time is running out."

"I've got all the time in the world," I said.

"No, you don't. The longer this goes on, the more agitated I will become. I could get careless. This gun could go off."

I knew he wouldn't give up his only leverage.

He glared at me from behind the young girl. "Bring the helicopter. I'll let Haley go when I'm sure that I'm safe."

As long as I was alive, he would never be safe. If he hurt Haley, I'd hunt him down wherever he went.

"How about a hostage exchange?" I suggested. "Let Haley go. You can take me instead."

He laughed again. "You're not my type. Too hard to manage. Too dangerous."

By this time, the patter of Tango One thumped overhead. Red and blue lights swirled on the street as more patrol units arrived. A crowd of curious neighbors gathered, and Paris Delaney and her crew pulled to the scene.

"You're going to be quite the celebrity when all this is said and done," I warned.

Nash peered through the window at the gathering swarm.

He backed away from me, moving clear of the window. Snipers had climbed onto the roof across the street and were lining up a shot.

"I get it. You want to get out of here and make your way to a non-extradition country so you can enjoy your billion dollars. Sounds perfectly reasonable to me. Help me help you do that."

Nash scoffed. "You're the last person that is going to help me."

"Right now, we have a common goal."

His face twisted with confusion.

"I want you to get everything that's coming to you."

He laughed.

Haley donkey-kicked him in the knee and dove to the ground.

I took the opportunity. With a clear shot, I squeezed the trigger twice before Nash could get a shot off.

The rifle hammered against my shoulder, and crimson spewed from the perp's chest. He tumbled back and fell against the nightstand, taking a lamp with him as he crashed down. It fell on top of him, adding insult to injury.

Nash writhed and moaned on the ground, gasping for breath.

Haley launched to her feet and ran across the bedroom to me.

She gave me a hug, and I escorted her out of the room, keeping an eye on Nash. I passed her off to the deputies behind me and advanced to the body. I kicked the weapon away, knelt down, and felt for a pulse in his neck.

He was gone.

The color had drained from his lips and skin, and his cold eyes stared at the ceiling.

He didn't even get to spend one dollar of his billion.

I rummaged through his pockets and found the USB drive and our cell phones. I slipped the drive into my pocket.

With the situation secure, I backed out of the room, and forensic investigators moved in. They collected his pistol as evidence. Dietrich snapped photos, and Brenda examined the remains.

I found Haley in the living room. "Are you okay?"

She nodded and gave me another hug.

First responders swarmed inside as I escorted her out of the house.

Reporters rushed to greet us, and cameras flashed.

"Deputy Wild, what can you tell us about the situation?" Paris asked.

"No comment at this time."

I ushered Haley past the horde of media and the crowd of curious neighbors.

Penelope waited for us at the sheriff's patrol car, and Haley ran into her arms. They gave each other a tight embrace.

Tango One circled overhead.

The morning sun had crested the treetops, casting long amber rays. The nightmare was over, and the daylight was here to wash away the darkness and the demons.

The sheriff drove us back to the station, and I filled out an after-action report using a little creative license. I surrendered my duty weapon and was put on administrative leave, as per protocol.

It didn't take the lab long to return ballistics on Carter Nash's pistol. It was the same one used to kill Haley's parents.

Penelope was cleared of any wrongdoing.

"Looks like you got your life back," I said to her in the hallway.

"I'm not so sure about that. I don't think anything is ever going to go back to normal for me. Or Haley, for that matter."

She put her arm around the young girl. The two were inseparable at the moment. She was all Haley really had.

It didn't take long for the men in navy suits with dark sunglasses to show up at the station.

Penelope tensed at the sight of the two men as they stepped inside and approached us.

"Officer Johnson, Special Activities. We need to do a debrief."

52

We sat in the conference room in cushy leather chairs. Officers Johnson and Jones remained stoic. They were clean-cut in their early 30s, with slicked-back hair and square jaws. They were puppets of someone higher up the food chain.

After we explained everything to them, beginning to end, Officer Johnson—not his real name—said, "As you're aware, this is a delicate matter. The utmost discretion is required."

"Discretion?" Penelope balked. "My entire group is corrupt. What are you going to do about my group chief, Ronan O'Connor?"

"He is being dealt with. It is regrettable that the situation has occurred, but the company is deeply grateful for your efforts to uncover these bad actors." He paused. "Rest assured, your reputation and status within the company remain impeccable. I think you will be pleased with your new position."

"New position?"

"I'm not at liberty to discuss that at the moment."

Penelope regarded him with suspicion.

"Now, to the matter at hand," Johnson said. "We'll need access to the program."

Penelope glanced at me.

"We were unable to recover the USB drive," I lied. "Nash mentioned that he planned to destroy it, along with the girl. I believe it's no longer in existence."

The two officers didn't look pleased.

"Are you sure?" Johnson asked.

"No drive was found on Nash or his associate," I said. "I doubt the two men that tried to dump us in the ocean were in possession of it. But if you'd like to fish them out of the water, be my guest."

The two officers exchanged a look.

"We'll need Haley to come with us. She'll be well cared for as she re-creates the program."

I looked at Haley. "Do you want to go with these gentlemen?"

Haley shook her head.

"There you have it, gentlemen. Haley is not going anywhere with you," I said. "This is over for her. This is where it ends."

Johnson's face tightened. "You're aware of the national security applications of this technology. Should it fall into the—"

"It's not going to fall into the wrong hands. She's not working for you or anyone else."

"We can't risk having an asset like that out in the open."

"She's not an asset," I growled. "I suggest you tell your superiors this is over." Then I made a thinly veiled threat. "If anyone attempts to harm her or take her against her will, they will have to deal with me."

Johnson looked stunned. "Of course, we can't compel anyone against their will." His eyes focused on Haley. "But should you decide you ever want to serve your country, please get in touch."

He pulled out a card from his pocket and slid it across the table.

"I think this debrief is over," I said. "I'm sorry you're going back empty-handed, but at least the program isn't in the hands of foreign intelligence or a terrorist group."

Johnson stared at me for a long moment. "Indeed."

There was another long pause.

"Well, I guess that about wraps things up," he said. "It goes without saying this conversation, and the events spoken of here today, never happened."

Officers Johnson and Jones pushed away from the table and stood up.

So did we.

There was another awkward silence. Johnson adjusted his coat, then marched out of the conference room.

Penelope smirked. "You don't back down for anybody, do you?"

I smirked. "It's not my style."

She smiled. "I think I like your style."

"What's next for you? Are you gonna take this *new position*?"

"I don't know what I'm going to do. I'm certainly going to take a little time off. I see a white sand beach and a piña colada in my future."

"I know a few good beaches. And I know where we can get a nice piña colada."

"Get a room, you two," Haley quipped with an eye roll.

We laughed and left the conference room.

Penelope planned on checking into the Seven Seas and unwinding. Haley would stay with her until she could coordinate with her aunt to take custody of her.

"I'll be in touch for that piña colada," she said.

"I look forward to it."

There were more hugs, and we said our goodbyes. Deputy Halford drove them to the Seven Seas, and I caught a rideshare back to the marina.

The morning's events had pulled all the media away from the celebrities. Diver Down was quiet when I arrived. I hustled down the dock, crossed the passerelle, and boarded the *Avventura*. I stepped into the salon, and the delightful aroma of bacon, eggs, and coffee hit my nose.

JD was in the galley whipping up breakfast. Logan, Brad, Dizzy, Styxx, and Crash all loitered around, looking pretty chipper for this time of the morning.

"Where the hell have you been?" Brad asked.

"Long story."

I grabbed a hammer from a storage compartment and hustled back outside. I smashed the drive against the asphalt in the parking lot. It was only a matter of time before someone, somewhere, recreated this technology.

I returned to the *Avventura*, dished up a plate, poured a cup of coffee, and took a seat at the breakfast nook. The gang listened with wide eyes and slack jaws as I regaled them with tales of high adventure.

I hadn't even finished the meal when Daniels called with more bad news.

53

There were several patrol cars on the street with lights flashing. The crowd of pedestrians had gathered, and traffic was backed up in either direction. An ambulance hovered nearby, red and white lights flickering. But at this point, nobody would be taking a ride in the ambulance.

Brenda and her crew were on the scene, and Dietrich snapped photos as forensic investigators chronicled evidence.

JD and I pulled to the scene in the jade-green Porsche. He parked at the curb, and we hopped out and hustled toward the chaos.

A mangled body lay in the street amid a pool of blood, arms and legs flailed about at unnatural angles.

Daniels looked over the scene with folded arms and a disgusted look.

The victim's face was bruised and swollen, barely recognizable.

"Hit and run," Daniels said. He pointed to a witness standing nearby. "She saw the whole thing. This guy was out for his morning jog when a white truck mowed him down. Witness says it wasn't an accident either. The truck deliberately swerved to hit the jogger."

I cringed. "Any ID on the victim?"

"Simon Sinclair."

My brow lifted, and my jaw dropped.

"You know him?"

"We spoke on the phone. He's an art appraiser. He was the first to raise concerns about potential forgeries."

The sheriff's face tightened. "Well, this isn't suspicious at all," he said, dripping with sarcasm. "I want you to figure this out. And pronto."

"I'm technically on administrative leave."

"Not anymore, you're not. You're reinstated. Get back on the case."

"You got it."

JD and I talked to the witness. She was early 20s with long, wavy blonde hair and a soft, approachable face. She was understandably freaked out by the incident. "It was horrible. They just ran that poor man over."

"Did you look at the license plate?"

"JZX something. I don't know. It happened so fast," she said excitedly, her cheeks flushed.

Daniels put out a BOLO on the vehicle.

I dialed Astrid.

"Are you calling to harass me again?"

"Simon Sinclair is dead."

Astrid gasped. "That's terrible. What happened?"

"You don't know?" I asked, incredulous.

"Should I? I haven't turned on the television all morning. Frankly, I find the news quite depressing."

"He was run down while out for a jog."

"You try to stay healthy, and then something like this happens," feigning empathy.

"This was no accident."

"Are you saying he was murdered?"

"That's a distinct possibility."

"You have any leads?"

"Not at this time. But I find it interesting that he was killed, given his position on the forgeries."

"So, he was your source?"

"I guess there's no harm in stating that now. Yes, he believed the Julian Krause that was in Cornelius Worthington's collection was a fake."

"We're all entitled to our opinions," Astrid said. "But I'll have you know, the paintings in my gallery have been authenticated by an independent appraiser that both parties agreed on."

I lifted a surprised brow. "That was quick."

"It didn't take long. A few samples were taken. Spectrometry was done. It is now the conclusion of multiple experts in the field that these paintings are genuine. I can't speak for anything else, and I don't know what Marcel was doing on the side. But I can say with confidence that there is nothing underhanded going on with my gallery. Now, if you don't mind, deputy, I have better things to do with my day than be accused of dealing in forgeries."

"I guess your name is clear. For now."

She hung up on me. I didn't really blame her.

"Something funny is going on here," JD said.

My next call was to Isabella. "I need you to monitor Astrid Blomqvist's phone."

"Your friend at the gallery?"

I filled her in on the situation.

"You think she might have a hand in this?"

"It seems Simon was the only one that maintained the paintings were fakes. Maybe somebody wanted to shut him up."

"Or maybe it's completely unrelated," Isabella said.

"It's a little too coincidental for my taste."

"I'll see what I can find."

I thanked her and ended the call.

The remains were bagged and loaded into the medical examiner's van.

Paris Delaney was on the scene, and her news crew captured all the gruesome footage. She asked me for a comment, but I declined.

We left the scene and headed back to the station to fill out after-action reports. I was rolling on zero sleep, and it was all starting to catch up with me. That, combined with the blood-boosting medication I was on, gave me a throbbing headache. I was dragging ass.

We headed back to the *Avventura*, and I caught a much-needed power nap.

I don't know how long I was out for, but it felt like I was in another dimension when JD banged on the hatch to my stateroom. "Get your ass up! I'm hungry."

He barged into the compartment, making way too much noise.

I peeled open a sleepy eye and yawned. "What time is it?"

"Time to eat."

"And you couldn't do that on your own?"

"I don't want to sit at the bar by myself."

I groaned and pulled myself out of bed.

The boat was quiet.

"Where are Brad and Logan?"

"They left. I think they said something about going shopping."

"Are they getting along now?"

"Seem to be."

We left the boat and ambled down the dock toward Diver Down. We were almost at the front door when Jack patted his pockets. "Shit. I left my phone in the car."

I stood by the entrance while he jogged to the Porsche. He opened the door, fumbled around inside, and grabbed his cell phone. He closed the door with that solid clunk you could only get from a classic German sports car.

He jogged back toward Diver Down. He was halfway back when the car blew up.

54

The blast knocked JD to the asphalt. The amber ball behind him rolled into the sky. Bits of blistering debris scattered in all directions. Twisted shards of metal, glass, and plastic. Flames engulfed the car, and black smoke billowed.

I rushed to JD's aid and looked him over for injuries.

"Are you okay?"

I helped him off the ground.

He stood up, grumbling, and dusted himself off. "Son-of-a-bitch!"

He stared at the car with a red face as it popped and crackled, the tires melting into the asphalt.

Teagan rushed out of the bar to join us. "Are you guys all right?"

We both nodded.

"I'm getting the impression somebody doesn't want us investigating the case," JD said.

"You think?" I snarked.

The muscles in his jaw flexed as he watched his pride and joy burn.

"A little polish and a tuneup. She'll be fine."

He glared at me.

I asked Teagan, "Did you see anybody tamper with the car?"

She shook her head. "But it's been busy today. I've been preoccupied."

I called the department, and it didn't take long until the parking lot swarmed with first responders. Red and blue lights flickered, and the bomb squad sifted through the rubble. There were thousands of tiny bits and pieces scattered all over the parking lot. It would take hours to sift through.

Daniels arrived and wanted answers. "You think this is tied to the art case? Or something else?"

"Hard to say."

Deputy Finch on the bomb squad joined us. "Pipe bomb. Probably tripped it when you opened the door," he said to JD. "Delayed fuse. Somebody wanted you sitting in the seat when it went off. You sure know how to make friends, Donovan."

"It's a special talent of mine."

Finch rolled his eyes and went back to combing through the rubble. He called over his shoulder, "I'll let you know what we find out."

The blast and debris had damaged neighboring cars, shattering windows, destroying body panels. More than a few angry customers congregated in the parking lot, wanting to know who was going to pay for the damages.

I did my best to assure customers they'd be taken care of.

A black Yukon pulled into the parking lot and avoided the horde of responders. The driver parked the vehicle in front of Diver Down, hopped out, and got the rear doors.

Brad and Logan climbed out of the vehicle with shopping bags from upscale boutiques in Highland Village. They looked at the chaos with stunned faces.

"What happened?" Logan asked when he joined us.

I caught them up to speed.

A look of shock played on their faces.

"No shit?" Logan said.

"No shit."

"That was a cool car, too."

JD frowned.

Paris and her crew arrived and gathered footage. She marched in our direction, looking for the scoop.

"Who did you upset this time?" she asked.

I shrugged innocently.

The cameraman was off gathering footage of the first responders.

"Was anybody hurt?"

I shook my head.

"Well, that's a relief." She paused. "You're keeping me busy today."

"What would you do without us?" JD asked.

"I'm not quite sure." A thin smile curled her plump lips. "I'm glad you two are still around."

Jack grinned. "We'll be raising hell for a while."

I gave a brief interview on camera, then JD and I stepped inside to finally get that bite to eat.

Investigators tried to find every fragment of the bomb. Most people think all the evidence is destroyed in a bombing, but it actually creates thousands of pieces of evidence. With any luck, we'd be able to track the purchase of the materials back to an individual.

We took it easy for the rest of the day. I needed to get some rest. My procedure was in the morning, so the evening was uneventful.

I was up bright and early the next morning and made breakfast at the crack of dawn. Nobody else was stirring, even though the night before was tame.

I chowed down, headed to the clinic, and checked in. I was ready to get this over with. They checked my vitals and did some additional blood work. The nurse stabbed a vein and hooked me up to a machine. I was given a magazine and a remote to the TV. I sat in the chair for several hours while they drained my blood, collected the stem cells, and gave what was left back to me. A process called apheresis.

It was a minor inconvenience.

When it was done, they gave me a meal and made sure I was doing okay before they discharged me. Of course, the nurse gave me specific instructions to take it easy for the next few weeks, told me to eat healthy and get plenty of rest.

I tried to keep a straight face.

When I got back to the boat, the guys were already kicking around ideas about the evening's plans. A night off had recharged their batteries. Mine was flashing red.

"How did it go?" Logan asked.

"Easy peasy," I said.

"I should do that."

"I think you should. You never know who you might help."

"Sometimes I don't think we appreciate how good we have it," Logan said.

"None of us do."

My phone buzzed. I took the call from the sheriff. "I need you and numbnuts to get over to the gallery."

My stomach tightened. "What happened now?"

"Somebody did a drive-by on your friend."

My brow lifted with surprise. "Astrid?"

55

The large glass windows of the gallery were cratered with bullet holes. Shards of glass twinkled on the sidewalk, reflecting the afternoon sun. Crimson stained the walkway near the entrance.

Lights atop patrol cars flashed and flickered. Dietrich snapped photos, and forensic investigators combed the scene.

"What happened?" I asked Deputy Faulkner.

"Looks like somebody doesn't have an appreciation for fine art. We found 9mm shell casings in the parking lot. Astrid's assistant was inside when it happened." He motioned to Joyce. "She saw the vehicle speed away and called 911. Said they had a machine gun. I'm guessing it was a Mac-10 or something similar."

"What about the vehicle?"

"Silver four-door sedan. Maybe a Honda or a Hyuki. She wasn't sure."

"How is Astrid?"

"EMTs and paramedics treated her. She was rushed to Coconut General." He gave an uncertain shrug.

I talked to Joyce inside. She trembled like she had guzzled a pot of coffee. With her brow knitted and sad eyes, she looked mortified by the situation. Her eyes were puffy and red from crying, and she blotted them with a tissue. She sniffled. "I was in the back when I heard the gunshots. I rushed to the window to see what was happening. It was probably a dumb thing to do, considering there were bullets flying around." She told the story just as Faulkner had described. "Astrid was just lying there on the sidewalk. I didn't know what to do."

She was so frazzled she didn't pay any attention to Logan and Brad. They had begged to tag along, and Logan had hired a driver for the four of us to get around.

Joyce sniffled again. "Do you think she's going to be okay?"

"I don't know."

Her face twisted with torment.

"Do you have any idea who might have done this?"

Joyce shook her head.

"Have you noticed anything unusual around the gallery lately?"

Her cautious eyes surveyed me. "I suppose you're speaking in regard to the alleged forgeries. Those claims have been debunked."

"How long have you been working at the gallery?"

"A few months now. I needed a job, and Astrid was kind enough to take me on."

"Did you know each other prior?"

"Socially."

"Are you full or part-time?"

"I help out here and there when she needs me. I answer phones, schmooze clients, set up events. I'll open or close the gallery when she needs me to. If I need a day off or to run an errand, it's not an issue."

"You don't find any of this odd? First Cornelius, then Simon Sinclair, now Astrid?"

"I find it really odd. It freaks me the hell out. I don't know what's going on. You're the cop. You tell me."

There was an awkward moment of silence. I didn't have any real answers for her.

"I should lock up and get to the hospital," Joyce said.

We exchanged information, then I rounded up the crew. We climbed into the black Yukon and hustled to the emergency room. Along the way, Logan asked, "Who do you think is responsible?"

"Yesterday, I was growing suspicious of Astrid. Today, I'm thinking maybe somebody else is pulling the strings, and she's just a pawn in all of this."

The emergency room was a never-ending sea of chaos. Triage nurses scurried about. Administrators tapped on keyboards. EMTs and paramedics rolled victims in on gurneys. The harsh overhead fluorescents made everyone look ill.

Walk-ins staggered about like the living dead. There were cuts and bruises, broken bones, dislocated shoulders, broken noses, and wheezing coughs. An elderly man sucked on supplemental oxygen through a nasal cannula.

There was nothing cheery about this place.

A flatscreen mounted to the wall was tuned to a 24-hour news channel, and Paris Delaney's coverage of the aftermath flashed on the screen.

A glance around the room was a depressing sight. Faces were twisted with pain, and the eyes of loved ones were filled with worry. An occasional announcement was made over the loudspeaker, paging a doctor. The place smelled like antiseptic, mixed with stale coffee and faint traces of blood.

I checked in with the receptionist and told her to update me on Astrid's situation. They weren't really supposed to release patient information, but she told me Astrid was in emergency surgery.

I told Logan and Brad they didn't have to stick around. This could be awhile. I didn't want to miss an opportunity to speak with Astrid if she made it out of surgery alive.

"This is part of the gig," Brad said. "We want the full experience."

"Suit yourselves," I said.

We found a seat near Joyce and settled in for the duration.

The movie stars drew curious stares, but a celebrity encounter wasn't a priority for most people in the waiting room.

I called Isabella and updated her on the situation.

"I've been monitoring her phone calls and looking over her call logs," she said. "There is nothing that stands out. Calls to various clients, appraisers, other gallery owners, a curator at the museum."

"Can you put any cell phones at the gallery at the time of the shooting?"

"Just her phone, one that belonged to Joyce Stevens, and the cell phones of people in neighboring shops. Looks like your shooters were smart enough to turn their devices off."

I thanked her for the info. "Let me know if anything turns up."

"You got it."

We waited over an hour for Dr. Parker to emerge. He pushed through the double doors, wearing teal scrubs and a surgical mask and cap. Traces of crimson stained his attire.

He spotted me, and I launched from my chair to greet him, along with the crew and Joyce.

"How is she?" I asked.

56

Dr. Parker had a grim look on his face. He was a difficult man to read. "She's got a long recovery ahead of her, but she should be alright."

"Oh, thank God!" Joyce said with a relieved breath.

"There was damage to her liver and descending colon. Extensive bleeding. I'll spare you the gory details, but it was a complex repair. She's in recovery now. She'll be there for about an hour or two. As long as she remains hemodynamically stable, we can move her to an intermediate care unit."

"When can I talk to her?" I asked.

"She's still a little groggy. Why don't you all go home? I'll have someone call you when she's up for visitors."

I gave a grim nod.

Dr. Parker looked at Logan. "I liked you in Rectifier. Not bad."

Logan smiled and nodded.

He marched back through the double doors, on to the next patient.

"What!? He didn't like any of my movies?" Brad muttered with a disappointed look.

Logan grinned. "Make better movies."

Brad's face crinkled.

We left the ER and headed back to Diver Down. I was ready for a drink, but that would have to wait. The sheriff buzzed my phone. "Henry Wilkins. That punk you arrested who was helping Liam Vance. I guess a few days in jail have softened him up. He wants to cut a deal. I talked to the state's attorney. He's willing to play ball with this guy if he gives us something useful. Get down to the station. I'll have this guy transferred from the pod."

"We're on our way," I said and ended the call.

I gave the driver our new destination, and we zipped to the station. Logan and Brad watched from the observation room as we talked to Henry in the tiny interrogation room.

The inmate looked frazzled. A few days in jail will do that to you. He had that crazed look about him, not adjusting to captivity well. Decked out in an orange jumpsuit with his wrists shackled about his waist, he was on the brink. Some people just aren't cut out for prison life. They often find that out when it's too late. "You gotta get me out of here."

"It's simple," I said. "You tell us where we can find Liam Vance."

"I want assurances."

"Look, I know you drove the car when Liam tried to take us out."

"You don't *know* anything."

I lied a little. "I pulled your phone records, and we talked to your neighbors. One of them will testify he saw Liam entering and exiting your house. Call logs show quite a bit of history between you two—calls and texts before and after he was on the run."

"Like I said, I'll tell you what you want to know. But I walk away."

"The state's attorney is willing to drop your charges to a third-degree felony—$10,000 fine, and you walk away on time served."

He thought about this for a long moment. "I don't want a felony on my record."

"You should have thought about that beforehand."

"Do you want Liam or not?"

"Do you want to go back to the pod and take your chances at trial? If convicted, you'll get hit with a first-degree felony, at minimum. You could be looking at 30 years in prison. Think about that. You wouldn't last three days."

Henry frowned and deflated. He was silent for a long moment as he hung his head. Finally, he said, "He's at the Mangrove Bay Marina aboard the Wind Chaser."

"Whose boat is that?"

"It's a friend's. He's in Europe for the summer and asked me to look after his boat. I gave Liam the keys."

"You're going to testify against him, too," I said.

Henry's face tightened. "So, are you gonna let me out of here?"

"Not until we have Liam in custody. You better hope this information is correct."

57

We hustled down the dock, weapons in the low-ready position.

The marina was relatively calm. There was a yacht party on the next pier. We passed by a 40-foot sailboat that swayed in its slip a little more than the others. Moans of ecstasy filtered out.

Somebody was having fun.

The tac team gathered at the stern of the *Wind Chaser*. It was a nice, new 33-foot SunDancer—sleek lines, perfect for laid-back cruising or adventurous sea crossings. The brand was renowned for its well-lit interiors, good ventilation, and comfy cabins.

We boarded the boat and flooded into the cockpit.

"Coconut County! We have a warrant."

There was no commotion on board.

With a cautious hand, I opened the hatch. It was unlocked. I angled my weapon into the cabin.

The space was empty.

I plunged down the ladder and cleared the corners.

The sailboat had a typical layout with a galley, a forward seating area, a forward V-berth, an aft head, and another aft berth.

The team flooded into the compartment and secured the area.

It was clear somebody had been living aboard. The sheets in the forward berth were rumpled, and there were pots and pans lying around. Dishes piled in the sink.

"Think that bastard lied to us?" JD asked.

"Always a possibility," I grumbled.

I climbed back up to the cockpit and glanced around. A few curious neighbors looked on.

I disembarked and hit the dock, heading back toward the parking lot.

JD and the tac team followed.

Logan and Brad waited for us in the Yukon with the driver, watching the raid from a distance. I didn't want those guys anywhere near the action.

I kept my head on a swivel, glancing around the marina for the scumbag.

The moans of ecstasy had stopped, and the 40-footer was no longer swaying.

A man climbed into the cockpit, wearing only board shorts. He lit a cigarette and inhaled a deep breath.

His moment of blissful relaxation was shattered when his eyes met mine. They rounded, and his body tensed. Liam recognized me, and I recognized him.

He launched from the cockpit and sprinted toward the parking lot, his bare feet slapping against the dock.

58

I chased after the bastard, my legs driving me forward, my chest expanding as I sucked in deep breaths. I had to admit, after the procedure and a week of blood-boosting meds, I wasn't exactly at peak performance.

Liam hit the parking lot and glanced over his shoulder to see how fast I was gaining on him.

I wasn't.

He raced past a parked SUV.

Logan sprung out from behind the vehicle and put his shoulder into the perp, knocking him to the ground. The two movie stars pounced and kept the scumbag pinned to the ground until we arrived.

I took over and slapped the cuffs around Liam's wrists and ratcheted them tight.

Paris Delaney and her news crew captured the whole thing on video. I suspected one of the celebrities had tipped her off. It turned into a hell of a PR opportunity.

I read Liam his rights, escorted him to a patrol unit, and stuffed him in the back. He was whisked away to the station where he'd be processed and printed.

The two movie stars beamed with triumphant grins as the camera focused in on them.

"That was a daring citizen's arrest," Paris said.

Logan smiled. "Just doing our civic duty. Giving back to the community."

I rolled my eyes.

"You could have been injured or killed."

"We really weren't in any danger," Logan said, feigning modesty.

"The fugitive was a suspected assassin," Paris said, playing it up for her TV audience.

Logan pointed to the tactical team. "Those are the real heroes. They deserve all the praise."

The camera lens swung to us.

"Deputy Wild, what do you think of their assistance in apprehending this dangerous criminal?"

"I think they took a big risk." Then I added, "But a ruthless assassin may have escaped otherwise. The county owes them a debt of gratitude."

I stepped out of frame, and Paris asked the celebrities a few more questions. They were happy to ham it up in front of the lens and take on the role of heroes, arm in arm, like best buddies.

"Has this experience affected the way you will portray these characters?"

"Absolutely," Logan said.

"It's given us a new and deeper understanding of just how difficult and dangerous the work of law enforcement is," Brad said.

And just like that, everyone had forgotten about Logan's little stunt in my Ferrari and the girl he punched.

His attorneys had made a quick settlement with the girl. She'd get a nice chunk of cash and would be prohibited from discussing it. Logan agreed not to press charges against her boyfriend. Everybody was happy.

We waited for the celebrities to finish, then climbed into the Yukon and headed back to the station. Logan and Brad were on cloud nine. They mingled around the main office, taking congratulations for their valiant efforts while we filled out after-action reports.

When the paperwork was done, we had a word with Liam in the interrogation room. He was smart enough to keep his mouth shut, but there was no getting out of this. We had acquired weapons from a previous raid on his condo that linked him to the crimes. Combined with the testimony of his accomplice, he'd be spending a long time in a small cell.

It was finally time for that long-awaited drink. But I would have to wait just a little while longer.

59

Astrid was in an intermediate care unit when we spoke with her. She was heavily medicated and looked like hell. Vitals displayed on the monitor beside the bed, and a drip of IV fluids ran into her arm, along with a metered drip of morphine.

She didn't look surprised to see us. Almost relieved. "I had a feeling you might be stopping by."

I smiled. "I just wanted to make sure you were doing okay."

"Bullshit."

I chuckled. "Well, I do have a few questions. I suppose this shooting wasn't the result of a disgruntled customer."

She looked at me and said nothing.

"This is the part where you come clean. Somebody tried to kill you, and I suspect they might try to finish the job. Let me help you."

She thought about it for a long moment. "This is the part where I tell you what you want to know, and in return, you give me immunity and provide protection."

I didn't really have the authority to enter into a deal with her, but I figured we could work out the specifics later. "Tell me everything you know."

She sighed. "Where do you want me to start?"

"Cornelius Worthington would be a good place."

"Cornelius was making a stink."

"About the forgeries?"

She nodded. "He threatened to go public. Simon Sinclair exposed one of the paintings."

"So you had Cornelius killed?"

Her face twisted with a scowl. "No. I didn't have him killed. I didn't have any control over that."

"Who did?"

She was silent for a moment.

"Do you have a silent partner in the gallery that I don't know about?"

"Not a partner," she said, dancing around it. "More like a mutually beneficial acquaintance."

"News flash. Getting gunned down in front of your gallery doesn't seem beneficial."

She frowned at me.

"Tell me about this *partner*." I had a pretty good idea of where this was going.

"It started out innocently enough."

"It always does."

"The gallery was struggling. Prices skyrocketed. My cost of acquisition went sky-high. People were hanging onto their assets. They didn't know what the future would bring, and they were holding onto artwork as investments. I had no product to sell. It was the craziest thing ever. I've never seen anything like it. I couldn't source any high-ticket paintings, and when I did, the cost was so high I couldn't clear much of a margin. That's when Vera Voss came into the picture."

"Vera Voss?"

"You remember her. You met at the museum."

I nodded.

"She made me an offer that was hard to turn down. She provided cash through a shell corporation to purchase nonexistent paintings. I paid invoices to another corporation to pay for said nonexistent paintings."

"You were laundering money."

"It was fine for a little while, but I needed actual paintings to document sales and account for these large numbers."

"And that's where Marcel came in?"

"He painted forgeries from gaps in a known artist's catalog. They couldn't be tracked down or verified. Who's to say what the value of those paintings were? I took pictures of the paintings and documented the sales. We worked hard to create a plausible original story for each painting. I took my commission off the top. Everybody was happy."

"Until Cornelius Worthington bought one of those forgeries," I surmised.

"It was too easy. The buyers were eager to have them. They saw them hanging on the walls in the gallery. I never intended to sell one to anyone else but Vera. But the demand was too great. People had to have them. Global supply was scarce, and I didn't have to give most of the money to Vera Voss with those sales. Sure, I was still laundering her money, but I was making a fortune with these on the side. I couldn't stop myself." Astrid paused. "I guess you could say I have an impulse problem."

"How many forgeries did you sell?"

"I don't know. I'd have to check."

"Ballpark."

"Hundreds."

That hung there for a moment.

"When Worthington started making noise, Vera got nervous. She's a little… crazy… to put it mildly. She is a control freak. She wanted to silence everyone in the chain. I couldn't stop her."

"Your appraisers were in on it?"

She nodded. "This is big business. And everybody wanted the gravy train to continue."

"You're willing to testify against Vera?"

"If you can guarantee my safety. She's not shy about shutting people up."

"I'll post a guard around-the-clock. You'll be safe."

She regarded me with skeptical eyes.

"You're doing the right thing."

She scoffed, then winced. The tensing of her abdominal muscles shot a jolt of pain through her body. "I'm just trying to survive."

"Aren't we all?" I paused. "Was Stacy in on the laundering?"

"I never told Marcel anything. I just put in orders for paintings."

"I'll need access to your books and anything else that can back up these allegations."

"You'll find everything you need on my laptop. It's all documented. But it might not be helpful. It will look legit."

"Where's your laptop?"

"At the gallery. But I don't know where my purse or my keys are."

"I'll track that down."

I called the sheriff and updated him on the situation. He said he would send a deputy over to stand watch.

A nurse told me EMTs had collected Astrid's personal belongings from the scene. "Hang on a minute, and I'll get that for you."

She returned to the room moments later and handed me a white plastic drawstring bag that contained Astrid's purse.

I pulled out the expensive cream-colored leather handbag that was stained with blood.

"My keys should be in there," Astrid said. "You can look through it. At this point, I don't care."

It was like entering a forbidden temple. Sacred ground. I rummaged through the bag and found her keys along with another item of interest.

60

Along with her keys, I found two phones. One was powered on, the other one off. It was most likely a prepaid cellular. I pulled it from her purse and displayed it. "Burner phone?"

She gave a guilty shrug, then winced from the movement.

"I need access to the device."

I powered up the phone. Astrid told me her passcode. Once I was past the security screen, I went to the recent call list. There was only one number that this phone ever dialed.

"I take it this number belongs to Vera's burner?"

Astrid nodded.

The encrypted messaging app, *Memo*, was installed on the phone. There were no messages in the device's history. They were automatically set to delete after a few hours. It was good protocol to wipe messages on a regular basis if involved in nefarious activities.

I handed Astrid the phone. "Try calling Vera. See what she has to say."

"She won't pick up."

"Let's just see what happens."

"She'll only call from a public place. One that can't be tracked back to her. I would usually go to a coffee shop or restaurant, and I never turned the device on when I was at home or at the gallery."

"I'll give you credit. You played it smart for a while."

She frowned at me. "You really want me to call Vera?"

I nodded.

"What do you want me to say?"

"Hint that you know she tried to kill you."

"You like to stir up shit, don't you?"

"It's a special skill."

Astrid dialed the number. As expected, it rang a few times, then went to voicemail. "Hi, Vera. It's me. A really odd thing happened to me today. Somebody tried to kill me. I can't imagine who. Give me a call when you get a chance. I'd love to hear your take on things."

Even after all she'd been through, Astrid still had a little snark in her.

We waited until a deputy arrived, then headed to the gallery. We cut through the police tape and searched the property but didn't find Astrid's laptop.

I used her key fob to gain access to her white Mercedes that was parked in the lot. After rummaging through it and searching the trunk, I still came up empty-handed.

We all climbed into the Yukon, and the driver took us over to Stingray Bay. Maybe Astrid had forgotten where her laptop was. It was understandable, given the situation. Her brain was a little foggy from the anesthesia and the pain medication. She'd been through a lot.

We pulled into the driveway at her McMansion. I hopped out, hustled to the door, and clicked the key fob to shut off the alarm. I slipped the key into the slot. After unlatching the deadbolt, we pushed inside and searched the home.

No laptop. No tablet.

I checked all the windows and doors. No sign of forced entry.

"You think somebody else got to that laptop?" JD muttered.

"Somebody who had a key to the gallery and the house," I said.

I called Isabella. "I need you to tell me everything you can about Vera Voss."

"Tyson, it's a Friday night. You were recently kidnapped, you donated stem cells, and you've been going nonstop for longer than I can remember. How about you take an evening off?"

"Your suggestion is duly noted."

"And ignored." She sighed, and her fingers danced across the keyboard. After a moment, she said. "Vera looks clean."

"Clean?"

"I didn't say she was clean. I said she *looks* clean. No criminal history. Her father was a wealthy entrepreneur. She was left with a sizable trust fund. Socialite. She gets written up in the gossip blogs from time to time."

"What is a rich socialite with a trust fund doing laundering money through an art gallery?"

"I'm afraid that's what you'll have to find out."

"I thought you knew everything," I teased.

"Some things are yet to be discovered."

"Can you use your magic and tell me where Joyce is?" I gave her Joyce's cell number.

Her fingers tapped the keys again. "Her phone is on Oyster Avenue at Volcanic. Maybe you might get a night out after all."

61

Volcanic was a chill, laid-back bar with good music and plenty of eye candy. As the name implied, there were faux volcanoes with glowing lava flows. The kind of volcanoes that once required a virgin sacrifice. The volcanic gods would be waiting a long time for a virgin in a bar like this.

The outdoor patio was lit with paper lanterns, giving the area a soft, relaxing vibe.

We grabbed a round of drinks, and JD lifted his glass to toast. "Good to have you back in the trenches!"

"Good to be back," I said.

The four of us clinked glasses.

I took a sip of the fine amber whiskey, and it felt like I had escaped from a dank dungeon of abstinence—that refreshing, smooth burn warmed my belly.

It didn't take long for the celebrities to draw a crowd.

I scanned the patio for Joyce and saw her at a Tiki bar on the other side of the outdoor space. She was with a young blonde with golden ringlets that hung to her shoulders. I made my way across the bar to join the two ladies. "Funny seeing you here."

Joyce looked a little stunned. "Deputy Wild..."

She looked like a deer caught in headlights.

"This is my friend, Kayla. Kayla, this is the deputy investigating Astrid's case."

She smiled and extended a manicured hand.

"Pleasure to meet you," I said.

Her blue eyes sparkled.

"I talked to Astrid," Joyce said. "She's doing well. As well as can be expected."

"I spoke with her earlier myself."

"Oh, good. Was she able to tell you anything?"

"A few things."

"I asked her if she got a look at the shooters, but she didn't want to talk about it."

I surveyed her carefully. She seemed nervous, but then again, most people get nervous talking to cops.

"We looked for her laptop at the gallery and at her house," I said. "Do you have any idea where that might be?"

"No. What do you need her laptop for?"

I shrugged. "We thought it might have information."

She looked confused.

"Nobody has contacted you about the laptop?"

She swallowed hard. "No." She was lying. "Who would contact me?"

"We believe there's evidence on the laptop that could implicate a certain individual in a money laundering scheme."

Her eyes rounded, and her brow lifted. "Money laundering?"

"You wouldn't happen to know anything about that, would you?"

"Like I said, I just answer phones and help coordinate events. I'm not involved in the business side of things."

She paused and exchanged a look with Kayla.

Her friend didn't know what to make of the situation.

"Listen, deputy. It's been a stressful day. I just want to have a drink and unwind. I don't want to think about this anymore."

"I totally understand. How about I buy you girls another round, and you can tell me about Vera Voss?"

She stiffened. "I don't know anybody by that name."

She made a mistake. I knew damn good and well she knew Vera. Everyone in that circle did.

"Oh, certainly you remember Vera. I believe I saw her at the gallery as well as the museum."

Joyce knew she was caught. "Kayla, would you excuse us for a moment?"

Kayla smiled. "Sure. I'll just go... powder my nose."

Kayla slinked away and meandered through the crowd, heading toward the ladies' room.

Joyce glanced around with nervous eyes. She leaned in and said in a hushed tone, "Look, I don't want to get involved. I don't know what was going on, and I don't want to know."

"So you do know Vera?"

"I said I'm not getting involved. And I'd prefer if you just walked away. I don't want anyone to see me talking to you."

"Did she contact you?"

The muscles in her jaw flexed. "What part of *I don't want to talk about this* do you not understand?"

She stormed away.

I figured somebody had gotten to her and compelled her to hand over the laptop. I had my doubts that she would ever cooperate. But I hoped, for her sake, nobody decided to come after her.

I returned to JD and the crew.

"Did you find out anything useful?" Logan asked.

62

Daniels called the next morning. "You want the bad news, or do you want the bad news?"

I groaned, still half asleep. I might have overindulged on my first night back in the saddle. Amber rays of morning sun filtered through the blinds. I peeled my eyes open and said, "What is it?"

"Your witness didn't make it."

"What!?"

"Sorry. She started bleeding during the night. They took her back to the OR and tried to stabilize her, but she bled out."

I felt a heavy weight on my chest. My relationship with Astrid was complicated. She got mixed up with the wrong people and made some bad decisions.

"I don't suppose you found that laptop," Daniels asked.

"No."

"Well, you're back to square one. Echols won't issue a warrant for Vera's arrest without a witness. And a dead witness can't testify."

I gritted my teeth and stifled the urge to shout a few obscenities.

"Get something on Vera Voss that sticks."

"I'm on it," I said with a disappointed voice.

"I'm sorry, Wild."

The sheriff ended the call, and I pulled myself out of bed. I showered, dressed, then staggered down to the galley to fix breakfast, still in a stupor.

This case was slipping away.

The smell of coffee and the sizzle of bacon drew a few customers into the galley.

"You guys are up bright and early," I said to Logan and Brad as they stumbled in.

"If you're up, we're up," Logan said.

"You guys are taking this seriously," I said, somewhat impressed.

"That's what we're here for," Brad said.

It seemed the two had turned over a new leaf.

I filled them in on the bad news.

"What happens now?" Logan asked.

"We dig up dirt on Vera Voss."

"How do we do that?"

"We put her under surveillance. Do a stakeout. See what turns up."

Their eyes lit up with glee.

"A stakeout?"

"Don't get excited," I said. "It's like watching paint dry."

My phone buzzed with a call from Penelope. "Hey, how's your morning?"

"It could be worse."

"That doesn't sound encouraging. I hope I'm not disturbing you."

"No. Not at all."

"Well, I just put Haley on a plane to Iowa. She's going to stay with her aunt. I don't think she's terribly excited about the prospect, but I think it will be good for her."

"She needs a good environment right now." I paused. "Did you tell her not to write any more software programs?"

Penelope laughed. "That kid is going to change the world someday."

"Hopefully, for the better."

"I have no doubt." She paused. "If I recall correctly, you should be off the wagon by now."

"Yes. I may have had a few drinks last night to celebrate."

"If you're up for it, I believe you owe me a piña colada."

I laughed. "I thought you owed *me* a piña colada."

"Either way, I'm pretty sure we can remedy the situation. Say 8 o'clock at Jellyfish?"

I cringed. "I'd love to, but..."

"You already have plans."

"I think we might be on a stakeout tonight."

"Oooh, a stakeout," she said in an intrigued voice. "You're back on another case?"

"No rest for the weary."

"If you need backup, let me know."

"Careful, I might recruit you."

"You've got my number. Use it."

I grinned. "I will."

"Out of curiosity, who's your target?"

"Vera Voss."

"What did she *allegedly* do?"

I gave her a laundry list of dirty deeds.

"I know you've got resources, but I'll see what I can dig up."

"I'd appreciate that."

"Well, you did help me out in a pinch. The least I can do is return the favor. Besides, I'm not used to having free time. I don't know what to do with myself."

I could think of a few things to do with her.

"When are you back on the job?"

"The job is there if and when I want it."

"Having doubts?"

She laughed. "You could say I'm questioning everything at this point."

"Understandable," I said.

"I'm weighing my options. Maybe I'll go into the contract world."

"I don't know if that's any better."

"Well, we can discuss the merits of our chosen professions another time. You know where to find me if you need me."

I ended the call. By that time, JD had staggered into the galley, and I filled him in on the situation.

After breakfast, we took the Devastator to Jack's house and picked up the Wild Fury van. We drove back to the marina and picked up Logan and Brad, then headed to the station where we swapped it out for the surveillance van. We changed the wrap at regular intervals. It was currently disguised as Coconut Electric. Utility vehicles could park for days without drawing much suspicion.

63

Vera Voss lived aboard an 82-foot SunTrekker yacht named *Glamour Goddess* in the Sandpiper Point Marina. We pulled into the lot and found a place to park that gave us a good line of sight to the superyacht. Sandpiper Point was home to luxury yachts, bluewater sailboats, and high-end sportfishing boats. The marina was popular with tech moguls, entrepreneurs, crypto types, and the occasional drug dealer.

The surveillance van had every imaginable gadget. Multiple ultrahigh-definition cameras, laser listening devices, and the ability to launch and pilot a drone. The inside was decked out with a computer terminal and large flatscreen displays. There was a small restroom for extended stakeouts. Still, with the four of us, it was pretty cramped.

JD manned the computer terminal and aimed the cameras at the *Glamor Goddess*. He zoomed in. The diabolical vixen ate a late breakfast on the sky deck. A wide-brimmed hat shielded her face from the sun. Oversized Chanel glasses covered her eyes, and a navy blue bikini showed off her svelte form.

Vera wasn't your typical crime boss. And without a witness, we had no proof of any wrongdoing.

It looked like she had a full crew. Stewards waited on her hand and foot. A chef prepared meals. Deckhands scurried about, cleaning and polishing the boat. It took a pretty penny to keep a show like that rolling.

Vera wasn't bad to look at, but it didn't take long for the stakeout to get boring.

"So, what do we do?" Logan asked. "Just sit around all day and watch?"

"Pretty much," I said.

A big guy walked through the boat, keeping an eye on things. I recognized him from the museum. Mr. Muscles stepped to the aft deck and glanced around the dock, then looked to the parking lot. He stepped back into the salon. He was, no doubt, one of Vera's security team. He wore a gray suit that barely contained his physique. He had a slick head and an upper torso that would give a comic book supervillain a run for his money.

Another security guard joined him in the salon. This guy was at the museum as well. He was a little shorter than Mr. Muscles and perhaps a little wider. Stubby had a face like a Mac truck. A real bruiser.

After a leisurely meal, Vera sauntered down to the bridge deck and changed into something more fashionable. The way the morning sun beamed through the tinted windows offered a silhouette of her form as she changed.

She emerged wearing a designer cream dress and heels.

Before long, the tall, musclebound security guard escorted her across the passerelle and down the dock. They climbed into a shiny black Escalade, the tires slick with protectant. The engine rumbled to life, and the duo pulled out of the lot.

I slipped behind the wheel of the surveillance van, cranked up the engine, and we followed, keeping our distance.

The Escalade twisted through the streets and made its way to Oyster Avenue. It parked in the lot behind Key Bean.

They climbed out of the SUV, and the bodyguard escorted Vera inside, keeping a watchful eye on the surroundings.

I pulled into the parking lot and circled around by the Escalade after they had stepped inside. JD slid open the cargo door, hopped out, and tried to act inconspicuous as he walked to the Escalade. He attached a tracking device to the underside of the bumper, then hopped back into the van.

JD pulled the door shut, slid behind the computer terminal, and pulled up the tracking device on a map.

"Is that legal?" Logan asked.

"Not exactly," JD said.

"Don't you need a warrant for that kind of thing?"

"Technically?"

"So, you guys just break the rules when it's convenient?" Brad said with a hint of judgment.

Jack frowned at them. "I don't know if you've been keeping score, but we're not exactly winning this game."

I drove out of the parking lot and turned onto Oyster Avenue. It took a couple passes, but I found a place to park at the curb across the street from the eclectic coffee shop. We could see directly into Key Bean.

Jack zoomed the camera lens in. The reflections on the glass windows made it a little harder to see, but Vera made several phone calls while she sucked down a tall latte.

The two stayed at the coffee shop for a half hour, then left. We followed them to the *Five Fathoms*. They pulled to the valet, and the attendant grabbed their doors. We lost sight of the duo when they entered.

I parked across the street. Jack hopped out of the van and hustled to the restaurant. The four of us piling into the eatery would draw too much attention, especially with the celebrities.

Jack returned 15 minutes later, pulled open the cargo door with a rumble, and hopped inside. "She's having lunch with a girlfriend. Muscles is at a table nearby.

"You know who the girl is?" I asked.

"Nope." He pulled out his phone and showed me a picture of the young blonde Vera dined with.

He texted the image to me, and I sent it to Isabella.

She texted back 15 minutes later. *[Cara Montgomery. Socialite. No criminal record.]*

"Maybe it's just a casual lunch," Jack said.

They were in the restaurant for a little over an hour and a half. The valet pulled the Escalade around, and Muscles escorted Vera to the vehicle, then hustled around and climbed inside. We followed them to the Highland Village Mall. It was an upscale center with boutique shops that catered to the ultra-rich, offering bespoke clothing, handbags, shoes, jewelry, and more.

Our stomachs rumbled, and Logan and Brad were getting pretty antsy by this point. They stayed in the van while I tailed Vera through the mall as she went on a spending spree. All the clerks knew her. They greeted her with smiling faces and dollar bills in their eyes.

I grabbed a couple sandwiches from the food court before returning to the van. We chowed down and kept an eye on the Escalade.

After Vera had spent an inordinate amount of money, she returned to the SUV with Muscles carrying the bags. He drove her back to Sandpiper Point.

We pulled into the parking lot as the big guy carried the boutique bags down the dock, following Vera across the passerelle.

I found a place to park.

With the joystick, JD adjusted the cameras and zoomed in.

We watched for the rest of the afternoon.

Not much happened.

In the evening, Vera met a young boy-toy for dinner at the Bluewater Bistro. Afterward, they hit a few clubs and ended up back at the marina on the boat.

It was the most interesting part of the evening. Vera and her young lover went for broke on the edge of the Jacuzzi on the sky deck. Moans of ecstasy drifted across the water. The glowing moon presided over the debauchery as stud-boy took her to pound town. Washboard abs and bulging biceps, treating her like a blow-up doll. She seemed to love every moment of it.

Vera liked to have her fun.

When the show was over, we headed back to Diver Down. That was enough for one day. We were all tired and stiff from sitting in that cramped van all day. I figured Logan and Brad wouldn't be eager to do another stakeout. To my surprise, they were willing to climb back into the van the next day and do the same thing all over again.

It was another day of much the same.

By the third day, we were all growing a little weary of the process, and I began to have my doubts that anything would turn up. Vera seemed well insulated from whatever underhanded activity she had going on. She had obviously been running a lot of money through the gallery, but Astrid had never indicated the source of Vera's illicit funds.

I figured Vera was in a bind. She'd need to find another front soon.

It was late afternoon when the savage vixen decided to go for a little cruise. Deckhands cast off the lines and disconnected shore power and water. The pilot navigated the boat out of the marina and hit the open swells.

We hustled back to Diver Down and raced down the dock to the *Avventura*. After we gathered a few supplies, we boarded the wake boat, and I cast off the lines. JD took the helm and piloted us out of the marina. He throttled up once we passed the breakwater, bringing the boat on plane. We raced toward Sandpiper Point, hoping to catch up with the slower superyacht.

The sun hung low in the sky, casting golden rays across the teal water, painting the sky with soft pastel colors. The engines howled, and the bow carved through the swells, spraying mists of seawater. The briny air swirled.

We were all excited about a little change of scenery.

It didn't take long to catch up with the *Glamor Goddess*. We kept our distance as it cruised out to sea.

We followed the vessel for 45 minutes. Vera lounged on the sky deck, drink in hand, soaking up the last rays of sun.

It wasn't long before the amber ball dropped over the horizon, and the swells turned black. The superyacht dropped anchor.

JD cut the engine, and the wake boat slumped into the swells, drifting with the current. The tiny craft pitched and rolled, and the evening breeze drifted across the boat.

I sat at the bow, watching the super yacht with IR optics.

The garage opened, and with the help of a davit, Mr. Muscles and Stubby launched a rigid inflatable tender. The outboard whined as they skimmed across the surface, disappearing into the night.

JD cranked up the engine, and we followed the tender.

64

The two goons cruised through the inky swells to Calypso Key. They entered the bay and rode in with the surf and beached the craft on the sandy shore. Muscles and Stubby hopped out, pulled the tender ashore, then disappeared into the tree line.

"What do you think they're up to?" JD said, knowing they were up to no good.

"One way to find out," I said.

JD navigated the boat to the other side of the island, and we came in against the wind. That would cut our sonic profile. He cut the engine, and we paddled into the shallows.

I press-checked my pistol, grabbed an AR-15, extra magazines, and donned a tactical vest. I pulled the charging handle and chambered a round with a clack. It was the unmistakable sound of impending ass-kickery.

I grabbed my helmet with night vision opticals and told the movie stars to stay put. "Paddle out, drop anchor, and wait for my signal. If you don't hear from us in 20 minutes, call the sheriff."

"It would be really good for our character research if we could tag along," Logan said.

"Yeah, I totally agree," Brad added.

"I'm glad you both can agree on something." I gave them a stern look. "Do not, under any circumstances, get out of this boat. You got me?"

They stared blankly at me.

"Do. You. Understand?"

They frowned, and Brad gave me a mock salute.

We hopped out, hit the beach, and advanced to the tree line. JD and I crept through the underbrush, the dappled rays of moonlight poking through the treetops.

In the distance, a generator rumbled.

We continued in the direction of the sound.

Calypso Key was a small island. You could jog around the damn thing in less than half an hour at a leisurely pace. It was thick with high grass, mangroves near the shore, and other verdant foliage. Crickets chirped, and mosquitoes buzzed around my ear. The muggy night air misted my skin, and the thump of my pulse drummed in my ears. My veins spiked with adrenaline.

We moved with silent steps like shadows through the underbrush until we came across a clearing. JD and I held up at the tree line.

Somebody had built a makeshift shack out of plywood on the other side of the meadow. The generator provided power.

I had no doubt we'd stumbled across a production factory. Even across the clearing, the chemical smell hit my nostrils. Noxious fumes that you didn't want to breathe. These types of pop-up labs were common in the jungles of Colombia, but I hadn't seen one before around here.

Judging by the acrid smell, this was a meth lab. Acetone, pseudoephedrine, red phosphorus, anhydrous ammonia, sodium hydroxide, and trichloroethane, among others. A volatile mixture that could explode with the slightest provocation. For every pound of methamphetamine, the process produced 6 pounds of toxic waste. Not particularly great for the environment.

We circled around, hugging the tree line, moving closer to the shack.

An operation like this would run round-the-clock, produce as much illicit narcotics as possible, then change locations. These things were constantly on the move. I had no doubt in a day or two, this would be gone.

Hell, it could be gone by morning.

Mr. Muscles and Stubby emerged from the shack, both with a black duffle bag in each hand. I caught a brief glimpse of the cook inside wearing a full chemical suit and facemask with a respirator. There were vials and beakers and burners and drums of chemicals.

The door closed, and Mr. Muscles and his compatriot lugged the bags toward the trail that led to the beach.

JD and I emerged from the tree line, weapons shouldered.

"Coconut County!" I shouted. "On the ground. Now!"

The faces of the scumbags tensed with scowls. They dropped the duffle bags with a crunch.

They exchanged a look, and in their eyes, I saw a moment's contemplation.

Pistols in their waistbands were an easy grasp. Would they take their chances? Or would they let this play out?

Better judgment prevailed, and they raised their hands in the air.

"On the ground. Face down. Put your hands behind your head."

The two goons exchanged another look, then complied.

JD kept them covered while I approached the shack. I kicked open the door and swung the barrel of my AR inside, taking aim at the cook.

Startled, he raised his hands that were covered with black industrial rubber gloves. He looked like a bumblebee in the yellow suit and black mask.

I held my breath, the stench from the chemicals overpowering.

"Out of the shack!" I commanded.

I waved him outside with the barrel of my rifle, and he complied. The bumble bee stomped toward his co-conspirators wearing thick black rubber boots.

I put flex cuffs around the trio, while JD kept them covered. With the goons secured, I unzipped one of the duffle bags. It was full of the crystalline red meth that had been plaguing the island.

We were feeling pretty accomplished.

But that sense of accomplishment was shattered when a voice shouted from the tree line, "Drop the weapons, pigs! Or the pretty boys get it."

I cringed and looked in the direction of the voice. Two thugs had Brad and Logan at gunpoint.

65

I glared at the movie stars as two thugs marched them into the clearing. These guys were clearly security for the island operation. One was tall and lanky. The other was shorter and wider, with a mustache. They were decked out in tactical gear with assault rifles, extra magazines, and wore jungle camouflage. They had been patrolling the island when they stumbled across Logan and Brad.

An operation like this was susceptible to pirates. Hard to get a bigger score than stealing from the source. They had to be ever vigilant in their defense of the lab.

"What part of *stay in the boat* did you not understand?" I asked.

Brad and Logan shrugged.

"We thought we could help," Logan said sheepishly.

JD and I stood there with our hands in the air. The goons collected our weapons, then cut Muscles, Stubby, and the cook free.

"Get back to work," Mr. Muscles said to the cook.

This was a business with no downtime.

The cook slipped back into the shack, pulled the door shut, and resumed his duties.

"What do you want to do with these clowns?" Mustache asked.

Mr. Muscles stared at us for a long moment, contemplating our fate. "Take a shovel and make them dig their own grave. Do it away from the lab so it doesn't stink."

"It already stinks around here," Mustache replied.

Lanky grabbed a shovel from the shack, and the two goons marched us across the clearing.

Mr. Muscles and Stubby grabbed the duffle bags and continued on their journey down the trail toward the beach.

We reached our destination, and Lanky tossed the shovel on the ground. "Start digging."

"Make it big enough for the four of you," Mustache said.

Logan flashed that million-dollar smile. "There's been some misunderstanding here. We're just doing character research for a role. We're not really involved in this."

Mustache gave him a flat look. "Really?"

"Really. I don't know if you've seen any of our movies, but..."

"I know who you are," he said, unimpressed.

"We're happy to sign autographs. Maybe you'd like us to record a birthday wish to a friend or loved one. We could do that kind of thing, you know?"

"Would you?" he taunted, feigning sincerity.

"Certainly," Logan said.

"That would be great. I'd love to get selfies with you two."

The two celebrities smiled.

Mustache handed his assault rifle to his comrade, then stepped in between the two celebrities, pulled out his phone, and took a smiling selfie. He looked over it after the picture was taken and seemed pleased. Then his smile faded. "Start digging."

He stepped away and took his rifle back from Lanky.

"Are you serious?" Logan asked.

"Do I look serious?" he said with a stone face.

"I thought we..."

"I don't give two shits who you are. You're in the wrong place at the wrong time. You should have listened to these guys and stayed on the boat," he said, pointing his thumb at us.

Logan and Brad looked stunned.

"C'mon, pretty boy. Start digging."

"I want a selfie," Lanky said.

Mustache glared at him, quashing that idea.

Lanky sulked.

After the shock wore off, Logan grabbed the shovel and plowed the blade into the soil.

He got a few scoops into it, tossing the dirt aside. "Why am I the only one digging?"

"Because there's only one shovel, dipshit."

"I think we should take turns. It's the only fair thing to do."

"Shut up and dig!"

Logan was flabbergasted.

Brad seemed almost amused.

Logan stomped the shovel into the ground and heaved a scoop of dirt. Little by little, a mound grew.

It wasn't long before Muscles and Stubby returned with angry looks on their faces. The two stomped across the clearing and joined us.

"What's wrong?" Mustache asked.

"Seems like these fuck nuggets cut the fuel line on the boat. Nobody's going anywhere at the moment." Muscles drew his pistol. "Go find the boat they came in on and bring it around to the bay."

Mustache and Lanky hesitated a moment.

"Go!" Mr. Muscles commanded.

Lanky and Mustache took off while Muscles and Stubby stood watch.

66

"Just out of curiosity, which one of you two shot Cornelius Worthington?" Logan asked.

"None of your fucking business," Mr. Muscles said.

"Oh, come on. What's the harm now? We're not getting off this island alive."

Muscles aimed his pistol at Logan. "The same person who's gonna put a bullet in you if you don't shut up and keep digging."

Logan got his answer, and so did we.

He dug the pit for the next hour. His hands were raw and blistered. Sweat soaked his shirt and beaded on his brow. It was the hardest he had worked in a long time. "Anybody else can feel free to take over at any time," he said, his voice thick with sarcasm.

"Toss me the shovel," I said.

He flung the shovel toward me.

It all happened in the blink of an eye. Faster than the wings of a hummingbird.

I snatched it.

In a fluid motion, I swung as hard as I could, smacking Mr. Muscles in the face.

Blood spewed from his nose, and the bastard lost a few teeth in the process. The back of the blade hit his skull with a loud gong-like ring, and the impact reverberated through my forearms.

The mountainous man tumbled back, and his pistol fell away.

Stubby had pulled out a pack of cigarettes and fumbled with his lighter at the time. It delayed his response.

Logan dove for the pistol, tumbled and rolled onto one knee, and fired two shots into Stubby before he could draw his weapon.

It was like something out of an action movie.

A movement that he had rehearsed a hundred times for the camera. Now, this was real life.

Geysers of blood erupted from Stubby's chest. He staggered back, drew his pistol, and took aim at Logan. Stubby squeezed the trigger. Bullets snapped through the air, narrowly missing the movie star.

Stubby hit the ground, and I swung again, batting the pistol out of his hand just about the time he ran out of breath.

Logan's eyes rounded, and he trembled, adjusting his aim at Mr. Muscles, who groaned on the ground, spitting fragments of his pearly teeth onto the dirt.

JD grabbed Stubby's pistol that I had batted away.

"Holy shit!" Logan exclaimed in disbelief. "Holy shit!"

I kept my head on a swivel. I knew Lanky and Mustache had heard the gunshots and would be heading in our direction soon.

"Give me the gun," I said to Logan.

He nodded, and I carefully took it from him.

He paced around, wiping sweat from his brow and running his fingers through his hair. "I just fucking killed somebody."

Bullets snapped through the air, muzzle flash emanating from the tree line.

"Hit the dirt!" I shouted.

We all dove to the ground.

The movie stars climbed into the pit, taking cover. I slid on my belly to the edge of the high grass and took cover behind a fallen tree. It wasn't much, but better than nothing.

Short bursts of automatic gunfire spewed.

Bullets rocketed through the night air.

I popped up and fired two shots in the direction of the muzzle flash, then ducked down again.

JD crawled to join me.

Across the clearing, the cook opened the door and peered out to see what was going on. An instant later, he had an AR angled out the door and blasted a few shots in our direction.

The scenario wasn't looking good. We had two pistols and a limited amount of ammunition.

67

Muscles regained his wits and drew a pistol from an ankle holster. He took aim at me.

Logan lurched out of the pit, grabbed his forearm, and pushed the gun away as he squeezed the trigger.

That got my attention.

The two wrestled for the gun on the ground. Muscles was damn near twice Logan's size. He bucked him off with ease.

Logan tumbled away, and Muscles took aim at the movie star.

I swung my pistol around and put two shots into the big ogre before he could put holes in the movie star.

Logan had a panicked look on his face, his eyes wide. He scampered to Muscle's pistol and snatched it, then slipped back into the pit with Brad.

Bullets crisscross overhead—Lanky, Mustache, and the cook still firing at us.

Logan angled the pistol over the edge of the pit and opened fire at the cook. I guess all that target practice he'd done during training for his movies paid off. He tagged the cook's shoulder, spinning him around. Blood stained the yellow PPE suit.

JD returned fire at Lanky and Mustache. They were attacking from the east. I scampered south, my belly to the ground. At the tree line, I took cover behind a thick trunk.

Bark exploded with bullet hits, spewing splinters.

I held up for a moment, then raced through the underbrush to another thick trunk.

More bark exploded as another burst of automatic fire pelted the tree.

I angled my weapon around and returned fire.

Then the craziest thing happened.

Brad climbed out of the pit and sprinted across the meadow toward the shack. It had become a war movie for these guys, and they were trying to out hero each other.

Bullets zipped through the air as Brad ran across the field.

All eyes were on him.

It gave me an opening to advance. I sprinted through the trees, arcing around until I was parallel with Lanky and Mustache. They had maintained their positions instead of continually staying on the move.

Brad reached the shack unscathed and grabbed the cook's AR. The meth chef writhed and moaned on the ground, clutching his shoulder.

Brad opened fire on Lanky and Mustache. The goons were taking fire from three different positions.

I crept through the underbrush and held up behind another tree. I angled my pistol around and blasted a few shots at the morons.

Mustache swung his rifle in my direction and sent a flurry of molten copper my way.

I ducked behind the tree, taking cover as more bark exploded, splintering the tree. Bullets crashed through the underbrush, hitting twigs and leaves.

JD blasted a few shots, catching Mustache in the chest. It flopped him to the ground. He twisted and writhed, gurgling for breath.

I angled my pistol around and fired twice at Lanky.

One bullet caught him in the chest, the second in the head as the barrel had risen. Chunks of skull and goo splattered the tree behind him as he fell back.

"Targets down!" I shouted. "Cease-fire. Cease-fire."

Gunsmoke hazed the air, and the jungle went quiet but for the sound of chirping crickets and the ringing in my ears.

I advanced through the underbrush to the perps and checked vitals.

They were both gone.

I collected their weapons and marched back to join JD and Logan.

Brad shouted across the meadow, "We've got a live one!"

He put pressure on the man's wound and tried to stem the bleeding.

We were all on an adrenaline high.

"Holy shit!" Logan said with wide eyes.

"Not quite like the movies, is it?" I said.

"It doesn't seem real," Logan said. "All the blood looks like a special effect."

We joined Brad and moved the cook out of the toxic shack to fresher air. His skin was pale and misted with sweat.

"Try to stay calm," I said. "Help is on the way. Today is your lucky day."

"I don't feel so fucking lucky."

"You're still alive, and you have an opportunity to testify against your employer."

I moved back toward the pit and searched Mr. Muscles's pockets for my cell phone. I found the stash of them, including his. I used FaceID to unlock Muscles's phone. It took a few tries because his face was bloody and mangled, but I eventually got in.

There were recent text messages on an encrypted app to another phone labeled *Boss Lady*. I figured that had to be Vera's burner. They were set to disappear, but the messages hadn't expired yet. I took screenshots and texted them to my phone.

Boss Lady had texted: *[Is everything okay?]*

Muscles replied: [Slight complication. Everything is under control.]

[What kind of complication?]

[Those two cops and their entourage.]

[Shit!]

[Don't worry. Nobody is ever going to find them.]

[Someone will come looking for the celebrities.]

[They can look all they want. They won't find them. It will be one of the great mysteries.]

[Don't fuck this up.]

[I appreciate the words of encouragement.]

I called the sheriff and updated him on the situation. I told him to send the Coast Guard to board and detain the *Glamor Goddess*. They could board and search any boat on the water without a reason or a warrant. I figured I had enough to bring Vera down, but I needed to connect her to the burner phone.

It took an hour for the first responders to arrive. Deputies swarmed the island. EMTs and paramedics attended to the cook.

A helicopter landed in the meadow, the rotor wash mowing down the high grass, swirling up a windstorm.

The EMTs transferred the cook aboard, and the red chopper lifted from the ground and disappeared into the night, rotor blades thumping.

Investigators swarmed the island, and Dietrich snapped photos. Brenda and her crew examined the remains. We left them to wrap up and hustled back to the wake boat.

The sheriff followed in his patrol boat as we raced across the swells to the *Glamour Goddess.* The Coast Guard had detained the vessel and searched it.

The small amount of cocaine on the boat was enough to put Vera in custody. The burner phone in her possession connected her to Mr. Muscles and the meth operation.

The Coast Guard transferred her into the sheriff's custody, and she was taken back to the station where she'd be processed, printed, and put into an interrogation room.

We followed the sheriff back to the station, the wind swirling. We all felt accomplished.

Paris Delaney and her news crew waited for us on the dock. Her cameraman recorded Vera as she was escorted into the station.

"Deputy Wild, can you tell us what happened on Calypso Key?"

I patted Logan and Brad on the back. "I think these guys can tell the story better than I can. They're the real heroes of the day."

I left the movie stars to bask in the glory of the camera lens. With proud smiles, they regaled Paris with the details of the event. It was a hell of a PR campaign. You couldn't buy better promotion than this for the upcoming series.

We'd gotten the source of red meth off the street, and I figured Vera would do a long time in prison. She was smart enough to keep her mouth shut during the interrogation, but I didn't think she'd get out of this one.

We filled out after-action reports and surrendered our duty weapons. We were put on administrative leave while the island chaos was investigated, and that was fine by me. I needed a few days off.

After we wrapped up, we headed back to the *Avventura* and celebrated with a cocktail on the sky deck. Logan lifted his glass to toast. "To wild adventures!"

We grinned, clinked glasses, and sipped the fine whiskey.

Their time in Coconut Key was drawing to an end. They'd head back to Los Angeles, then would return when production ramped up.

They were kind of a pain in the ass to deal with, but they weren't bad guys. I might even say they grew on me a little.

A little.

After all we'd been through, I figured they'd do the TV show justice. They had enough real-life experience to draw from.

"Brad and I pitched in, and we got a little surprise for you two," Logan said.

JD and I perked up with curiosity.

Sly grins curled Logan's and Brad's faces. If I didn't know better, I'd say the two of them had almost become friends.

We'd have to wait until the morning to see what kind of surprise they had in store. I could only imagine what they had cooked up.

"I've been meaning to ask you," JD said to Logan. "The boat in that pirate movie…"

"Curse of the Caribbean."

"Yeah."

"We just finished the sequel."

"Who built the boat?"

"I don't know," Logan said. "I can find out."

"Are you going to make a third movie?"

"Depends on how the sequel does?"

"What's going to happen to the boat?"

Logan shrugged. "The studio had it built just for the film. Might become a backlot tour item, but I doubt it."

Jack had that look in his eyes.

"Why do you ask?"

"I might know somebody who's interested in buying it."

Logan surveyed him with curiosity, and JD began telling tales of our treasure hunt.

My phone buzzed with a call from Penelope. "I saw you on the news. Looks like you got your situation handled."

"It got a little tense there for a moment, but it all worked out."

"I guess congratulations are in order."

"It's definitely a reason to celebrate. We're enjoying a cocktail now. You should join us."

"I could be persuaded," she said in a coy voice.

The evening was looking up.

Ready for more?

The adventure continues with Wild Skin!

Join my newsletter and find out what happens next!

AUTHOR'S NOTE

Thanks for taking this incredible journey with me. I'm having such a blast writing about Tyson and JD, and I've got plenty more adventures to come. I hope you'll stick around for the wild ride.

Thanks for all the great reviews and kind words!

If you liked this book, let me know with a review on Amazon.

Thanks for reading!

—*Tripp*

TYSON WILD

Wild Ocean

Wild Justice

Wild Rivera

Wild Tide

Wild Rain

Wild Captive

Wild Killer

Wild Honor

Wild Gold

Wild Case

Wild Crown

Wild Break

Wild Fury

Wild Surge

Wild Impact

Wild L.A.

Wild High

Wild Abyss

Wild Life

Wild Spirit

Wild Thunder

Wild Season

Wild Rage

Wild Heart

Wild Spring

Wild Outlaw

Wild Revenge

Wild Secret

Wild Envy

Wild Surf

Wild Venom

Wild Island

Wild Demon

Wild Blue

Wild Lights

Wild Target

Wild Jewel

Wild Greed

Wild Sky

Wild Storm

Wild Bay

Wild Chaos

Wild Cruise

Wild Catch

Wild Encounter

Wild Blood

Wild Vice

Wild Winter

Wild Malice

Wild Fire

Wild Deceit

Wild Massacre

Wild Illusion

Wild Mermaid

Wild Star

Wild Skin

Wild…

CONNECT WITH ME

I'm just a geek who loves to write. Follow me on Facebook.

TRIPP ELLIS

www.trippellis.com

Made in United States
Orlando, FL
10 January 2025